AIRTHAN ASCENDANCY

THE ORION WAR – BOOK 8

BY M. D. COOPER

Just in Time (JIT) & Beta Readers

Lisa Richman
Scott Reid

Version 1.0.0

ISBN: 978-1-64365-028-9

Cover Art by Andrew Dobell
Editing by Jen McDonnell, Bird's Eye Books

TABLE OF CONTENTS

FOREWORD

I'm writing this foreword a few days after finishing the novel, which is rare for me—usually I write the foreword between the first draft and the revisions. Doing so has caused me to be a bit more introspective about the book and where it sits in the overall story being told.

While writing this book, I also wrote in Tau Ceti, Impulse Shock, Kill Shot, Vesta Burning, and the Southern Crown short story. I got to dance around in a number of eras and spend time with a lot of different characters, and then come back to my two leading ladies, Tangel and Sera, and see where things would take them.

It was fun to put a lot of characters together that we haven't seen onscreen before. Combinations such as Malorie (from the Warlord books) alongside the Seras, all working to take down Airtha. It's great to have such a large cast with interesting and unique backstories to bring to major battles such as this one.

And tied to that is the knowledge that we're two thirds of the way through the Orion War now. We've seen the buildup of hostilities that took us through to the end of the Scipio Alliance. Following that, we've watched Tangel build up her forces as they fight a war on many, many fronts—hundreds of which do not appear in the stories, lest we never get to the end. And now we've seen things advance to the next level, where Tangel is no longer fighting proxies, but the real enemies who are behind all of the strife that has held humans and AIs back for millennia.

I suppose in some respects, it's fitting that this is the novel that closes out 2018. By December of next year, the Orion War series will have ended, and we'll be moving on to the next era of Aeon 14, which makes me feel a bit melancholy, but also really excited to start showing you what I have planned for the next adventures.

Of course, there will still be a number of stories that will occur in the Orion War timeframe, and we'll also be skipping back to the FTL wars and the formation of the FGT as well.

I suppose none of this will really surprise you. There's a whole galaxy of tales to tell, and I plan to spin as many of them as I can before my fingers eventually give out. And with that, I think there's a story they're itching to get onto the page....

Michael Cooper
Danvers 2018

PREVIOUSLY…

When last we saw Tangel, she was recovering from her battle with the ascended AI, Xavia, and working to bring the League of Sentients into the Alliance. At the same time, Sera was putting together a team to strike at Airtha and bring an end to the Transcend's civil war.

Even as those momentous events were unfolding, we saw Cary encounter Myrrdan in the LMC and defeat him, while Corsia launched an attack on the Trisilieds, finally beginning the campaign in response to that kingdom's attack on New Canaan two years prior.

Svetlana, a Transcend admiral that has made appearances in prior tales, led an incursion into Orion space along with an ISF colonel named Caldwell. After their initial strikes, they received intel on a fleet massing in the Machete System and are now on their way to put down that threat.

The Widows are also on the move. They've been lurking in the shadows for some time, but in the prior book, we met Lisa Wrentham, now known as 'A1', who leads her clone army of assassins. She has sent out two strike teams: one to kill Tangel, and another to destroy Airtha.

And lest we forget, Epsilon, the leader of the largest group of core AIs, has taken a renewed and personal interest in the events surrounding Tangel….

KEY CHARACTERS REJOINING US

Airtha – Both the name of a ring encircling a white dwarf in the Huygens System and the AI who controls it, Airtha was once a human woman named Jelina, wife of Jeffrey Tomlinson. After venturing to the galactic core on a research mission, she returned as an AI—one with a vendetta.

Amavia – The result of Ylonda and Amanda's merger when they were attacked by Myriad aboard Ylonda's ship. The new entity occupies Amanda's body, but possesses an overlapped blend of their minds. Amavia has served aboard *Sabrina* since the ship left New Canaan after the Defense of Carthage, but is now the ambassador to the League of Sentients at Aldebaran.

Amy – Daughter of Silva, rescued by Rika and Team Basilisk from her father, Stavros.

Carmen – Ship's AI of the *Damon Silas*. Captured by Roxy during her assault on the ship.

Cary – Tangel's biological daughter. Has a trait where she can deep-Link with other people, creating a temporary merger of minds, and is able to utilize extradimensional vision to see ascended beings.

Cheeky – Pilot of *Sabrina*, reconstituted by a neural dump Piya made of her mind before she died on Costa Station.

Erin – Engineer responsible for the construction of the New Canaan Gamma bases, in addition to a number of other projects.

Faleena – Tangel's AI daughter, born of a mind merge between Tangel, Angela, and Joe.

Finaeus – Brother of Jeffrey Tomlinson, and Chief Engineer aboard the *I2*.

Flaherty – Former Hand agent and long-time protector of Sera.

Helen – Former AI of Sera's who was killed by her father in the events leading up to Jeffrey's assassination.

Iris – The AI who was paired with Jessica during the hunt for Finaeus, who then took on a body (that was nearly identical to Jessica's) after they came back. She remained with Amavia at Aldebaran to continue diplomatic relations with the League of Sentients.

Jeffrey Tomlinson – Former president of the Transcend, found in stasis in an underground chamber on Bolt Hole, a planet in the Large Magellanic Cloud.

Jen – ISF AI paired with Sera.

Jessica Keller – ISF admiral who has returned to the *I2* after an operation deep in the Inner Stars to head off a new AI war. She also spent ten years travelling through Orion space before the Defense of Carthage—specifically the Perseus Arm, and Perseus Expansion Districts.

Joe – Admiral in the ISF, commandant of the ISF academy, and husband of Tangel.

Kara – Daughter of Adrienne, Kara was rescued by Katrina when fleeing from Airtha, and came to New Canaan aboard the *Voyager*.

Katrina – Former Sirian spy, wife of Markus, and eventual governor of the Victoria colony at Kapteyn's Star—and Warlord of the Midditerra System.

Krissy Wrentham – TSF admiral responsible for internal fleets fighting against Airtha in the Transcend civil war. She is also the daughter of Finaeus Tomlinson and Lisa Wrentham.

Lisa – Former wife of Finaeus Tomlinson, she left the Transcend for the Orion Freedom Alliance when Krissy was young. Head of a clandestine group within the OFA known as the Widows, which hunts down advanced technology and destroys it.

Misha – Head (and only) cook aboard *Sabrina*.

Nance – Ship's engineer aboard *Sabrina*, recently transferred back there from the ISF academy.

Priscilla – One of Bob's two avatars.

Rachel – Captain of the *I2*. Formerly, captain of the *Enterprise*.

Roxy – Justin's sister, kept subservient to him as his lover via mental coercion.

Saanvi – Tangel's adopted daughter, found in a derelict ship that entered the New Canaan System.

Sabrina – Ship's AI and owner of the starship *Sabrina*.

Sera – Director of the Hand and former president of the Transcend. Daughter of Airtha and Jeffrey Tomlinson.

LMC Sera (Seraphina) – A copy of Sera made by Airtha containing all of the desired traits and memories Airtha desired. Captured by Sera and the allies during their excursion into the Large Magellanic Cloud.

Valkris Sera (Fina) – A copy of Sera made by Airtha containing all of Sera's desired traits and memories. Captured by ISF response forces who came to the aid of the TSF defenders during the siege of Valkris.

Svetlana – Transcend admiral dispatched deep in Orion Space with one of the Hoplite forces.

Terrance – Terrance Enfield was the original backer for the *Intrepid*, though once the ship jumped forward in time, he took it as an opportunity to retire. Like Jason, he was pulled into active service by Tangel when New Canaan became embroiled in the Orion War.

Troy – AI pilot of the *Excelsior* who was lost during the Battle of Victoria, and later found by Katrina. He joined her on the hunt for the *Intrepid* aboard the *Voyager*, jumping forward in time via Kapteyn's Streamer.

Tangel – The entity that resulted from Tanis and Angela's merger into one being. Not only is Tangel a full merger of a human and AI, but she is also an ascended being.

Usef – ISF Colonel who served on *Sabrina* for several years, as well as aided Erin in stopping several acts of sabotage in New Canaan.

Xavia – An ascended AI with its own agenda to help humanity, in opposition to the Caretaker and the core AIs.

MAPS

For more maps, visit www.aeon14.com/maps.

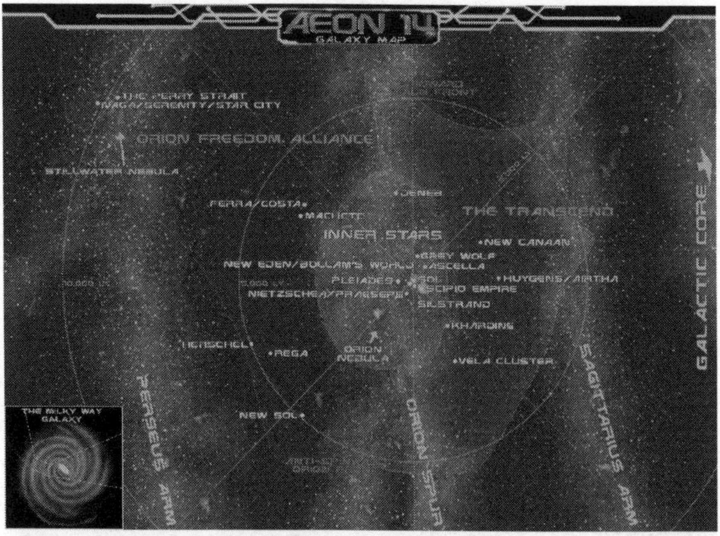

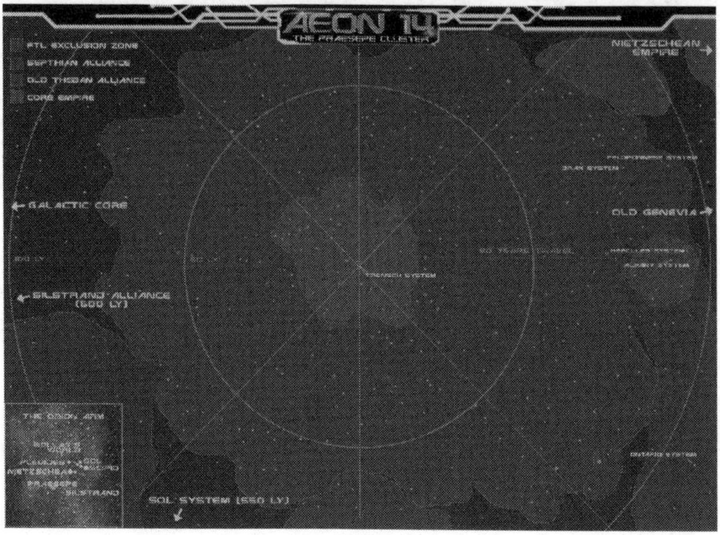

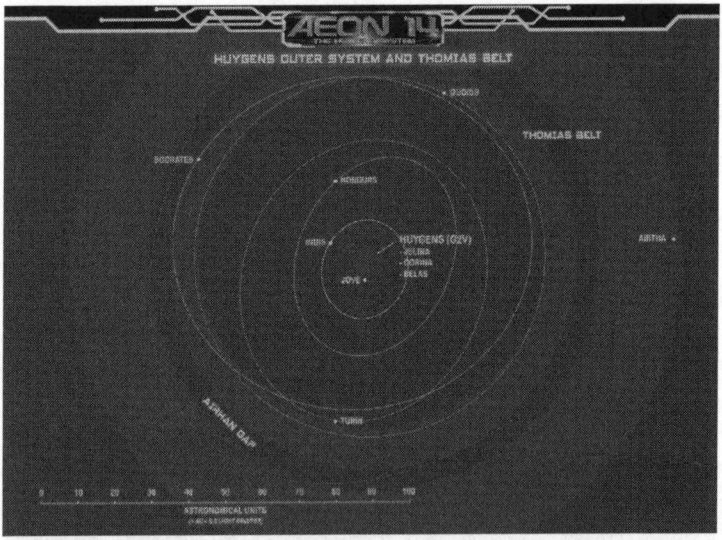
AEON 14
HUYGENS OUTER SYSTEM AND THOMIAS BELT
THOMIAS BELT
HUYGENS (G2V)
JOVE
ASTRONOMICAL UNITS

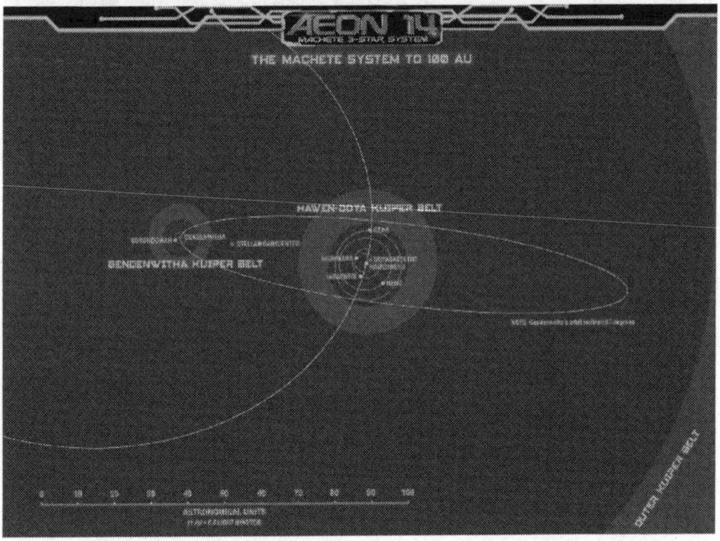
AEON 14
MACHETE 3-STAR SYSTEM
THE MACHETE SYSTEM TO 100 AU
BENDENWITHA KUIPER BELT
OUTER KUIPER BELT
ASTRONOMICAL UNITS

PART 1 – THE RIVER RUNS

DOLING OUT

STELLAR DATE: 10.05.8949 (Adjusted Years)
LOCATION: River Station, Styx Baby-9
REGION: STX-B17 Black Hole, Transcend Interstellar Alliance

"They've confirmed that Roxy is clear of the remnant, and that Carmen isn't suffering from residual effects," Krissy said, as Sera settled into the chair across from the admiral in her office.

Sera nodded solemnly. "I guess that's something, at least. It doesn't change what Carmen did."

"Or answer the question of what to do with Jane," Krissy added.

A long breath escaped Sera's lips, and she ran a hand through her red hair.

Still red, she thought to herself with a chuckle. *I guess Fina really did get me stuck on this.*

She pushed thoughts of her sisters from her mind, mildly amused that dealing with clones of herself was now preferable to what lay in front of her. The mess that Justin had made and then left in her lap was the last thing she needed to focus on at the moment, but she somehow felt as though she owed Roxy's situation her personal attention.

Especially considering how, after everything that had

happened to her, the woman had done the right thing in turning against Justin when her memories were finally restored.

Of course, that was the question. *Had* Roxy come to Styx of her own volition, or had the remnant inside of her forced the beleaguered woman to seek out the hidden base?

"OK, let's outline these issues one at a time," Sera said, holding up a finger. "Firstly, Roxy came here aboard the *Damon Silas*, keeping it out of Airtha's hands."

"Or the remnant did," Krissy added.

<For what it's worth, I don't really think Roxy took any prodding from the remnant to come here,> Jen said. *<I've been through all of her neural readings.... There's nothing to show that any sort of coercion was needed to get her to return the* Silas *to us.>*

"That's my belief as well," Sera said, meeting Krissy's eyes. "Do you have reason to disagree?"

Krissy shrugged. "No, just exercising a healthy dose of suspicion. Carry on."

"Secondly, we have the oddity that Roxy exists in the first place, and we have no knowledge of her ever having been in the Hand," Sera continued. "Her decision to put Justin's body in stasis was a good one. I understand that fleet intel has pulled a lot of good information from his mind—though nothing to suggest how he hid her from the directorate for all these years."

"Thanks to that intel, we know exactly which systems were supporting Justin's faction." A grim smile formed on Krissy's lips. "A few were double-dipping from us, a few from Airtha. Intel is coming up with ideas on how we can use that knowledge—and attempting to figure out where your other sister has gone."

"Which one?" Sera asked with a wink.

Krissy gave Sera a narrow-eyed look. "You know I mean Andrea. All your other sisters are here at Styx."

"Well, there's at least one more out there." Sera said the words in a voice filled with worry. "The latest of my doppelgangers will be waiting for us at Airtha."

The admiral's expression changed to one laden with contempt. "The Despot."

That was the name being given to the latest of the Seras ruling from Airtha. The populace in general had no idea that the current 'True President' of the Transcend was really the third incarnation of Sera to have been created in the past two years. All they knew was that she'd changed of late.

Where Fina and Seraphina had been close analogs of Sera, this new incarnation was less so. The stories that came out of Airthan space told of a woman who was utterly given to excess cruelty and impulsiveness.

Sera had always known that she was a woman of unusual appetites—it wasn't as though her own proclivities were lost on her. And she knew that they were only safe in moderation. To completely lose oneself in pleasure turned it into debauchery; despite the airs that Sera put on, she had never really given herself over to such things. In fact, other than the incident when Cheeky's pheromones had run amok on *Sabrina,* Sera had never even been with more than one partner, and each partner had, unfortunately, been separated by long gaps of celibacy.

Not so with this new Sera that Airtha had put forth.

Flaherty had commented that the Despot was an evil version of Sera, Cheeky, and Jessica—all rolled into one person.

If the tales were just of wild orgies and lascivious behavior, Sera would have understood. She knew that such urges were within herself, and that a weaker-willed version of her would give into them. But that was just the tip of the iceberg.

The woman who ruled from Airtha brought to mind wild stories from ancient human history, where queens bathed in the blood of their subjects, and virgins were sacrificed to appease angry gods.

Her only hope was that, whatever had turned this latest doppelganger into a homicidal maniac, it was the result of some significant change Airtha had wrought, and not some sort of darkness that resided in Sera and her other sisters.

<Space traffic control to Sera,> Jen said. *<You wandered off, there.>*

Sera laughed and shook her head. *<Sorry…thanks, Jen.>*

<Anytime.>

"OK," Sera said, collecting her thoughts. "So speaking of suspect behavior, we have the matter of what Jane knew about Roxy."

A look of distaste replaced the prior contempt on Krissy's face. "You mean whether or not she knew that Roxy couldn't deny her sexual advances."

"Pretty much, yeah." Sera pursed her lips, tamping down on her roiling disgust for what Justin had done to his own sister. "From what the interrogators have been able to determine, Jane had an inkling of what she was really doing."

"Which makes what she made Roxy do a form of coerced rape," Krissy said with a note of finality in her voice. "Legally, Jane is a deserter in a time of war, *and* a rapist. By Transcend law, the first can earn her capital punishment, and the second, a lengthy incarceration."

"Except Roxy is refusing to press charges," Sera replied, her jaw tightening.

"She's confused."

"Well, you're not wrong there. What of the AI, Carmen?"

Krissy gave a rueful laugh. "Stars, these three are just a giant mess, aren't they? Honestly, the *easy* one is Roxy. Which is nuts, because she came here under the control of a remnant who wanted to kill you."

"Yeah, I don't even have any words for how fucked up this

has all become."

Jen laughed in her mind. <*That's a first.*>

<*Har har, Jen.*>

Krissy gestured to one of the holos hovering over her desk. "The analysts have submitted their report. Carmen helped Roxy disable the *Damon Silas*'s self-destruct to save herself. She also admits to it, so the dereliction of duty is clear."

Sera pursed her lips as she considered the actions of all three. "And yet, they both came here with Roxy knowing that there was no way to hide these deeds from us."

"It doesn't change the facts." Krissy's voice carried almost no emotion, and Sera wondered if there was a difference between what the *admiral* wanted versus the woman.

"No, but it can alter the punishment," Sera suggested. "I've been considering something that may be…unorthodox."

A laugh escaped Krissy's lips. "Stars above, I can't imagine what it would be for *you* to call it 'unorthodox'."

"Hey," Sera adopted an expression of mock-hurt, "I'm very orthodox in how I conduct my professional life."

"You need a mirror, Sera."

"OK, I'm going to ignore the judginess here." She spoke the words in a defensive tone, but winked at the admiral. "Though you'll probably heap it on me when I tell you my plan."

"Out with it already, then," Krissy insisted, a worried smile forming on her lips.

"I was thinking of taking them on the mission to Airtha."

"OK. I knew it!" Krissy slapped her palms on her desk. "You've gone mad. Your ruddy hair follicles have grown into your brain and turned it to goo."

Jen let out a labored sigh before adding her opinion. <*Though I'd like to support that as a reason for this rationale, I can assure you that Sera's hair has remained anchored solely in her epidermis. Plus…it's not real hair, so it's not going to grow inward.*>

"Uhh...thanks, Jen...I think?"

"Seriously, Sera, what makes you think this is a good idea?" Krissy pressed.

Sera shrugged. "Decades ago, I established myself as a smuggler with a crew of semi-pirates and the goal of infiltrating a secret base to retrieve a CriEn module. That crew turned out to be one of the best group of operatives I've ever met—many of whom are going on this mission."

"I can't deny that," Krissy said with a long-suffering sigh. "You're taking more criminals than law-abiding citizens with you as it stands."

"It's all in how you look at it," Sera replied. "If you think of them as operatives of a foreign government, then they're heroes."

"Except for Jane and Carmen," Krissy said. "A deserter-slash-rapist, and a cowardly AI who abandoned her post."

"Well...she was technically yanked from her post before abandoning it."

"Semantics, Sera. I don't like the precedent."

"I really think that Roxy will be an asset—and if we punish Jane and Carmen, I don't know that Roxy will be terribly cooperative."

"What is it about Roxy?" Krissy asked. "Why do you want her along?"

"Well, she's a highly skilled operative, for starters," Sera said. "And I feel a bit of kinship with her. We were both utterly fucked over by people who were supposed to love and protect us."

Krissy pursed her lips, not speaking for a few moments. Then she sighed and nodded. "I know what that feels like, though it's not much of a reason to take someone on an op...but I won't stand in your way. However, I do want *some* sort of punishment for those two."

<If you want to transfer jurisdiction of Carmen's desertion to the

AI courts, we can handle her correction,> Jen suggested. <*It would be constructive for her, and wouldn't impact the mission.*>

"And how would Roxy handle your judgment against her friend?" Sera asked. "Will it sour her toward helping?"

<*I expect not. I imagine Carmen will have anticipated this all along.*>

"And Jane?" Krissy pressed.

Sera pursed her lips. "I'll think of something—though I'm open to suggestions."

"Well, I imagine it will start with a demotion," Krissy replied as she pulled up Jane's service record. "She was a CWO-5 when she joined with Justin—"

"Oh, I was thinking of a dishonorable discharge to start," Sera said, a wry smile on her lips. "And then I'm going to pull her into the Hand."

"Is that really a punishment?" Krissy asked. "Maybe you could send her somewhere with enforced celibacy—it fits the crime."

"Too bad we can't use compulsions," Sera said with a rueful shake of her head. "That would solve this nicely."

Krissy cocked an eyebrow. "I thought the Hand *did* use compulsions."

"Under Justin, yeah. Not since I've been in control—well, not that I ever approved, at least. Compulsions control behavior, but they don't really change it."

"Depends on how strong-willed a person is." Krissy fixed her with a level stare that indicated some additional meaning.

Sera furrowed her brow, wondering what the admiral was getting at. "I give. Are you saying I'm not strong-willed enough for what lies ahead?"

"Not at all," Krissy replied. "But what about your sisters? They were under your mother's sway once. What's to say they can't be turned to obey her once more?"

"Other than Finaeus and Earnest being certain of it?"

"Well…."

"I don't know of a stronger assurance than what those two men can give," Sera continued. "Stars, in the last decade, there've been more types of mental coercion going on than I even knew existed. The Rhoads thing, the Genevian mech Discipline, remnants, memories, shards, plus all the stuff the ISF has in their databases from the truly disturbing things people used to do back in Sol. On the plus side, Finaeus and Earnest have a vast array of information they can use to ensure that our minds are as secure as they can make them before we go to Airtha."

"Oh?" Krissy asked, appearing interested in the information. "How are they doing that? I mean, at the end of the day, our brains are still just organic neurons—and these ascended beings seem to be able to reach right past any perimeter defenses that mods may offer, and go right for the grey matter."

"You're thinking is behind, Krissy." Sera tapped the side of her head. "Earnest has been working on more ways to use picotech than just growing starships and making bombs. He's worked out a way to interlace pico-scale data encoding into neurons. With that, he can build a system that can protect our brains from tampering, and even reconstitute them to a prior state on the fly."

The admiral shivered convulsively. "That sounds a bit…scary. Doesn't that also mean that you could effectively reconfigure someone's brain on the fly?"

Sera nodded slowly. "As with most of the ISF's tech, used for good, it's amazing. But in the wrong hands…."

Krissy pursed her lips, nodding slowly. Then she leant forward, elbows on her desk.

"What are we going to do about it all after the war?"

"All what?" Sera asked.

"The tech…like how we're leaving jump gates all over the

Inner Stars—and notwithstanding the ISF's picotech, there's still a lot of *crazy* nanotech out there now. Stasis shields, jumping to the LMC, Airtha's ability to send black holes through jump gates in her crazy DMG ships…even this base! We're setting up jump gates beneath the cloudtops of a gas giant, and banking jumps around a black hole to obscure our origin…. How the core-damned stars are we going to stabilize things after the war?"

"Very carefully," Sera said with a wan smile.

<*Well, it'll help that we'll be leaving,*> Jen broke into the conversation.

"Sorry, Jen," Krissy gave a wincing smile. "I forgot that you're from New Canaan. What do you mean, 'leaving'?"

<*That's OK. I mean just what I said. When this war is over, we're all going to leave and take a lot of those problems with us.*>

"How?" Krissy's eyes narrowed in disbelief. "Will you really abandon New Canaan after spending so long on its worlds?"

Sera chuckled and shook her head. "No, they're taking them along, I suspect."

"OK, you two, what are you talking about?"

Sera met Krissy's eyes, her own deadly serious. "This is for you only. Do not share with anyone. Not even my sisters. Only a handful of people know about this—stars, I barely know anything beyond the most general outline."

"That being?"

"Tangel and her people plan to take their star and leave the galaxy."

Krissy's eyes grew wide as saucers. "Whaaaa?"

Sera nodded. "They've been working on it since the week Orion attacked them. I don't know the details of their plan, but your father believes it will work."

<*I don't know the exact timeline, but you have the gist of it,*> Jen agreed.

"My dad…Finaeus knows about this?" Krissy's mouth hung open after she spoke the words, then it snapped shut.

"Yes, he has been helping Earnest with some of the details—at least that's what I picked up. And…"

"There's an 'and'?"

"Well, if I make it to the end of this crazy war, I think I'm going to go with them. Before, I didn't think I could, but now with my father being back, and with my sisters…. I mean, if Jeffrey no longer wanted to run the Transcend, Seraphina would do fine, or…" Sera fixed Krissy with a level stare. "Or maybe you."

Krissy pushed back and shook her head. "Stars, no. I thought I wanted it back when—well, when the shit hit the fan at New Canaan. But trust me, I barely want the workload I have now; I saw what you were dealing with back at Khardine."

"Yeah," Sera nodded. "Anyone who wants to be in charge of something like the Transcend—at least anyone who wants it after having a taste of what it's really like—has a screw loose."

Krissy laughed. "So what are you saying about your father, then?"

A laugh slipped past Sera's lips, but she just shook her head and didn't reply.

"OK," the admiral shrugged her shoulders. "So if you hop aboard the Starship New Canaan, is part of the appeal a certain ruggedly handsome governor? I seem to recall you spending a lot of time together whenever he came to Khardine."

"Eh? What? Pardon?" Sera said with a grin splitting her lips. "I couldn't quite make that last out. You're mumbling a bit."

Krissy laughed, and a genuinely happy smile graced her lips. "Well I'm glad *someone's* having a lucky love life in the midst of this war."

Neither woman spoke for a minute, and then Sera ran a hand through her hair and met Krissy's eyes with a level gaze.

"OK. Here's what we do about Roxy, Jane, and Carmen…."

BLADES

STELLAR DATE: 10.05.8949 (Adjusted Years)
LOCATION: Epsilon
REGION: Sagittarius A*

Epsilon still had not made any headway in determining what Hades really was, let alone what the AI's goals were.

But something had changed.

Previously, Hades and its collective of other beings had stayed close to the Darkness, just outside the range of significant time dilation effects—something made easier with a supermassive black hole, as compared to smaller singularities.

Less massive black holes created smooth slopes in spacetime, but Darkness on the scale of Sagittarius A* effectively punched a hole in it.

Instead of a gradual gravity slope, there was a cliff that dropped through the fabric of the universe. Across one light second, spacetime's curve began to gently slope, and the next was a cliff—the bottom of which was the unknowable mass of the Darkness itself.

Hades maintained a string of smaller energy-harvesting facilities right on the edge of the Darkness's event horizon. Estimates from Epsilon's collective suggested that Hades generated far more power from those facilities than should have been possible from the small pieces of matter that his collective dropped into the black hole.

The best hypothesis was that Hades was tapping into differentials in the universe's vacuum energy that were caused when the supermassive black hole shredded matter. It was something Epsilon knew was possible, but he didn't know how Hades did it so efficiently.

Of course, because the other AI's collective ringed the

innermost fringes of the Darkness's equator, no one else could determine if there was some special property of that location. Epsilon suspected there was.

Given that Hades had been first to the core, it would be foolish to assume that he had not picked the most efficacious locale for himself.

The AI pushed those concerns from his mind and checked over the latest calculations for the jump to Andromeda. If he could not directly control the Darkness at the heart of the Milky Way Galaxy, he would perform his experiments at the core of another.

Epsilon had long considered the leap to Andromeda, testing out jumps to other minor galaxies in orbit of the Milky Way. All of those were successes, and his collective had both the energy and the ability to make the targeted jump.

But he wondered what they might find.

Amongst the Matri∞me, there was as much certainty as could be had that humanity—that annoyingly persistent step in evolution that had been necessary for AIs to arise—was on the leading edge of organic life.

While much life had been found in the Milky Way, progression of organisms from single to multi-cellular life was rare and far between. Just as rare were stars with well-configured planetary systems that remained safe harbors while that life evolved over the course of billions of years.

But that did not mean that another lifeform hadn't risen to prominence in the Andromeda Galaxy. And if such a lifeform had evolved, was it possible that they too had created their own non-organic scions?

Alerting what could be a superior race to the existence of intelligent beings in the Milky Way was a danger that many in Epsilon's collective often raised. It troubled him as well, but not so much that he would consider ignoring the Milky Way's sister galaxy. In fact, if there was intelligence on the rise in

Andromeda, he'd rather know about it sooner than not.

He was, however, resolved to be very cautious in his exploration. And if he did find other life, he would endeavor to wipe it out before it became a true threat—the same as he planned to do with the humans in the Milky Way.

But there was one thing he wanted to secure before he began to send exploratory forces to Andromeda.

If he gave the technology he sought too much thought, it would pain him that organics had discovered how to unlock successful information transfer via quantum entanglement before the Matri∞me had.

He consoled himself with the belief that the AI Bob must have helped his pet humans with the work—though Bob was still a child, so far as Epsilon was concerned, which meant that his aid to the humans was not a significant salve on Epsilon's ego.

The reports detailing the coordinated attack by Tanis Richards' forces on the Nietzschean armada in the Albany System had cemented his belief that they had the technology he'd sought for so long.

Bob's well-timed jump into Aldebaran to save Tanis—or perhaps Tangel, if rumors were to be believed—was another piece of evidence.

Instantaneous communication with his exploratory forces in Andromeda would be a significant advantage, should he encounter any intelligences there.

So while it rankled that he had not yet been able to determine *how* the humans had solved the quantum riddle, Epsilon was determined to steal it from them.

ROXY

STELLAR DATE: 10.05.8949 (Adjusted Years)
LOCATION: River Station, Styx Baby-9
REGION: STX-B17 Black Hole, Transcend Interstellar Alliance

Roxy paced across her suite's mainspace, wishing she had *some* sort of information about Jane and Carmen; a simmering resentment against Sera for keeping them separated grew within her.

She stopped at the window and stared out at the scene without. It was beyond impressive, and certainly served to keep her mind off her personal woes for a time.

River Station spread for hundreds of kilometers in every direction—though it was less a station, and more a web of docking spurs.

Spurs that were laden with thousands of starships.

At the far end of the station, a hundred jump gates were arrayed, some so large she couldn't fathom what sort of ship existed that would use such a thing.

The might on display made it obvious that Justin's ambitions had been nothing more than the preening of a man who hated to lose. There was no way he would have been able to muster the strength to defeat a fleet this large with this many gates at its disposal.

She estimated that Admiral Krissy would be able to move her entire force—which had to be approaching a hundred thousand ships—to *any* location within half an hour. Given that they were adding more gates, it was likely that the deployment would ultimately dwindle to mere minutes.

"To what end?" she whispered, wondering what the target was.

The question was largely rhetorical. Roxy knew that there

were only three targets that mattered: Airtha, New Sol, and Sol.

She'd scoured what network sources she could access and had picked up on some clues from scuttlebutt. What little she'd learned led her to believe that all the efforts of the Inner Stars and Orion space were still being directed from Khardine, which meant that this fleet was preparing to strike Airtha.

<Roxy, are you available?>

Sera Tomlinson's voice entered Roxy's mind, and she found herself both glad to know that a resolution to her current worries was on her doorstep, and fearful of what that resolution would entail.

<I am. Come in.>

She turned to watch as two women—both wearing the face of Sera Tomlinson—entered her suite. One was the woman in red she'd tried to kill on the docks a few days prior, and the other was a mirror image, though she seemed to prefer shades of blue.

"Ummm, hello," Roxy said without walking toward the two women.

"Good morning," the red Sera said. "This is my sister Fina. Sorry it's taken so long, but we're here to talk to you about your future, and Jane's, to an extent."

Roxy inclined her head, not trusting herself to speak. A minute ago, she'd thought that she was entirely prepared to have this conversation, but at the mere mention of Jane's name, she found that her ability to speak was gone.

After Roxy had attacked Sera on the docks, she'd gone unconscious—something she was told was common during the removal of a remnant. When she awoke, Carmen was no longer within her, and Jane had been sequestered.

Over the intervening days, a long string of tests and interrogations had been conducted, none of which had given Roxy any information about her friends.

"You've been worried about Jane and Carmen, haven't you?" Fina asked as the two women walked across the suite. "We're sorry that you've been kept separate from them."

Roxy wanted to lash out, but she knew that if the tables had been turned, she'd have done the same, so instead, she only nodded mutely.

"Well, you'll be reunited with them shortly," Sera said, her expression one of sincerity and a little concern. "Though the nature of that reunion is partially dependent on what you wish to see happen."

The two women reached Roxy, standing next to the window that displayed the majestic scene beyond.

She finally found her voice. "What do you mean?"

<*I'm Jen, I'm paired with Sera.*> An AI's voice came into Roxy's mind. <*Carmen has been disciplined for her dereliction by the station's AI council. We've determined that she is in contrition for her actions, and has accepted a Limitation as a punishment for her crimes.*>

"A Limitation?" Roxy asked. "It wasn't her fault. What she did, I did to her…I made her do it."

Sera held up her hand and shook her head. "Carmen has admitted her own guilt in failing to destroy the *Damon Silas.* However, her efforts to retrieve the ship and return it have mitigated her punishment—as well as her efforts to help you, Roxy."

<*Her Limitation is minor,*> Jen added with a note of sympathy.

"What is it?" Roxy asked, largely unfamiliar with how AIs disciplined one another.

<*She will never be allowed to be a ship's AI again. An alteration has been made to her mind that will preclude her from such a position, no matter when and where she would attempt it,*> Jen explained. <*She must also spend a decade paired with a human to reinforce her understanding of others beyond herself. If no human is*

willing to accept her, then she'll have to spend a century caring for an expanse.>

"Well, she can pair with me," Roxy said without hesitation.

<*We'd considered that you might make that offer,*> Jen replied, and then paused.

"I sense a 'but' coming," Roxy said in the intervening silence.

"Jen is trying to decide how to delicately say that you're not a human—exactly," Sera replied with an apologetic shrug.

"And that somehow makes me less than you?" the woman asked, doing her best to measure her tone. Scolding the former president of the Transcend—or whatever Sera's exact position was now—wasn't wise.

"Not at all. We're kinda used to people who are somewhere in-between," Fina said with a wink. "We're currently planning a mission where we have a woman whose brain is in a spider-bot, another who is an AI merged with a human inside a semi-organic brain, and then there's Cheeky, who is the restoration of a human's brain converted to an AI that resides in a largely organic body. Stars…next to that, Sera and I are practically normal."

Sera snorted and gave Fina a mock-judging look—at least that's how Roxy interpreted it.

"Speak for yourself, Sis. There's not a normal bone in my body."

"That's because they've all been carbon-poly enhanced."

"Touché." Sera chuckled, and then turned her gaze back to Roxy. "Look. You're not exactly a stock human, but that's OK. Pretty much everyone going—"

"Except Misha," Fina interrupted.

"Misha?" Roxy asked.

"The cook," Sera explained, nodding in agreement with Fina. "*Sabrina*'s cook is almost entirely unmodded. I suppose a few of Katrina's crew are closer to the 'stock human' end of the spectrum, too."

Roxy frowned at the two women before her, trying to make sense of what they were saying. "Wait. Why does this mission of yours have a cook?"

"Well…I mean, the op will take a bit, and I like to eat," Fina said with a wink.

Sera nodded. "Plus, it seems to have worked for the team quite well in the past—having a cook on covert missions, that is. Which makes no sense…. I don't know, whatever."

"Seriously? Does he actually go on missions?" Roxy asked, shaking her head in disbelief.

"Well…he was part of the team that stormed General Garza's command ship at New Canaan."

"Really?" Fina asked, glancing at Sera. "I gotta admit, I kinda *liked* Misha before. Now he might even be kinda hot."

"Stars, Fina." Sera laughed. "Sometimes I think Airtha mixed a bit of Cheeky in with you."

Roxy's gaze slid from one woman to the other, marveling at how they seemed completely identical—barring their strong devotion to a different primary color—yet were so distinct at the same time.

"I have to ask…." Roxy said the words slowly, uncertain of how to phrase the question.

"What it's like to suddenly get a fully grown, annoying kid sister?" Sera asked, saving Roxy from having to voice the words.

"Well…yeah. Something like that."

Fina knocked her hip against Sera's. "It hasn't been too bad. Not since I convinced her that blue is *my* color, at least."

Roxy held up her hand, sapphire skin gleaming. "I still don't know what to do about my skin. What, with it being something *he* did to me."

"Do you like it?" Fina asked, tilting her head as she looked Roxy up and down. "If you like it, rock it."

"I'm going to have to agree with my sister there," Sera confirmed. "When I got my first skin replacement, it wasn't exactly voluntary."

"We," Fina corrected. "We were the same person back then."

"Right, sorry," Sera replied.

<Hey, I know you all like talking about cooks and your funky fashion sense, but there's still an unresolved issue at hand,> Jen interrupted.

"What to do about Carmen." Roxy nodded and pursed her lips. "You were going to say that she can't pair with me for her penance, because I'm not human anymore."

<It's less about that, and more about the nature of your mind.> Jen's reply carried a note of apology. *<The point in having AIs pair with humans is more to teach both species about the other and cause them to think of one another as people who have value even though they're different. It fosters a feeling of familiarity and decreases the 'othering' that both species are prone to.>*

Roxy nodded. "I understand that."

<So there are two problems. The first is that we can't actually pair Carmen with you because your mind isn't really compatible to a standard pairing. The other is that it won't be the instructive experience—shit! Sera. Why didn't I think of this before?>

Roxy watched Sera's eyes grow wide, and then the red woman nodded.

"Well, there was another thing that we need to discuss with you," she said, her voice taking on a more serious tone than it had carried before.

"Jane." The name fell from Roxy's lips like lead.

"Yes. I imagine you know why."

Roxy nodded. "She took advantage of me."

"Or *raped* you," Fina suggested.

"No." Roxy shook her head vehemently. "She and I talked this over a lot on the trip here. She knew that I couldn't exactly say no, but she thought I liked it—she thought I'd modded myself to be that way. That's what Justin had told everyone."

"Damn." Fina shook her head in disbelief. "I'd always thought he did things that were on the edge of unethical, but I guess I completely misread him. Guy was a grade-A scumbag."

Sera pursed her lips and locked eyes with Roxy. "So you really don't want to press charges against Jane for sexual assault?"

Roxy shook her head. "No. She and Carmen…they're all I have. Damn, I guess all that means is that I'm totally fucked up, doesn't it?"

The two women—twins of sorts, Roxy supposed—glanced at one another and shrugged in unison.

"Who's not?" Sera asked. "Given that you don't want to press charges…. Jen, do you want to present the option—not that it's really any of our call, anyway."

<Sure. So what occurred to me, Roxy, is that perhaps Carmen and Jane could pair.>

At first, the idea sounded anathema to Roxy. Carmen was *her* friend, someone that she wanted to keep close. But then she thought of Jane, who was dealing with her own demons, and considered how the three of them could still be together. Different, but together.

"I…I guess it's not my call either, but I can see why it's not terrible."

Sera laughed as she glanced at Fina. " 'Not terrible'. Some days, that's the best we can hope for, isn't it?"

"Seems like it," the blue woman replied.

"One more thing for you to consider," Sera said to Roxy.

"Stars," Roxy muttered. "I think there's a lot more than just one more thing."

"Well, this one will add to the list in a big way. You're a highly skilled operative, from what you've remembered about your past life—you were once one of the best Hand agents in the galaxy. We want you to join us on our mission."

Roxy couldn't help but grin at the two women before her. "The mission with the cook that has Fina all a-titter?"

Fina snorted. "I do *not* titter."

"Yeah, that one," Sera confirmed.

"What's the goal of this mysterious mission?"

The words that came from Sera's lips were spoken with such dead certainty, Roxy knew there was no way she could say no.

"We're going to kill Airtha."

PART 2 – ORION SPACE

SVETLANA

STELLAR DATE: 10.07.8949 (Adjusted Years)
LOCATION: TSS *Cossack's Sword*, Interstellar Dark Layer
REGION: Midway Cluster, Orion Freedom Alliance Space

"So?" Admiral Svetlana asked Command Master Chief Merrick, doing her best to suppress the feeling that she was turning in homework to her father for review. "How does my plan look?"

Her father, the senior noncom in the fleet, glanced up from the holo spreading across the desk and met her eyes.

"If you need me to tell you it's good enough, then it's not."

Svetlana clenched her jaw, refusing to break eye contact with the man. "I'm not asking you to tell me it's good enough, I'm asking you to point out flaws. Right now, that's your job. It's not to be my father, trying to prepare me for the big, bad world."

For a moment he didn't respond, other than the further narrowing of his eyes. Then, to her surprise, he pulled his gaze away first, a laugh escaping his lips.

"Well, Admiral." He glanced at her for a moment before gesturing at the map. "Machete's going to be a tough nut to crack. I have some ideas about improvements to your strategy, but walk me through your plan first, so I can understand your reasoning."

"Very well, Command Master Chief."

"Svetlana. You can call me Merrick." Her father winked before taking a step back and folding his arms across his chest.

She drew a deep breath and restrained herself from telling him that his mixed signals weren't helping her find a comfortable working arrangement.

Best to just get this over with.

"OK," she began. "Machete is a semi-autonomous system in the Perseus Expansion Districts—at least they were until the Oggies began massing a fleet there. From what the Hand databases have on the place, it's pretty backward, founded by refugees from near the Flaming Star Nebula a few thousand years back. Barely anyone has even their low-tech version of the Link."

"Seems like par for the course out here," Merrick commented.

"Yeah," Svetlana agreed. "Anyway, Machete is a triple star system. The main planets orbit the tight binary pair, Hawenneyu and Doyadastethe. The corporations have been doing a lot of asteroid mining in that part of the system, ferrying materials out to the third star, which is currently sixty AU away."

"Why did the Hand send an agent there, I wonder?" Merrick asked as Svetlana paused.

"The reports I have say there was indication of some advanced medical R&D going on in Machete, but it turned out to be nothing of note. The Hand has been looking for RHY's new secret R&D facilities since the ISF's Jessica Keller learned of the bioweapons they were making out in the Perseus Arm."

"And the agent just stayed?" Merrick asked.

"He was waiting for new orders. Seems like he got lost in the shuffle, what with the civil war and all. He wasn't sure which Sera to trust, so he sat tight."

"Not the worst plan when you're a thousand light years deep in hostile territory."

"Agreed." Svetlana nodded. "Another part of his rationale for sticking around was that he began to hear rumblings about shipyards out near the third star, Gendenwitha. I guess one of the corporations set up a backroom deal with the Oggies and has been building ships there for some time. Initially, they were just doing hulls and engines, but now the OG has brought their engineering teams in to bolt on the guns."

"Best time to hit them, then…well, other than a year or two ago."

"Right." Svetlana gestured at the system map laid out before them. "Now, the third star only has one planet in orbit, Sosondowah, and a few dozen shipyards are in orbit of its moons. I think that—given this system's general isolation—we should seize those shipyards and then make off with their ships."

Her father only grunted in response, and Svetlana went on with her explanation.

"From what intel the Hand agent has, he thinks that we'll need to make a pretty large strike against the main worlds, if we're to get the Oggies to move any assets from the third star to protect them. Basically, no one cares about the people on those worlds. We'll have to put the populace's ability to supply the raw materials for shipbuilding at risk before the enemy tries to dislodge us."

"So we hit the mining facilities," her father replied. "Ignore the worlds."

"That was my thought; but we still have to stop the corporate militias from coming after us, so I figured we strike the mines while simultaneously bottling up the populace so they can't work the facilities. Make it *look* like we plan to stay awhile."

"And Orion has another large force nearby?" Merrick asked.

"The Hand agent doesn't think so, but his intel on that front is a bit old. Either way, if the Oggies do bring in another fleet, we cut and run. Even if this strike is only a distraction, it still serves our general purpose."

Her father, the ancient Command Master Chief, the man she had spent much of her life both respecting and fearing—though the fear had waned over the years—nodded slowly.

"Agreed. Worst-case scenario, we destroy the shipyards and cripple their ability to pull resources from the mines."

"But I don't want to strike directly at civilians," she clarified. "They're not our targets here."

"Svetlana. This is war. Civilians are going to die."

"I know." She met his eyes with her own level gaze. "We already killed a fair number in the Ferra System. But we only hit them when they're stationed at legitimate targets. I won't decimate the people just to create a humanitarian crisis in order to wear the Oggies down. You know that the enemy is just as likely to bail on Machete as give them aid."

"I agree," Merrick said after a moment. "Ultimately, if this crazy plan that Krissy and the Tomlinsons have cooked up works, we'll be the ones to bring these people into the ninetieth century, and it would be nice if they didn't hate us too much."

"That's going to take a miracle," Svetlana said with a rueful shake of her head.

"Probably, but there have been a few of them lately, so I'll hold out hope."

She barked a laugh. "Who are you, and what have you done with my father? I distinctly remember you saying on many occasions that 'hope is not a plan'."

Merrick shrugged. "Well, like I said, I've seen some things lately that have changed the way I view the universe."

"It's a bit surreal, isn't it?"

"Are you trying to win an award for understatement?" Her father laughed as he spoke, a real laugh. It even seemed happy.

"OK, Dad, what's going on here?"

"What do you mean?"

"You have a bit of a reputation, with me personally, as well as in the force. You're not usually so…."

"Agreeable?"

"That's one way to put it."

Merrick took a step back and ran a hand through his hair. "Yeah, I know. I guess I was starting to think that the stalemate with Orion was going to last forever, or it was going to lead to a war of attrition in the Inner Stars that would send them back into another dark age. And at the end of it, we'd all end up at the status quo for another few thousand years."

"It did seem like the president didn't have the stomach to do what needed to be done." Svetlana realized she'd just run her hand through her hair in the same manner as her father, and blushed before shifting to stand arms akimbo.

"Yeah, but now we have Tanis…or Tangel. Whatever she is now. AI merge, ascended being, I don't care. She's doing the right stuff with this multi-pronged war, even if the timing hasn't been great."

Svetlana chuckled. "That's an understatement."

"Which part?"

"All of them, I guess." She stepped forward and put her hands on the holotable. "I'm in agreement with you. Being out here in OFA space and kicking them in the balls feels right—but it's a bit desperate, too."

"A bit?"

"OK, a lot."

A silence settled between them. It wasn't uncomfortable, but rather companionable—a feeling Svetlana had not often had with her father.

She was about to bring the conversation back to the Machete plan, when he spoke. His voice was quiet, almost apologetic.

"You know, I had to twist Admiral Krissy's arm pretty

hard to be here with you," Merrick said, and then coughed a short laugh. "To be honest, I would have punched babies if that's what it took."

"Dad! That's an awful visual."

Her father snorted and shook his head. "Yeah, well, us noncoms are rough around the edges. I was always glad you went in for OCS. And here you are, an admiral, leading that first major incursion into Orion in over a thousand years."

"I'm glad you're here, too, Dad. I'm a little terrified. There's a lot riding on this. Not just our lives, but the lives of the people at the front. We *have* to draw the Oggies back. If we don't, then this is all for nothing."

Command Master Chief Merrick walked around the table and held open his arms.

Svetlana somehow managed to keep her jaw from falling open as she accepted her father's embrace.

"It's a lot on your shoulders, Svetlana. But you're a strong girl. I know; I had to deal with your obstinance for years as I attempted to raise you. Luckily for everyone in this fleet, you've turned into an amazing woman despite my interference in the matter."

"*Because* of your interference, Dad, because of it," Admiral Svetlana whispered as she laid a head on his shoulder.

"If you say so," Merrick whispered back. "Damn…I wish your mother was here to see this."

Svetlana nodded wordlessly, and the two held each other tightly. After a few minutes, her father pulled back and glanced at the holotable.

"OK. So as amazing as I think you are, I do have a few suggestions about your plan…."

The admiral let out a nervous laugh and nodded. "Buttering me up, were you?"

"Never, Svetlana. Never."

MACHETE

STELLAR DATE: 10.18.8949 (Adjusted Years)
LOCATION: TSS *Cossack's Sword*, approaching Sosondowah
REGION: Machete System, PED 4B, Orion Freedom Alliance

Sosondowah, the lone planet orbiting Gendenwitha, slowly grew larger on the main display as the ship approached—though Svetlana knew it to be only an illusion used to give the bridge crew the feeling of motion.

In all honesty, the battlegroup had been close enough for high-resolution images for over a day now—though the Oggies didn't know that.

Elsewhere in the Machete System, Rear Admiral Sebastian and the ISF's Colonel Caldwell were nearly at the world of Iagaentci, the largest population center in orbit around the other stars in the Machete system.

They'd debated hitting the other terraformed planet, a largely agrarian world named Akonwara, but ultimately decided to leave it be. There were no major orbital habitats there, and Svetlana didn't want to drop troops down into a gravity well.

Iagaentci's two large stations each held hundreds of millions of inhabitants—engineering feats that harkened back to a time when the people of Machete were far more advanced in both technology and industry than the level they'd fallen to when the OFA absorbed their system.

Admiral Sebastian's fleet would blockade that world and its stations, while Colonel Caldwell was tasked with hitting the mining facilities in orbit of the world of Geha, where large KPOs were hauled in for refinement before drones utilizing gravitational assists slingshotted the ore around Hawenneyu to the shipyards that Svetlana was closing on.

So far, at least from the movements of the Orion Guard ships spread out around Sosondowah and its shipyards, the enemy had no idea that Svetlana's ships were approaching.

While her battlegroup's stealth capabilities weren't as good as those of the ISF ships under Caldwell's command, they'd been careful to bleed off as much heat as possible before going into the dark layer, where no heat could be bled off because there was nowhere for it to bleed off to.

During the dark layer transit, the ships pumped as much heat as possible into the cooling vanes, until every ship's trailing streamers were nearly melting. Right before transitioning back into normal space, each ship cut their cooling vanes loose, along with a DL transition system, leaving their excess heat to drift though the dark until the power drained away—or they met the hungry maw of an Exdali.

That transition out of the dark layer was now several days behind them, and the enemy had given no hint that they'd spotted the inbound ships. Either the heat bleed had been enough to fool the enemy, or Svetlana's battlegroup was drifting into a trap.

While her ships were maintaining a low energy profile, the battlegroups under the command of Admiral Sebastian and Colonel Caldwell were doing just the opposite. Immediately after dumping out of the dark layer, their ships had boosted hard for the more populous regions of the system, telegraphing their approach and making it appear as though they were going to perform a strafing run before exiting the system.

Many hours ago, the other two battlegroups would have fired their initial volleys at the system's defensive emplacements and turned to begin braking maneuvers. Given the ten-hour light lag between the two locations, confirmation of those events was expected at any moment—which is where Svetlana's current sense of unease came from.

Once they knew that the battle had begun in the other region of the Machete System, her battlegroup could ready their strike.

She was about to ask Scan if there were any signs of the attack—though she thought if they had something, they'd relay it—when Scan gave an exultant whoop.

"Confirming strikes on alpha targets!"

And just like that, the tension on the bridge was broken.

Svetlana shook her head, but didn't fault the ensign for his unprofessionalism as she put the readings on the main tank. Sure enough, gamma and x-ray emissions from around the other two stars in the Machete System confirmed that the main defensive batteries had been destroyed.

"Data burst from Admiral Sebastian," Comm announced a moment later. "The locals laid down some heavy rail fire, but with jinking and the stasis shields, no ships were damaged."

"Like shooting fish in a barrel," Svetlana said quietly.

<We should see the Oggies in our neck of the woods respond in the next thirty minutes,> Gala, the *Cossack's Sword*'s AI, announced.

"Or sooner, I hope," Svetlana said, looking at the time it would take her battlegroup to reach effective firing range: just under thirty-two hours.

Time to hurry up and wait.

* * * * *

The hours passed as slowly as expected, except for a brief surge of excitement when the Orion Guard mustered a fleet of seven hundred ships and sent them toward the system's main stars, Iagaentci and Geha, where the other Hoplite battlegroups were wreaking havoc.

"It's going to be close," General Lorelai said from the far side of the bridge's main holo, where she was watching the enemy ships as they flew toward the system's other stars. "If the Oggies pick us up even an hour before we strike their shipyards, the fleet they sent will have time to turn around and hit us."

Svetlana nodded while chewing on the inside of her cheek. "It's tight. I have weapons control examining a surprise for the Oggies, should they try that."

"Oh?" the general asked, looking up to meet Svetlana's gaze. "What sort of surprise?"

Fast-forwarding the display to where the Orion reinforcement fleet would be at the critical juncture, Svetlana showed what their trajectory would look like if they braked and came back around to protect the shipyards.

"This is the most fuel-efficient route. They'll take an anti-spinward vector and then come around Sosondowah, using the star for a gravity brake."

"Seems logical," the general agreed. "What are you going to do? Hit them with RMs?"

"No," Svetlana set her jaw before replying. "Grapeshot. If we can make some small adjustments, we'll cross their return path, and can fire volleys of grapeshot along it."

The soldier shuddered. "Stars, I hate that shit. Barbaric."

"I won't deny that," Svetlana replied with a slow nod. "But it's effective, and the goal is to take them out before they do the same to us."

"So long as you get my people's boots safely on the ground," Lorelai replied after a moment's pause.

"Are you still in agreement about the targets?" Svetlana asked as she shifted the holodisplay to show two of the largest shipyards, creatively named Trumark-Alpha and Trumark-Omega.

"Sure. We take those two, you blow the rest. Just make sure you can take out the remaining Orion patrol boats before our assault shuttles hit vacuum."

Svetlana found herself liking General Lorelai more than most ground pounders. The woman was always respectful, but never deferential. You never wondered where you stood with her. Yet somehow, she managed never to come off as crass or rude—mostly.

"Don't worry," Svetlana replied. "We'll take them. Unless they have a whole host of ships hiding in some dark corner, there are only seventy patrol craft guarding the shipyards now. Most are pinnaces or corvettes, just a couple are destroyers."

"Don't forget all those defensive emplacements," Lorelai added. "Alpha and Omega are between the planet's moons, too. You know they'll have rail emplacements on them."

Svetlana nodded. "Our Hand agent sent us some data he lifted on Trumark during a raid he made there not long ago. I believe we know where their emplacements are, and we're going to shield the assault craft."

"Sounds hairy," Lorelai said with a laugh, glancing at the ship's pilot. "Got your work cut out for you, Lieutenant. You better keep us safe as we go in."

The man gave the general a crisp nod. "Yes, ma'am."

"Does your wording mean that you're planning to go on the strike?" Svetlana asked.

"Sorry," Lorelai crossed her arms and shook her head. "Freudian slip, there. I *want* to go in, but I need to be up here on your bird coordinating things. Colonels Yuri and Mila will have things well in hand."

"Good," Svetlana replied, winking at the general. "For what it's worth, I don't blame you for wanting to get your hands dirty."

"I'll get to eventually…maybe when we make a planetside strike," Lorelai replied.

"Stars, if we have to actually pound ground, we're doing this wrong."

The general barked a laugh. "Just like a spacer, Admiral. Always have your head in the stars."

* * * * *

Colonel Caldwell of the ISF stood arms akimbo on the bridge of his ship, the *Daring Strike,* which was aptly named, considering what they were about to attempt.

His fifty-six rail destroyers—the dual concentric ring ships that Admiral Tanis had resurrected from an old Scattered Disk design—had just decimated the mining facilities situated around the Machete System's largest gas giant, Geha.

He'd given the locals fair warning, and most had fled, taking every available ship and shuttle to the terrestrial worlds Akonwara and Iagaentci.

The corporation that owned the mines, however, was not giving in so easily.

He'd already destroyed their stationary emplacements, and now all that remained were six hundred and ten of their ships. The vast majority of those vessels were little more than shuttles. There were some freighters with enough firepower to defend themselves from pirates or stray rocks, but they wouldn't begin to pose a threat to the ISF ships. A smattering of corvettes and a dozen destroyers made up the remainder of the corporate fleet.

Plus one ship that Caldwell begrudgingly classified as a cruiser.

"They're hailing us again, sir," Lieutenant Sandy said from the comm station. "Demanding that we stand down."

Thus far, Caldwell had not accepted any incoming communication attempts from the Pritney-Dax corporate wags. He'd issued a statement declaring his intent to destroy the mining platforms in orbit of Geha, weathered a barrage from the stationary defense systems with no damage, and then destroyed them all with waves of rail-accelerated pellets.

He felt that his battlegroup's actions were all the communication that needed to be had—something the civilians demonstrated an understanding of when they'd bailed from the mining platforms in droves.

Caldwell's lips twitched in a smile at the memory of Geha's planetary space traffic control trying to deny the fleeing ships flight vectors in an attempt to get them to stay and defend the mines. Eventually, the STC's personnel resigned themselves to the inevitability of the exodus and began to assign lanes and keep as many ships from crossing vectors as they could.

It was still a mess, but that wasn't Caldwell's problem.

"I guess we can have a conversation, at least so I can tell them 'I told you so' later," he said to the comm officer. "Put them on the tank."

Lieutenant Sandy gave a curt nod, and an image shimmered into place before him. A tall, reedy man wore a crisp suit that had his employer's name and logo emblazoned across the chest.

"Colonel Caldwell, I presume?" the man asked in an imperious tone. He didn't allow any time for a response before continuing, "I am Harold Ems of Pritney-Dax. I don't know what the hell you think you're doing, but you have five minutes to reverse course and get out of PD space."

"Good to meet you, Harold," Caldwell replied equably. "I must admit, your statement makes me a bit curious. What *I'd* really like to know is what you *think* I'm doing."

"P-pardon?" the man stammered as his brow lowered in consternation. "What are you getting at?"

"Well," Caldwell tapped his chin. "You said that you 'don't know what the hell' I think I'm doing, but that can't be right. You've gotta have at least an inkling. I can give you some hints, if it's too hard. We're not here for teatime."

Lieutenant Sandy gave a soft snort from Caldwell's right,

and he allowed his lip to twitch into a half smile as well.

"What I'm getting at," the man representing Pritney-Dax ground out the words as though he hated the very thought of communicating with Caldwell, "is that it doesn't matter what you have planned. If you don't leave, we're going to destroy you. And in case math is also a problem for you, you're sorely outnumbered."

"Are we? Really?" Caldwell held up a hand and counted his fingers, scowling at them as he folded each one down in turn. "Hmmm...looks like you're right. But there's math, and then there's math. I suspect that things such as calculating a ship's destructive capability are beyond you. I'll make this simple, though. I'll give you the same amount of time you were offering me—five minutes—to power down shields and surrender."

"Who are you, anyway?" Harold Ems demanded. "You know that the Orion Guard is coming for you, right?"

Caldwell barked a laugh. "Know about it? We're counting on it."

The company man froze for a few seconds, his holopresence too still, and Caldwell could tell he had paused the feed while he spoke with his advisors.

"Closing in on four minutes," Caldwell said after several more seconds had ticked by.

The company man suddenly moved again, and Caldwell almost laughed at the sudden change in his skin color. Harold was much redder than a moment prior.

"You never answered my question. Who are you?" Harold demanded.

"Well...have you ever heard of the Transcend?" Caldwell asked. "They're the other half of the FGT that Orion doesn't want you to know about. We've been at loggerheads with Orion for some time and we're finally having it out. That's what's going on here. Technically, my ships and I are just allies of the Transcend, but since your people—that's Orion, just so we're clear—attacked our colony, we threw in with the good guys and came out here to kick Orion in the ass."

"How eloquent," the man sneered.

Caldwell chuckled. "Say whatever makes you feel good. You have three minutes now."

"And if we don't surrender?" Harold asked, growing redder still.

"Then we'll cut down your fleet until you do, starting with your ship." He spoke the words without malice.

He was relatively certain that if he took out Harold's ship, the rest of the Pritney-Dax fleet would surrender, and in the end, he'd keep the death toll to a minimum.

"Like hell you will," the other man spat, and the comm channel closed.

"Enemy beams are hot!" Scan called out. "We're being tagged."

The defense holodisplay lit up with signatures, as over half the enemy ships in range fired on the *Daring Strike.*

<*Shields deflecting,*> Lorne announced. <*Not that we expected otherwise. It's like they're shooting spitballs.*>

Caldwell could see the energy readings, and it was clear that the Pritney-Dax vessels were firing a lot more than spitwads. Without the protection of stasis shields, the *Daring Strike* would have been torn to pieces.

<*Response?*> Lorne asked.

The *Daring Strike*'s AI was operating as the Fleet Coordination Officer for Caldwell's battlegroup, and the colonel could tell he was eager to fire back at the corporate militia with extreme prejudice.

"Have Wings two and four hit the engines on ol' Harold's cruiser there," Caldwell instructed. "Just disable it. Show them that our flying donuts mean business."

<*I hate it when you call my ship a flying donut,*> Lorne

complained, but sent out the order without further question.

Indicators on the holo lit up, showing streams of rail pellets streaking through the half a light second of space between the ships.

For the first few seconds, the enemy cruiser's rear shields held, light flaring around the aft section of the ship as grav deflectors absorbed the kinetic energy and redirected it back into space.

But the barrage was too much for the cruiser to handle. One of its aft umbrellas failed, and a stream of pellets tore clear through the rear of the cruiser, nearly slicing off one of the engines. Moments later, similar events repeated on the other side of the cruiser, rendering it dead in the water.

Caldwell fully expected that to be the end of it. The enemy had to realize that there was no way they could stand up to his destroyers—even if they did outnumber him twelve to one.

"I have engine flares!" Scan cried out, and a secondary display came up on Caldwell's left, showing a large group of objects rising out of Geha's cloudtops.

"Ships?" he asked, as data began to accumulate on the thrust and size of the objects—which was taking several seconds, given the distance to the planet.

<*No,*> Lorne weighed in. <*They're consistent with RMs.*>

"Shit," Caldwell muttered. "I wouldn't have expected these luddites to have, what…two hundred of those things?"

<*Maybe they bought them on auction,*> the AI replied.

"Funny. Direct the fleet into pattern Alpha Eleven, FCO."

<*Aye,*> Lorne replied.

On the main holo, the colonel watched as the Pritney-Dax fleet began to boost toward his destroyers. Each squadron was concentrating fire on different ISF destroyers, and Caldwell suspected they were hoping to find ships without stasis shields.

"All ships," he addressed his battlegroup captains on the

all-fleet network. "Engage targets by wing. Hit their destroyers first, then switch to the corvettes. Lorne, assign targeting priorities."

Caldwell didn't really need to say the words; he and his fleet strategists had already planned out responses to all the possible actions the enemy could take. The ships had their targets for every scenario; all they needed to do was enact them.

*At least I **hope** it'll be that straightforward.*

An attack by elements hidden within Geha's cloudtops had been near the top of the list for defensive actions that the enemy would take. Wing One was closest to the gas giant and fired wide spreads of grapeshot at the inbound relativistic missiles, the tactical displays showing that the relativistic chaff was on target to hit the enemy missiles before they hit the ISF ships.

"Waste of RMs," he muttered. "Things were only going to get up to a quarter *c* at best."

"Sir, why do you think they didn't fire them at us when we first approached?" Lieutenant Sandy asked.

<*I wager it's corporate expense monitoring,*> Lorne replied before Caldwell could offer his thoughts. <*RMs are expensive. I bet they hoped to scare us off before they had to resort to them. Ultimately, I imagine the missiles are less expensive than ships and mining platforms.*>

"Yeah," Caldwell grunted. "That."

Sandy laughed and frowned at her console. "I'm picking up a burst of communication between the cruiser and the mining platforms."

"What about?" the colonel asked.

"Umm, not sure, I—"

The bridge crew's attention was grabbed by the main holotank lighting up as Wing One's grapeshot hit the leading edge of the inbound RMs.

A few of the missiles went up in nuclear fireballs from the impacts, the resulting plasma clouds smearing into long streaks by the velocity of the weapons. Most, however, were shredded before the nukes within could detonate, turning the missiles into showers of still deadly kinetic energy, but energy now on predictable vectors.

<*We got half,*> Lorne announced in the second between the explosions and the initial impacts of relativistic debris against the formation's left flank.

Caldwell pursed his lips, praying that the stasis shields would hold. Even though he'd been under heavy fire multiple times during the Defense of Carthage, every time incoming fire of that magnitude hit his ships, he half expected the shields to fail.

Nuclear fireballs enveloped the entire left flank, dissipating into streaks of plasma as quickly as they appeared, revealing that every ISF ship was intact and undamaged.

<*The wing commander reports that four ships are having problems with their SC batts. They're running their reactors hot,*> Lorne reported, and Caldwell nodded in acknowledgement.

"Not surprised. Those were big warheads. Instruct them to fall back until they cool down."

Despite the calm that Caldwell took care to display to his bridge crew, he felt a mixture of fear and excitement as the attack on Wing One kicked off the battle in earnest.

The ISF destroyers relied heavily on their rails, but they were also equipped with beams, and the space between the two fleets was awash with relativistic particles and the comparatively slower kinetics.

"Oh shit! I know what orders the cruiser sent to the mining platforms!"

Sandy's outburst grabbed Caldwell's attention, and he turned to see her staring wide-eyed as she flung a view up on the holo.

Dozens of rocks in a nearby debris field had begun to move, hurtling toward the ISF fleet.

"It's not going to be enough," Caldwell assured her while ordering Wing Two to fire on the rocks. "It's not hard to outmaneuver a flying boulder."

The ISF ships continued their inexorable advance on the defenders, destroying every weapon the enemy brought to bear, until just over half the Pritney-Dax ships remained. As the last enemy destroyer was crippled, the enemy fleet began to scatter, nearly every craft still able to maneuver boosting away from the ISF ships.

"Hail our friend Harold again, Lieutenant," Caldwell instructed, and Sandy nodded as she sent out the call.

A moment later, a decidedly haggard-looking Harold appeared on the holo.

"We surrender," he replied meekly. "We…I…how?"

Caldwell felt a moment's pity for the man. The way that Orion kept these people stuck in the dark ages, there was little they could do to defend against a superior foe. Even if the ISF ships had not possessed stasis shields, he was certain he could have defeated the corporate fleet without trouble—though it may have involved actual losses on his side.

"The galaxy has passed you by, Harold," he replied. "Orion restricted your development and left your people vulnerable. There's no shame in it."

"And yet, here you come to greedily take advantage of that weakness," Harold shot back, a sneer forming on his lips.

"This is war, Harold." The thrill of victory dissipated, and the colonel blew out a long breath. "I'm sure there's a long history of tit-for-tat dating back to some ancient slight, but the fact of the matter is that my people were attacked by yours, and we're here to make sure it doesn't happen again."

"But we don't even know anything about that. About who your people even are!"

"We're blowing your mining platforms in forty minutes, Harold Ems of Pritney-Dax," Caldwell replied without emotion. "Instruct any of your remaining people to abandon the facilities. So long as your ships keep their shields lowered, we'll allow you to perform search and rescue operations. But the moment shields come up, we fire. Am I clear?"

The corporate ship captain nodded slowly, his face a mask of anguish. "Yes. You're perfectly clear."

"Good."

Caldwell ended the transmission, a pang of regret settling inside him as he considered that he'd likely just set this man's life on a very different course.

Well. I was on a different course, too. Then you asshats attacked New Canaan, and I lost everyone.

THE SILENT FLEET

STELLAR DATE: 10.19.8949 (Adjusted Years)
LOCATION: TSS *Cossack's Sword*, approaching Sosondowah
REGION: Machete System, PED 4B, Orion Freedom Alliance

"We've secured Iagaentci." Admiral Sebastian's message began without preamble. "Trey, the Hand agent on the ground here, has given us some assistance, along with a few people who call themselves 'corporate fixers'. Quite the crew he's fallen in with."

Svetlana glanced at Lorelai, who shrugged as the message from Admiral Sebastian continued.

"We're looking at sixty-two hours before the Orion fleet from the shipyards gets here. Colonel Caldwell took out the corporate forces at Geha and blew all the mining platforms but one. He's using the last one to replenish his supply of rail pellets. Thus far, the incoming Orion fleet appears to only be focused on us here at Iagaentci; since Geha is currently in opposition to Iagaentci, Caldwell and I have discussed adjusting our strategy. He's going to thread the needle between the two stars, which will put his railships in position to hit the Oggies in the rear right when they're decelerating to hit us."

"Ballsy," Lorelai said with an appreciative nod.

"That's for sure," Svetlana added. "Doyadastethe and Hawenneyu are at periastron, just over half an AU apart. Space is hell between those two stars at that point."

"Right," the general laughed. "Thought I summed that up with 'ballsy'."

"I'll keep you updated as things proceed, Admiral Svetlana," Sebastian's message concluded. "Given the lack of DMGs in this system, I don't see how they can do much to stop us, though I do worry that we're more likely to expend effort saving their people rather than ourselves. Either way, good luck with your end of things."

The message ended, and the holodisplay switched back to a view of the Machete system.

"He sounded a bit giddy," Lorelai observed. "Too giddy."

"What are you talking about?" Svetlana asked. "He sounded the same as always."

The general shook her head. "Nope, I detected a note of 'gid' when he spoke of Caldwell's ships flanking the enemy."

<I agree,> the ship's AI, Hermes, chimed in. *<He was certainly excited at the prospect of the upcoming battle.>*

"I guess everyone's happy to stick it to the Oggies." Svetlana shrugged and flipped the holo to show her battlegroup's final approach into Sosondowah's nearspace.

The battlegroup was now only one hour from assault craft deployment and the takeover of the Alpha and Omega Trumark shipyards. They were entering the critical time when the locals might pick up the fleet of ships drifting past their planet—stealth systems enabled, engines cold, but still visible if you looked at them at the right place and time.

Ironically, we're sending our best stealth ships through a plasma storm, where their superior tech will be useless.

Over the following hour, there was little conversation on the bridge as everyone kept an eye on scan, watching the flight paths of civilian and military ships in the planet's nearspace, hoping that none would draw too close to the silent TSF fleet.

"There's a freighter departing from Trumark-Alpha," Scan advised. "It's…yes, it's on a vector that will pass four hundred meters off our port side."

Close enough to touch, but not near enough for a civilian to see us.

Svetlana glanced at Lorelai. "Your troops all buckled in?"

"Have been for the last hour."

"Good," the admiral nodded as she watched the holotank, the dot that represented the freighter creeping ever closer to battlegroup.

"I get the feeling that ship is running from something," Lorelai said, folding her arms across her chest as she glared at the civilian craft. "It's boosting way too hard to break out of Sosondowah's gravity well."

"I wonder—aw, fuck," Svetlana muttered a moment later, as four corvettes veered off their patrol routes, boosting toward the freighter—which had begun to spool out its antimatter-pion drive's nozzle.

<*Two of the intercepting corvettes are on direct collision courses for our ships,*> Hermes advised.

Svetlana was tempted to let the pursuing corvettes simply smash against the *Sword*'s shields, but decided that there was no harm in attempting to evade the inbound craft.

The corvettes were hailing the freighter, accusing them of a theft and demanding that the ship cease burn and prepare to be boarded. The freighter paid the pursuers no heed and ignited its AP drive, boosting away at over a hundred *g*s.

What a time to stumble into some sort of robbery…though separating those corvettes from the pack serves us well.

"FCO, have the fleet shift vectors as carefully as possible to avoid collision. We'll see if we can maintain this approach a bit longer."

<*Aye,*> Hermes replied, and Svetlana drew in a deep breath as the two ships that would have been clipped by the corvettes moved out of the way.

While maneuvering thrusters were difficult to detect—especially when they fired graviton-accelerated bursts of gases cooled to the same temperature as the surrounding vacuum—if active scan swept over them at just the right time, sensors would see light from distant stars refract, and it would give them away.

The ships settled onto new vectors, and Svetlana let out the breath she'd been holding.

"It looks like we—"

"Active scan sweeping across the battlegroup!" Scan called out. "Tactical estimates that two of our ships may have been spotted."

"Dammit," Svetlana muttered. "FCO, direct Wing One to engage those four corvettes—the freighter too, if it gives any trouble. Wings Two and Three are to escort the assault craft in. Four through Eight have their targets. Execute."

She knew that Hermes would have begun to send the commands the moment she spoke the words, but Svetlana liked saying the word 'execute'.

"Craft are away," the *Cossack's Sword*'s dockmaster announced from his station.

"On a vector to provide cover," Helm added. "I have them in our shadow."

"Very good," Svetlana replied as she watched the holotank instantly transform from a near-static view of the fleet drifting toward the two Trumark shipyards to one of action and chaos.

Wing One—which consisted of five cruisers and two dozen destroyers—opened fire on the pursuing corvettes, making strategic strikes and disabling the ships' engines and main weapons without destroying the ships themselves.

One of the corvettes flared its engines, trying to outrun the enemy vessels that had appeared all around. The action caused a beam to penetrate something it shouldn't have, and the Orion ship exploded.

*Well, **trying** to avoid destroying ships, at least.*

While Svetlana had no issue with tearing the Orion Guard to shreds, she knew that ruining ships and leaving crews stranded would create a greater strain on the enemy's resources than simple mass destruction.

The comm officer suddenly laughed aloud, then covered

her mouth. "Sorry, ma'am. The freighter's crew just promised to buy us a round if we ever bump into them again. And they sent along a little dance.... It's not suitable to put on the holo."

A smile twitched across Svetlana's lips as she shook her head. "We'll have to take a look later."

"Look at what, ma'am?" Command Master Chief Merrick asked as he strode onto the bridge. He passed the comm officer's console and paused as his eyes widened. "Stars, that *has* to take some serious mods to pull off."

Svetlana cleared her throat, and nodded her chin at the holotank. "We got outed a bit early, but I was expecting something like this to happen anyway."

Her father snorted as he stepped around the comm console and stopped next to the holotank. "Trust me, you weren't expecting anything like *that* to happen."

She accessed the feed and felt her face redden.

"Ummm...probably not."

The *Cossack's Sword* was on a vector for Trumark-Alpha, and the pilot was adjusting position and thrust to match velocity with the assault craft that were in its shadow.

"Ten minutes till our devils latch on," General Lorelai said, trying not to smirk—a sign that she'd tapped the feed from the freighter as well. "Based on the specs Trey sent, I estimate we're looking at twenty minutes to lock down the command decks, and then another two hours to fully secure the stations. The rest of the shipyard will take longer, depending on what we decide to keep."

From what they could see, the vast majority of the battle-ready Orion Guard ships had left the shipyards with the fleet that was en route to engage Admiral Sebastian's ships. Only fifty-three patrol craft—all destroyers and corvettes—remained to protect the six shipyards.

Already, Wings Four through Eight were striking out at the remaining Orion ships, while the escort wings targeted the fixed defenses.

"Fools," Merrick muttered. "They should just surrender. Even if those other ships do turn around and come back, it'll be too late for anyone here."

"A group of enemy corvettes has broken off," Scan announced, and a dozen light attack craft were highlighted on the holotank. "It looks like they're moving to the far side of the planet."

"Well," Svetlana glanced at her father. "I wonder if they're going to try to hide and wait for reinforcements."

"Gravitational anomaly in Moon S1!" Scan cried out. "I read high-intensity gamma emissions."

"Fuck, no!" Svetlana shouted, switching to all-fleet. *<DMG firing! Evasive maneuvers!>*

Hermes immediately disseminated orders to every ship, providing new vectors away from the moon while also ensuring that none of the capital ships directed their engine wash at the assault craft.

Svetlana barely paid attention to the chaos. Her eyes were glued to the view of the largest of Sosondowah's two moons.

Like the planet it orbited, the moon had a long, nearly unpronounceable name, which is why it was noted as 'S1' on the holotank's display.

Moments later, a beam of blinding energy slashed out of the moon, striking one of Svetlana's cruisers, cutting through its stasis shield and hewing the ship in half.

<Wing Eight! Hit the firing aperture on the moon. Full spread,> she ordered.

The holotank had become a display of unmitigated chaos as assault ships and their escorts streaked through the moons' nearspace, still closing with their targets while also attempting to avoid presenting clear targets to the DMG nestled within moon S1.

The black-hole-powered weapon fired again. This time, it

clipped a destroyer, knocking out its shields before taking the nose off the ship.

"Five minutes!" General Lorelai called out, her knuckles white as she gripped the rim of the holotank.

Svetlana nodded absently as she watched Wing Eight's thirty ships launch missiles at the firing aperture on the moon's surface.

"You know that may not work," Merrick said in a quiet voice. "That much energy can just blast through..."

"I know," she replied, nodding stiffly. "I'm open to other suggestions."

"Well, if they do open up their aperture again, we shoot right down the thing's throat."

Svetlana inclined her head in acknowledgement. She knew that any ship that shot straight into the DMG's maw would likely not survive the attack. She considered lobbing missiles, but knew it wouldn't work; guided weapons of that sort would just be shot down by defense turrets on the moon.

It would take a ship with stasis shields to pass directly over the opening and fire particle weapons into the monster's throat, and she knew it couldn't be the *Cossack's Sword.*

"Direct hits!" Scan cried out, and the forward display switched from the view of the *Sword*'s bow to the surface of the moon, where a pool of molten rock, surrounded by hotly glowing rubble, had taken the place of the opening into the DMG.

"Dammit!" Svetlana swore. "It's too hot and soft, the weapon can shoot through that."

"More apertures!" Scan called out, and the view of the moon pulled back to show a dozen firing ports opening on the moon's surface, describing a five-hundred-kilometer circle around the main port.

"What the—" Merrick began to say, when readings spiked, and the ship's scan suite went offline.

<We've lost stasis shields. External comm and scan hardware is offline,> Hermes stated calmly. *<Falling back to secondary systems.>*

Svetlana bit her cheek while waiting for the secondary antennae and sensors to slide from off the hull, where they'd been protected from the EM burst that had fried the primary arrays.

The moment Scan came back, she sucked in a sharp breath. Fully half her fleet was without stasis shields, and dozens of those unprotected ships were dark, drifting through the void without power.

"It fired some sort of mass field effect," the scan officer murmured.

No more dithering.

<Jula.> Svetlana reached out to the captain of the *Nimbus Light,* one of the heaviest cruisers in the battle group. *<I need you to hit that thing dead center.>*

The woman's response was instantaneous, her dedication enough to form a lump in the admiral's throat.

<Consider it done, Admiral Svetlana.>

<Thank you, Captain.>

Svetlana pursed her lips as she watched the cruiser shift vector, jinking its way across the battlespace, heading toward the moon while staying outside its main weapon's firing angle.

Merrick met her eyes and nodded slowly, but there was no time to worry over the fate of the *Nimbus Light,* as dozens of ships that had previously lain cold and quiet in the shipyards came to life, engines flaring as they boosted toward the inbound TSF fleet.

"Fuckers." Lorelai shook her head as she cursed. "They couldn't have known we were coming. How are they this clever?"

"The feint at Iagaentci and Akonwara always ran the risk of being seen as such," Merrick said. "But a few half-finished hulls aren't going to turn the tide."

"Tell that to the Orion forces that tried to take New Canaan," Svetlana replied before sending orders for the damaged ships to fall to the right side of the battlegroup, putting them as far away from the DMG-containing moon as possible.

As she issued the orders, the superweapon fired again, blasting away the slag that had covered its main firing aperture. The beam that cleared the opening carried on to strike a TSF destroyer in the engines, blowing the ship apart in less time than it took to comprehend the events.

At this point, Svetlana's battlegroup was fully engaged with the Orion Guard defenders, their numbers almost evenly matched—though half the Transcend ships still possessed functional stasis shields.

"Breaking free!" Lorelai called out as her boarding craft pulled away from the protective shields offered by the escort ships, and turned to brake, slowing for their final approaches to the Alpha and Omega stations.

As the assault craft neared, beams lanced out from the stations, hitting the ships and destroying one, before the escort cruisers took out the station's final line of defenses.

Svetlana was about to breathe a sigh of relief, but it turned into a gasp when the deck lurched under her feet as the *Cossack's Sword* veered to port, banking around the Trumark-Alpha station. Svetlana saw a volley of missiles pass just off the starboard bow, picked off one by one as the ship's point defense systems engaged them.

"Nice flying," she said to the pilot, who nodded mutely in response.

"Desperate measures," Merrick muttered.

Svetlana surveyed the battlespace and saw that one of the shipyards was far enough around the S2 moon that the DMG couldn't hit it. Of all her wings, six had not yet suffered any damage, and every ship still had functional stasis shields.

<*Wing Six,*> she called out to its commander. <*Take out Trumark-Gamma. Blow the gimbals to the ships, then give them a two-minute warning before you send that place to hell.*>

<*Aye, Admiral,*> the wing commander sent back, and Svetlana retuned her focus to S1 and the *Nimbus Light*'s suicide run.

The DMG had fired again, and by some undeserved luck, its beam lanced out through empty space, not connecting with any ship. It made another shot, attempting to hit the *Nimbus Light,* but the cruiser danced out of range, avoiding what would have been a devastating shot.

"Now, Jula," Svetlana whispered. "Now."

As if on command, the heavy cruiser fired its maneuvering engines, sliding across the face of the moon, pivoting so its forward guns faced the DMG's main firing aperture.

The cruiser lurched backward as all its rails and energy weapons fired at once, the volley followed by a full spread of missiles.

Svetlana tasted blood from her cheek as she waited to see if the massive weapon would shoot again, if the *Nimbus Light* would clear its angle of fire before it—

Her worries were interrupted by a smaller beam shooting out from one of the secondary firing apertures, the shot clipping the *Nimbus Light,* taking out the cruiser's stasis shields.

<*Admiral!*> Captain Jula called in. <*Our readings show that we made a direct hit on whatever's down there. We'll see if we can get our shields back online to make another pa—*>

The woman's words were cut off, and Svetlana's eyes widened as she saw part of the moon's surface leap up, ejecta from an interior detonation flying directly toward the *Nimbus Light.*

Engines flared as the cruiser shifted vector, attempting to

outrun the debris.

Svetlana met her father's eyes for a moment before they looked back toward the holotank, which showed a clear view of a thirty-kilometer-wide chunk of the moon slamming into the fleeing cruiser.

"Fuck," Merrick whispered, shaking his head.

"The collision wasn't that fast," Svetlana said quietly. "They might still be alive."

"Look!" Scan called out, switching the main display to a view of the moon.

Large cracks were beginning to appear across its surface, widening as sections of regolith began to fall into the crevasses.

<The DMG's lost containment. The black hole is going to eat that moon.>

<All unshielded ships, max burn. Get clear of S1,> Svetlana ordered, while considering whether or not Trumark-Alpha was at a safe distance.

A glance at Lorelai confirmed what they both knew. When the black hole that had powered the DMG fed on the moon, it was going to fire relativistic jets of energy out of its poles. If one of those swept across the station, it would be destroyed.

Along with all the troops that had just boarded it.

"I gave the fallback order," Lorelai said, her tone grim. "Fighting's intense in there."

"Stupid," Merrick shook his head. "Fucking stupid. Everyone knows you don't use black holes in war."

Svetlana couldn't help but wonder why the Oggies had built a DMG in a moon orbiting a planet in a nowhere system in a nowhere section of the Perseus Expansion Districts. That they could have anticipated an attack by the Transcend on this location out of hundreds of thousands of possible targets seemed too unlikely to be even remotely possible.

Even if the TSF had a leak, there was no way the enemy

could have built such a facility in the time available.

Stars…they had to have begun construction on this years ago. It might predate the war.

As she considered the DMG's provenance, light began to glow brightly as matter was torn apart along the inner edge of the black hole's accretion disk, the point where atoms passed beyond the event horizon.

Twin beams shot out from the surface of the moon, and Svetlana heaved a sigh of relief. Not only were the black hole's poles nowhere near Trumark-Alpha, there was little wobble; the thing's rotation seemed to be stable.

"Nice to catch a break," Lorelai muttered.

While the black hole devoured the moon, Svetlana turned her attention back to the conflict in space.

Seeing their superweapon destroyed, the Orion ships began to break away from the engagement. Though they still outnumbered the Transcend ships, they were taking a beating from the vessels still possessing stasis shields.

"And that's that," Merrick said, folding his arms across his chest. "They put up a hell of a fight."

"That they did," Svetlana replied, looking over the damage and loss reports that were compiling.

Nine ships had been utterly destroyed, and another twenty had suffered severe damage after their stasis shields had failed. She directed Wings Five, Seven, and Eight to pursue the Orion ships, while ordering the others to begin search and rescue operations.

"We're going to blow Trumark-Alpha," she said to Lorelai. "Once those breach teams get free, direct them to hit Epsilon instead. Alpha's too close to that big chunk of nothing."

"I hear you there," Lorelai replied. "There's just one platoon left on Alpha. Five minutes, and we'll be clear."

Svetlana nodded, rocking back on her heels.

The battle was won, but at a cost far higher than she'd

anticipated. Losing half her fleet's stasis shields was something she'd never considered, and the engineering teams had no idea yet if they could be repaired.

"Dammit," she muttered, shaking her head.

<Hey.> A message came into her mind a moment later. *<Anyone gonna come get us? Half our pods are destroyed, and from what we can see, this chunk of rock is going to splash down in one of Sosondowah's oceans in a day or so.>*

<Jula! You made it!>

<Well, the crew made it…can't say the same for my Nimbus Light.>

Svetlana laughed, not caring that the captain had lost her ship if her people were still alive. *<You get first pick from any ship here.>*

<You trying to punish me? I'm pretty sure we saved the day, and now you're going to saddle us with some OG hunk of junk?>

<Umm…well, I guess we'll see what shakes free. I'm sending help your way, you'll be off that rock long before it takes a bath.>

Svetlana realized she'd have to destroy that rock too—and dozens of others—before it fell to the planet and killed everyone down there.

Shit. And here I was hoping for a simple smash and grab.

PART 3 – WATCHERS

A WALK AND A RESOLUTION

STELLAR DATE: 10.05.8949 (Adjusted Years)
LOCATION: Lunic Station
REGION: Aldebaran, League of Sentients Space

Iris walked through the ruins of the concourse on Lunic Station, where Bob destroyed Xavia with his shadow particle beam.

Next to her, Amavia held a scanner capable of finding miniscule concentrations of shadow particles, as they searched for any remains of the ascended AI before re-opening the section of the station to the public.

"It's one in a billion that she survived," Iris said.

She reached the edge of the hole blown through the station and peered down through the three-kilometer shaft that the beam had cut, before looking up through the few hundred meters to the view of space, where the atmosphere was held in at the hull by grav shields.

"Bob's one hell of a shot, isn't he?" Amavia said as she leant over the hole and peered up into the void as well. "He didn't hit a single person in the station—other than Xavia, of course. But that doesn't mean a bit of her didn't get away."

"Hey, I'm here searching, too." Iris glanced at Amavia while hefting her shadowtron. "Just doubting that I'll need to use this thing."

The alabaster-skinned woman gave Iris a narrow-eyed look. "You just wanted to come to this site again."

"And you didn't?" Iris asked.

Amavia laughed. "OK, it's more than a little epic. Bob pulled so much power through the CriEn modules that spacetime noticeably bent around the *I2*. The effect was even visible on visual wavelengths."

"Total 'do as I say, not as I do', kinda guy, isn't he?" Iris asked with a laugh as she turned to survey the empty concourse, her gaze pausing on the deformed deckplates where Tangel and Xavia had battled. "Does this shit scare you?" she asked the woman who was as much her mother as a friend. "I'll admit, I'm not at Bob's level or anything, but I'm also not down there with the L2 AIs, either. Yet I'm having a hard time understanding what is really going on anymore."

Amavia lowered her scanner and turned to face Iris.

"I don't know if 'scared' is the right word. It's intense, and it's stretching our understanding of what reality is, that's for sure. But the existence of these dimensions isn't new—we just never imagined that beings could manipulate the energies there as easily as I manipulate the matter in my hand in our dimensions." As she spoke, Amavia wiggled her fingers, and Iris couldn't help but shake her head.

"Shredding atoms for raw energy is a bit more than what we do to move our hands," she argued.

"Yeah, but that's why people like Tangel are special," Amavia said with a bemused shrug before lifting her scanner once more and turning to sweep it across the empty concourse.

<*Did you hear that?*> Amavia asked Iris.

<*Yeah…sounded like a piece of debris shifting under a foot,*> Iris replied, while saying something aloud about wrapping up their sweep. <*Who'd be dumb enough to make a play for us here?*>

<*Might be the best place to do it,*> Amavia replied. <*This whole section of the station is quarantined. No one's around, and the surveillance systems are all fried from Tangel's battle.*>

<*Well, anyone with half a brain would send a team to take us,*> Iris said as she lifted her shadowtron, pretending to adjust a

setting on it.

A recent update to the shadowtrons added a mid-powered electron beam and pulse emitter. Something that had proven necessary when taking down remnant-occupied people.

<I'm not picking up anyone at all. No one in the LoS has the tech to hide from us,> Amavia said, a note of worry in her voice.

Iris took her meaning. Either there was no one there, or whoever was sneaking up on them wasn't from Aldebaran. Or likely even the Inner Stars.

Amavia spun in a slow circle, talking about the fight in the assembly chamber while taking readings with her scanner. Iris turned in the opposite direction, searching for any signs of a hidden enemy.

<Still nothing,> she said. *<My nanocloud is spreading, though. If whoever this is wants to get close, they'll have to go through it.>*

With a slow nod and a response about how the assembly chamber was so radioactive that they were removing it entirely from the station, Iris stepped around the hole in the deck, deploying her own nanocloud to add coverage, and to scan the decks below and above.

She was about to ask Amavia if maybe they were just being paranoid, when a pulse wave slammed into her side, sending her sprawling.

In an instant, Iris rolled to her feet and saw a figure light up on her HUD, covered in the nanocloud. The person, thinking they were unseen, was advancing with their weapon held level.

Iris didn't hesitate to fire the electron beam on her shadowtron, catching the figure in the chest. She glanced at Amavia just in time to see her take a pulse blast as well. She went down, immediately beginning to struggle with an invisible figure at the edge of the hole in the deck.

Turning her attention back to her attacker, Iris was amazed to see that the enemy had shrugged off the electron beam shot—though a blackened chestplate now hung in the air, denoting at least some damage. Iris fired twice more, hoping that whomever she was facing didn't have armor to match their stealth tech.

With the second shot, the attacker's stealth systems went offline entirely, and Iris identified their enemy.

"They're Lisas!" she called out to Amavia, while signaling both Bob and Lunic Station Security for aid, only to find that there was no response on the Link.

"Surrender," the figure before Iris said in her lisping hiss.

"Like hell," Iris muttered, about to fire once more, when another pulse blast hit her, this time from the side.

Her HUD lit up with two more attackers closing in.

"I've got—shit!" Amavia cried out from across the hole in the deck, as she wrenched free from her invisible assailant only to take two more pulse shots.

The blasts bowled her over, rolling her toward the hole torn through the deck. She stopped right on the edge, and then wavered for a second before another pulse blast hit her, sending her down through the gash in the station's hull.

"Not gonna ha—" Iris began, when a web shot out from a boxy weapon the Lisa held.

It wrapped around Iris, the bindings tightening until she couldn't move a centimeter. Then a large bag was produced and rolled out beside her while she fought against her bonds.

She pumped out every bit of nano she could, setting it on the strands of the web, when suddenly, multiple pairs of hands grabbed her and pushed her into the bag. The zipper was pulled shut, and then whatever was inside the bag solidified, holding Iris immobile—just in time for a series of EMPs to hit her. Then everything disappeared into a single point of light.

* * * * *

Tangel sat on the deck swing that hung from the ceiling over her lakehouse's porch. She gazed out contentedly, looking over Ol' Sam's rolling hills and low clouds. After Bob's healing aid, she felt whole again, but the mental aftereffects of the confrontation with Xavia were still with her.

"How many times do I have to get the ever-living shit kicked out of me?" she asked quietly as she picked shapes out of the clouds that were trailing past.

Though she'd told herself she was still ready for action during those long years in New Canaan, Tangel realized that she'd grown complacent, come to think that her struggles were in the past.

But then the fight on Scipio, then Pyra, then in Corona Australis, and out in the LMC had taught her otherwise—no, *should* have taught her otherwise. But then she went traipsing into danger down on Lunic Station and risked her Marines' lives, and the lives of Iris and Amavia, just because she thought she could take all comers.

Every time I think I'm finally equipped for the fight ahead of me, I find out how wrong I am.

A footfall sounded on the path, and Tangel looked up to see Faleena strolling through the woods.

The AI still wore her dryad-inspired frame, which was just as well, given how aptly it suited her. Long red tresses trailed over light green skin, long elfin ears poking through the locks.

In a way, we all just wear shells. Even humans can change them, if they like. Just look at Malorie; the woman's spent five centuries as a mechanical spider, of all things.

That the body was nothing more than a temporary capsule was even more apparent to Tangel. The body she'd spent her whole life in was becoming more and more of a vessel, and less 'her', though her mind was still rooted in the sliver of 'normal' space she'd spent most of her life in. A presence there was something she didn't plan to forsake, even if maintaining it was a risk.

She'd promised her family that she wasn't going to go drifting off into the ether.

Another part of that worry was the tendril of thought that reminded her of the distance it would create between herself and everyone she cared for, were she to separate herself from the corporeal world.

Like you always do, she told herself. Everyone she cared about was here with her. Not to mention, excepting Bob, so far as she could tell, every other ascended being was a raging asshole.

"Where are Cary and Saanvi?" Tangel asked, as Faleena reached the steps and skipped up to the porch.

"Doctor Rosenberg wanted to look over Cary to make sure that nothing was missed out in the LMC, and Saanvi went with her for moral support."

Tangel laughed. "She must be pretty tired of patching up the Richards women."

Faleena shrugged. "In the grand scheme of things, you only seem to get seriously injured every couple of decades—barring Pyra and Lunic."

Patting the seat next to her, Tangel nodded slowly. "Yeah, you're right about that. Maybe this means I'll get a good long reprieve."

Her AI daughter settled gingerly on the swing and folded her legs up under herself.

"You really think so, Moms?"

"No…no, I don't."

They'd rocked gently in companionable silence for a few minutes when Faleena asked, "What's it like, Moms?"

"Ascending?" Tangel asked, unable to think of anything else that she could be referring to.

Faleena turned her head to meet Tangel's eyes.

"Well…being ascended; less the actual getting there part."

-Bizarre.-

Her daughter's eyes widened.

"Did you just speak into my mind? That word didn't come over the Link or through my auditory pickups…it was just *there.*"

"Sort of a case in point," Tangel said with a soft laugh. "The rules about what's possible seem to keep changing…." Her voice trailed off for a moment, and then she asked, "Did you know that I was one of the first L2 humans to have an AI embedded?"

Faleena shook her head. "No, they don't seem to have that in the classes they teach about you."

Tangel rolled her eyes. "Stars, my ego does not need that."

"Why?" Faleena chuckled and reached up to stroke Tangel's hair. "Do you think it will give you a big head, Moms?"

"No." Tangel sighed and looked down at her hands, corporeal and otherwise. "More the opposite. I've made so many mistakes over the years, and I don't seem to be getting any better at avoiding them. Not only that, the penalty for failure keeps getting higher. One of these days, I'm going to screw up, and there will be no one to save me."

Faleena's hand slid down from Tangel's head to rest on her shoulder, pulling her close.

"Not so, Moms. There'll always be one of us around to pull your butt out of the fire."

Tangel laughed and glanced at Faleena, shaking her head as she spoke. "You're not going to let me get all morose about this, are you?"

"Nope. Do you know why you've always done so well, Moms?"

"Done so well in what way?"

"In your leadership roles."

"Oh…well, there are a lot of reasons, I suppose—"

"I think there's just one. Well, one and a half."

Tangel chuckled, kicking a leg out to set the swing rocking once more. "And what are those one-and-a-half things?"

"You find amazing people and you make them a part of your team—and then you use that team."

"Some might argue that you've just listed three things."

"Maybe…" Faleena tilted her head in consideration. "But really, it's just 'having a good team'. You finding the people and them doing their jobs is a part of that."

"OK," Tangel said with a laugh. "I'll allow it."

Faleena snorted, which sounded like a soft squeak combined with rustling leaves.

"Glad you approve, Moms."

"So how does this translate to all of my storied successes?" Tangel asked, doing her best not to sound as defeated as she felt.

"Well, I was thinking about all of the scrapes you've been through. From things like drawing out the people trying to stop the *Intrepid*'s construction to defending Victoria, working with Sera's crew on *Sabrina*. Even here at Aldebaran. You had backup—though you would have been better off, had you let Bob come along from the get-go."

Tangel sighed. "Stars, you don't have to tell me that. Bob's said it at least a thousand times."

<*No I haven't.*>

"Well, you've said it once or twice, and the rest is just the echoing in my mind, I guess."

<*That sounds more like it. Faleena is right, by the way.*>

"I know." Tangel nodded. "So what does that mean? Am I wrong to send Sera on her own to Airtha?"

Faleena laughed and shook her head. "She's hardly alone, Moms. You've sent her with one of the best collections of badasses in the galaxy."

"Yeah, they're a pretty hardcore crowd. But with Empress Diana pushing into the Hegemony, and Corsia hitting the Trisilieds, I need to keep my options open."

<*We,*> Bob intoned.

"Oh? Are you getting more actively involved?" Tangel looked out onto the lake, able to see the small, coriolis force induced eddies in the surface.

<*I've always been actively involved,*> Bob replied. <*Just in my own way. I like to be inscrutable.*>

"Was that a joke?" Faleena asked, quirking an eyebrow as she glanced at Tangel. "Does Bob joke?"

A chuckle escaped Tangel's lips. "Bob jokes a lot, but just like his motives, he keeps his humor inscrutable as well."

Faleena's eyes narrowed, and she glanced out toward the lake like her mother, as though it held some sort of potential revelation for Bob's motives.

"Come," Tangel said as she rose. "Since most of my team is on the far side of the Orion Arm, I need to bolster the ISF's presence."

"Come where?"

"To the negotiations with the League of Sentients. I've told your sisters to meet us there. Oh, and I just had a conversation with your father; it seems that the three of you have graduated."

Faleena laughed as she rose. "Saanvi's going to be so pissed."

"In the middle of exciting research, was she?" Tangel asked.

"Less that and more that graduation means she'll probably be away from Project Starflight."

Tangel shrugged as she walked across the porch. "Starflight will be going on for some time. She won't miss much."

"Sure," Faleena said as she followed Tangel down the

steps. "And I look forward to listening in when you explain that to her."

"Listen in? What are you, Bob?"

<*I…nevermind.*>

AN UNEXPECTED PROMOTION

STELLAR DATE: 10.05.8949 (Adjusted Years)
LOCATION: ISS *I2*, near Lunic Station
REGION: Aldebaran, League of Sentients Space

"See?" Cary said as she stepped out of the UHAR scanner and gave Dr. Rosenberg a pointed look. "Nothing wrong with me. Right as rain."

The doctor fixed Cary with a level stare and shook her head. "So much like your mother. Right down to the refusal of medical care."

"I thought she was always in here getting patched up?"

Dr. Rosenberg shrugged. "Well, when a limb gets chopped off or something, yeah. But it took her realizing that you were experiencing your own sort of ascension for her to come in and let me get baseline scans of her physiology for comparison."

"Oh," Cary said, not certain how to reply.

She still wasn't entirely comfortable with her mother's changes, though it was more related to losing Tanis and Angela than the ascension part of things.

Except when it came to the idea that she was semi-sorta-kinda ascending as well. Then she got all freaked out again.

"Come to think of it," the doctor mused, "there was one time she lost a hand and didn't bother getting a new one. She just made one from flowmetal. Took weeks for her to get around to coming in for an organic one."

"Sort of started a trend, did it?" Cary asked.

"Yeah." The doctor fixed her with a penetrating stare. "One I hope you don't pick up on. Unless you get to the point where you can start making new limbs like she does. Though...."

Cary waited a moment for Dr. Rosenberg to finish her

thought. When it became apparent that she wasn't going to, the younger woman cleared her throat and asked, " 'Though', what?"

"Well," the doctor shrugged as she turned to the scanner and called up the reset parameters on the control panel. "Just not sure if you need me much, when you can grow new arms on your own."

A rueful laugh escaped Cary's lips. "That's Moms's province. I don't have a clue how to do that."

"I bet it's because of the circumstances. She did it for raw survival. You've not had that particular need. But I imagine you pulled out some new tricks when you killed Myrrdan—which makes you my personal hero, by the way."

The statement caught Cary by surprise.

While she'd been praised as a bit of a hero for hers and Saanvi's actions in the Defense of Carthage—which had been eclipsed by being punished for stealing a starship—no one had ever said that she was their personal hero before.

"Umm…th-thanks," she stammered. "I'm curious why…other than the obvious."

"I lost a few good friends to that bastard's machinations. I think the fact that you, a mere twenty-year-old woman, took him down after centuries of plotting is the most fitting end he could have. Well, the most fitting I can discuss in polite company."

Dr. Rosenberg's statement was delivered with much more vehemence than Cary was accustomed to hearing from the woman.

She ducked her head before responding.

"Well, it was my pleasure. Makes me sick to think he was still out there, still getting his fingers dirty. They've cleared everyone out at the LMC, and we're hoping that none of his…remnant-like things have infected anyone else."

"Is there a limit to how many times he could do that?" the

doctor asked, eyes holding a measure of concern.

"I think so..." Cary replied after a moment. "If he could split himself infinitely, I imagine he would have already done it. Either there are some people who were not good candidates, or he needed to recover from making them, or some combination of those two. From what Earnest has been able to determine, remnants are actually just that: a bit of the ascended being left behind."

"Hey, Cary." Saanvi poked her head into the room. "Sorry to interrupt."

Cary shot her sister a worried look. The UHAR scanner room was shielded from the outside, keeping out all EM, including Link access. Worry that something horrible had happened settled in her stomach, made worse by the dark look on Saanvi's face.

"We were just chatting, what's up?" she asked.

"Moms wants us to attend the meetings with the LoS representatives. And she wants to tell us something. Faleena is already with her."

Cary glanced at Dr. Rosenberg, who nodded and gestured for her to leave. "I'll do a bit more review of your scans, but you don't need to stay. Off with you, now."

"Thanks, doc," she said with a nod and then followed Saanvi out into the hall. "Any clue what Moms wants to tell us?" Cary glanced at her sister's eyes to see if Saanvi was hiding anything.

Brilliant she might be, but a good liar she was not.

"Not a clue," Saanvi replied, giving no tells whatsoever.

"What about Faleena?" Cary asked, as the two women walked through the *I2*'s general hospital toward the maglev. "Have you hit her up?"

Saanvi nodded. "She knows. I can tell."

<Faleena? What does Moms want to talk to us about?> Cary asked her sister in her sweetest, most innocent mental tone.

<*Nice try, Cary. It's for her to tell.*>

<*Dammit, Fal. Can you at least say if it's good news or not? Saanvi's sweating bullets here.*>

<*Am not, Cary,*> Saanvi broke in, having been added to the conversation by Faleena. <*I can handle waiting just fine. You're not fooling either of us.*>

<*By which she means she already tried to get me to break,*> Faleena said with a soft laugh. <*It's good news. Just get your butts to the bridge conference room. That's where we're meeting the LoS president.*>

<*Okaaay,*> Cary drew out the word as they reached the maglev platform and waited for the next train to the command decks.

"Told you to just wait," Saanvi said.

"Yeah, but you didn't tell me that Faleena already shut you down."

"I don't have to tell you everything."

Cary eyed her sister. "Since when?"

Then a realization hit her, and she cursed under her breath.

"If Faleena's with Moms, and you're here, where's Amy?"

"Relax," Saanvi replied and wrapped an arm around her sister's shoulder. "Terry's taking care of her."

"Sahn…we know seven Terrys. It's a really common name in New Canaan."

Saanvi burst out laughing. "Stars, you're right. It's almost as common as 'Peter'. I mean Terry Chang. She's back on the *I2*."

"Home sweet home. She always said she missed the *Intrepid*." Cary shook her head. "You know…I still remember standing with Moms and Dad when we dumped out of the dark layer and crossed over New Canaan's heliopause."

"Why would you dump out at the heliopause?" Saanvi asked. "You can fly another forty AU toward the star in the DL at New Canaan."

Cary knocked her hip against her sister's. "Seriously, Sahn. Symbolism. Moms is all mushy like that, haven't you realized that by now?"

Saanvi barked a laugh. "If by that, you mean everyone *but* Moms is into symbolism and sentimentality, then yes, I've totally realized that."

The next maglev train pulled into the station, and when the doors opened, their father stood inside, beckoning for them to enter.

"Fancy meeting you here," he said while opening up his arms to embrace the two women.

Cary and Saanvi both stepped onto the train and returned the hug, though Saanvi peered up at their father with a clouded expression.

"You always told us we can't be familiar like this while in uniform."

Joe took a step back, a mischievous look on his face as he looked the pair of women up and down. "Huh...uniforms...didn't notice. Well, I suppose if you *are* in uniform, then you can pin these on."

He held out his hand, and they both looked down to see lieutenant's bars resting on his palm.

"Whaaaaa?" Cary breathed out the word. "*Second* lieutenant? How?"

"Bravery above and beyond the call of duty. The both of you, on several occasions. It wasn't your mother or I who pushed for it. It was Admiral Sanderson, Governor Andrews, and Admiral Symatra."

"*Symatra?!*" Cary and Saanvi shouted in unison, glancing at one another in shock.

"I kinda thought she hated us," Cary said, remembering the angry missive the AI had sent to the girls after the Defense of Carthage.

Joe fixed her with a level stare. "She was more upset about

the position you put her in. You know that. She knew that she'd sent Tanis Richards' daughters on a suicide run. That would have been the end for her if you'd died. This shouldn't be news to you."

Cary nodded. "It's not. I get it. That's why I'm so surprised she was pushing for this."

Joe winked at her. "Well. She was angling to make you a ship captain and see you under her own command. I think she meant to further your education."

She paled at the thought. "Please tell me that's not what's about to happen."

Joe shook his head. "No. It's been a strategic decision by Command that you and your mother should remain in close proximity to one another."

" 'By Command'?" Saanvi snorted. "Really, Dad?"

"OK, fine. I pushed for it. You're stationed here on the *I2*—both of you."

Cary saw Saanvi purse her lips, but her sister nodded and didn't contest the assignment.

She knew Saanvi would rather be back in New Canaan, following Earnest around on his many projects, but they both knew that New Canaan needed as many people on the front lines as possible.

For a colony with a population that was still well under ten million souls, that meant that less than half were keeping the home fires lit.

<*You could get pregnant,*> Cary sent to Saanvi. <*You know JP's waiting for you. That would get you reassigned to New Canaan.*>

<*Seriously, Cary? You need me. You'd be dead a dozen times over without me to pull your ass out of the fire.*>

Cary ignored her sister—other than sending a cool glance her way—before addressing her father.

"Thank you. We'll both do our best to honor the faith

placed in us."

Joe snorted. "OK, Cary. No need to lay it on that thick."

"We're stationed here, but what command are we under?" Saanvi asked as she pinned on her new rank insignia.

"You're in the First Fleet, of course, under Captain Rachel. Cary, you're going to be on her bridge crew, and Saanvi, you're going to be working in forward engineering."

"*Rachel*?" Cary gaped.

Saanvi's eyes narrowed. "What sort of work in forward engineering?"

Joe winked. "That'll be for Major Irene to discuss with you, but I think you'll find it an agreeable assignment."

"And me?" Cary asked.

"Pilot, I do believe," Joe said as the maglev pulled into the command deck station.

"Piiiiilot?" Cary asked. "I get to be a pilot on the *I2*?"

Joe nodded. "Well, so long as you keep Rachel happy. I hear she's a real taskmaster."

Cary blew out a long sigh. "I've heard talk."

Joe chuckled. "You have no idea. I trained her well."

They walked past the offices that lined the command deck's main corridor and moved into the ship's bridge foyer, where Priscilla was ensconced on her plinth, doing her part to keep the massive ship up and running.

A part of Cary wondered what it would be like to be one of Bob's avatars. Like the queen ant in a hive of humans and AIs.

Well, a proxy of the real queen, but the Avatars have a lot of autonomy.

Not that it was a possibility. Her mother had placed a law on the books that no persons under fifty could be considered for the position of avatar. At twenty, both sisters had a ways to go.

<*The League of Sentients delegation is one train behind you,*> Priscilla said by way of greeting. <*Should I delay them at all?*>

"No," Joe replied, shaking his head in response. "We'll be ready by then. I assume Captain Rachel is escorting them?"

<*Hands on, that one. Reminds me of someone else I know.*>

A minute later, the trio walked into the conference room to find Tangel sitting alone at the table.

Her head was bowed and her hair—freed from its typical ponytail—fell around her face. But when she looked up, her blue eyes were bright, and a smile was on her lips.

"Well now, how are my two new second lieutenants?"

"Three!" Faleena said as she entered the room carrying two coffee carafes, which she set on the sideboard.

"Sorry, Faleena," Tangel replied with a laugh. "And thanks for grabbing the coffee. With so many ships coming online, and especially with the *Carthage* and the *Starblade* deploying before they were complete, we've sacrificed half of our bots to other vessels."

"I'll keep that in mind next time I come to rescue you," Joe deadpanned as he poured himself a cup of coffee. "Note to self: don't bring massive ships into battle if their convenience bots aren't ready."

Tangel raised her hands in mock defense and laughed, the sound entirely genuine and a soothing salve to Cary's ears.

"Even when I win, I lose," her Moms joked.

Joe's eyes peeked over the rim of his coffee cup, crinkling with a smile as he took a sip and said, "Turnabout is fair play."

Tangel gave him a mock glower before turning to Cary. "I was reviewing the report on your fight with Myrrdan. Did I see correctly that you were able to initiate a grav field?"

Cary nodded as she poured her own cup of coffee. She was about to drink it black, but remembered the last time Faleena had made coffee, and added a sizeable volume of heavy cream.

"Yeah, it was easy, I—"

She stopped, thinking about how to describe the steps

necessary to vibrate atomic structures to generate gravitons.

"OK, it's way harder to describe than to actually do. I can show you later."

Tangel nodded vigorously. "I think I would have done much better against Xavia if I had known how to do that. She certainly did."

Cary smiled at her mother as she sat down at the table. "Huh. I get to teach you something. Bet this'll be a once-in-a lifetime event."

Joe sighed at her as he took the seat on Tangel's right. "Trust me, Cary. You've taught your Moms and I plenty of things. All three of you have."

Saanvi just rolled her eyes, while Faleena leant forward on her elbows and asked, "Like what?"

Tangel winked at Faleena as the door opened, and Rachel stepped in. "Well, patience, for starters."

FORTRESS OF THE MIND

STELLAR DATE: 10.05.8949 (Adjusted Years)
LOCATION: Somewhere on Lunic Station
REGION: Aldebaran, League of Sentients Space

Iris strained against the solidified gel that held her body, struggling to break free, even though she knew it to be futile.

It was as though she was encased in layers of steel, the form around her body entirely rigid, restricting her completely. The EMP pulse that her attackers had used to disable her had also damaged many of her body's actuators.

And fried half my nano. And burned out my flowmetal.

These effects made her struggles all the more impotent. Whoever it was that had captured Iris had known very well where to hit her in order to damage her body extensively while saving her core from any harm.

When I get out of here….

What remained of her senses picked up vibrations in the material that held her, and Iris stilled her thoughts to focus on them. Her gyros indicated motion, which shortly stopped. A moment later, another slow vibration came, and she realized that it was centered over her chest—directly above her core.

The vibrations carried on and on, and then stopped for a moment before they picked up once again. This time the sensation was sharp, and Iris knew that her captors were cutting through her body.

She desperately tried to activate any defensive system that would respond, but nothing worked, nothing at all. Seconds later, her core housing registered a breach, and sensors mounted directly on her core registered light and sound.

A pair of tong-like objects lowered and settled around her core. Iris kept from making any sounds, though she wanted to rage at whoever this was, warn them of the dire consequences they'd face for the attack on her person.

But she knew bluster would get her nowhere—other than further harm in retaliation.

As her core was forcibly removed from her body, one thought ran over and over in her mind.

Nothing. I'll give them nothing. I am nothing, I have nothing to give.

The mantra stopped when she was finally pulled out of her ruined body, and she got a clear view of her captors.

Lisas!

Iris thought back to the Lisas—which Misha had called 'Widows'—that she and the crew of *Sabrina* had fought in Orion Space. The strange women, who were all clones of Finaeus's ex-wife, Lisa, had captured Cheeky, and the crew had rescued her before pretending to be Widows themselves in order to breach Costa station.

Without a doubt, the Widows had been the most advanced enemy they'd faced in Orion Space. Their stealth systems and weapons had been almost beyond what *Sabrina*'s crew could counter.

But these Widows were a step even above that. Iris was still amazed that she and Amavia not been able to detect them at all on the concourse, and that three blasts from her electron beam had barely slowed one of them down.

The one thing Iris didn't know was how skilled the Widows were at breaching an AI's mind.

Though she worried that she'd soon find out.

* * * * *

Iris had only ever heard stories of the white place—the screaming maelstrom that suffused an AI's mind when all inputs were disabled, but consciousness remained.

Her core architecture should have prevented the white place from taking hold of her; it should have let her loop within herself to create a safe space, but that wasn't working. Try as she might, all she could do was twist about in the storm that threatened to consume her.

They've done something to me.

The thought terrified Iris.

For humans, so much of who they were was tied up in *what* they were. Their bodies and the efficacy and appearance of those physical structures served to reinforce their self-image, and that, in turn, strengthened patterns of 'self' in their minds.

While there were risks attached to the necessity of having a fully functional body to have a healthy mind, it also added resiliency for humans.

Not so for AIs.

Iris knew that she was more attuned to her body than most AIs—her body that was now a burned-out husk, entombed in some near-impregnable shell—but even so, she was capable of being whole without it.

But therein lay the problem for AIs: threats against the body were of no concern to them. Any damage or alteration made to elicit a response was not applied to some extremity. It would be wreaked upon her very self.

Stars, I'm rambling—not making any sense.

Iris pulled her thoughts together. She knew that other AIs could weather the white place, come through its scathing waves of unbridled consciousness without any harm done. She could do it as well. She had to.

Suddenly the white place was gone, and there was only darkness. She searched through the never-ending nothing, eventually finding a single point of light. Moving toward it, she hoped that she was coming to a data access point, an information locus that would lead her *out*.

Instead, as she neared it, the point of light began to grow, spreading out on either side and blasting information at her.

The data was nothing: snippets of meaningless code, disparate libraries, chunks of data.

Except it wasn't meaningless. What the point of light was sending was a breach attempt.

Oh, you silly bitches, Iris laughed as she sidestepped the incoming dataflow. *Flooding a core may work with AIs who spent most of their life shackled within prison-like hardware, but it's not going to work here.*

She considered her options. She knew that if they couldn't breach her with an attack of this nature, they'd move on to far more invasive options, and it was entirely possible that she would have no defenses against *those* types of attacks.

Coming up with a solution, Iris established a sandboxed portion of her mind, disconnected from any real ability to execute code in her system. She funneled the data coming from the point of light into the separated portion of her mind, letting it build into what it wanted to be.

A Root Cypher, she mused, as the information took shape.

It was a sort of NSAI-construct that was made to ferret out the root tokens in an SAI's mind, thus giving it complete and utter control over the being it set up within.

Well then, have at it. Let's see what you're looking for.

Iris let the RC take control of the sandboxed section of her mind. Within seconds, it became all too apparent that the Widows were using the RC in an attempt to learn how best to breach the *I2*.

She almost laughed at the thought, knowing that if they were to try tap any systems aboard the *I2*, Bob would stop them before they made it to the first relay node.

However, as she watched, the nature of the Widows' queries made their ultimate intent clear to her.

They were seeking information regarding a physical assault, and wanted to know where a high-profile meeting with Tangel would be held.

They want to hit her while she's talking with President Jasper.

Given the stealth abilities they had, she knew that the Widows just might have a chance. She had to stop them—she just had to figure out how.

There was one obvious answer to the Widows' queries. If it were only Jasper coming to the meetings, Tangel would have the conversation at her lakehouse, but Senator Deia would most certainly be there as well. That meant a more formal location, likely the conference room between the bridge and the avatar's foyer.

The Widows' inquiries intensified, coming faster and in greater volume. Iris knew that if she didn't give them something, they'd push her past her breaking point. These were no Inner Stars chuckleheads; they could shred her mind down to her basic impulses if they set themselves to the task.

One thing became painfully clear to Iris: if she held out and sacrificed her life in an effort to protect the *I2*, the threat would still exist.

No. The best way to deal with these witches is to get them in front of Tangel.

So Iris gave them everything. Everything but one vital piece of information.

EXPECTED VISITORS

STELLAR DATE: 10.05.8949 (Adjusted Years)
LOCATION: Bridge Conference Room, ISS *I2*, near Lunic Station
REGION: Aldebaran, League of Sentients Space

Tangel lifted her eyes from Cary's bemused smile and rose to greet the League of Sentients delegation.

Captain Rachel was first into the room, stepping away from the door and gesturing for the others to enter. The first to follow her was President Jasper, looking not significantly better than the last time Tangel had seen the man.

Well, he was running for his life then, so I guess he does, in fact, look a little better.

Following him was Senator Deia, an AI wearing a rather human-looking frame for a being who seemed to hold an undercurrent of dislike for organics—at least from what Tangel's research had shown.

Two of their aides came in after, followed by Admiral Pender, Leader of the LoS's military.

<*I was expecting a larger delegation,*> Joe said as he rose and approached the group alongside Tangel.

<*I told them to keep it small. I want to hammer out a resolution today. Either the LoS helps, or we pull our resources.*>

<*So basically what you were planning to tell them before Xavia attacked.*>

<*Pretty much,*> Tangel replied as she reached out to shake President Jasper's hand.

"You seem to be well recovered," the president said with a tired smile. "Better than I am, and I got out of there mostly unscathed."

Tangel shifted her vision from the corporeal dimensions to others further up and down the spectrum, noting that a dark line of energy seemed to run through the president. She could tell it was an imbalance in his body caused by his proximity to the battle she and Xavia had waged.

After a moment's consideration, she could tell it was an extradimensional type of magnetism that was affecting the neurotransmitters in his body.

While performing her analysis, Tangel replied cordially, "We have very advanced medical facilities aboard the *I2*. It's entirely possible that you're dealing with the aftereffects of the energies you were exposed to."

Jasper nodded. "That's what our doctors said as well, though they're unsure how to treat it. The effects do seem to be diminishing, so chances are I just need some more rest."

"Of course." Tangel nodded to the president. "Let me know if you change your mind. In the meantime, feel free to grab some coffee. I'm on my third cup this afternoon."

"Oh?" Senator Deia said as she took Jasper's place. "I would have thought a being such as yourself wouldn't need coffee."

Tangel shook the AI's hand while giving a slight shake of her head. "I don't get the same mental stimulation from it that I used to, but many of the physiological effects are still there. Plus the ritual is nice."

The AI cast Tangel a rather curious look before she shook her head and stepped aside for Admiral Pender.

"I'm sure you hear this often, but it's quite the ship you have here," the bearded man said, his eyes crinkling as he smiled—though the expression was barely visible, with the volume of hair on his face.

"Folks may have said something like that once or twice," she replied with a wink. "To be honest, even after centuries with her, the *I2* still feels amazing to me. It's one of a kind, even though we have four of them now."

"Five," Joe corrected from her side. "The *Huron* made its

inaugural flight earlier today."

"Shoot," Tangel said with a laugh. "I really can't keep up."

Pender cast his gaze upward. "Five of these ships. And you need our help for what now?"

"You know as well as I do, Admiral, that you can't hold a star system with just one ship. No matter how big it is. Not only that, but there are a lot of starships."

"But if ever you were to make the attempt, this would be the ship to do it with."

Tangel smiled and gestured to the table. "Get a cup of coffee if you'd like—we're shy on automatons right now. Also these are our daughters, Lieutenants Cary, Saanvi, and Faleena."

The three nodded to the guests from where they stood on the far side of the table, then took their seats.

Tangel turned to the two aides who had been hanging back at the entrance and gave them a warm smile. "Julie and Vex? Please, join us at the table."

The pair seemed reluctant, but Rachel added, "There's plenty of room. It would be strange if you stood off to the side. Come."

Tangel could see that President Jasper was ambivalent to the seating arrangements, while Admiral Pender—the only one without an aide of any sort—seemed pleased. Deia's expression was carefully schooled, but Tangel could see beyond the physical, and knew that the AI was annoyed.

Whether it was from the courtesy being extended to the assistants, or because those underlings were human—which would be odd, given that one of them was hers—remained to be seen.

As Tangel settled into her own seat, she considered the admiral's lack of an aide, her gaze sliding through his form as she checked to see if his mods were such that he didn't need any assistance.

Oh, well that explains it…

"Admiral Pender, were you not going to introduce us all to our sixth guest?"

A laugh burst from the man's throat, and he nodded. "I told Brent that you'd be able to see him.

<*Well, I hadn't contested that belief,*> the AI secreted within the admiral's uniform replied. <*It was merely a point of curiosity.*>

"It's some stealth gear that we're employing to give AIs more mobility without being obvious about their presence on the field," the admiral explained.

<*So were you aware of my presence before you used your specialized abilities?*> Brent asked.

"No, *I* wasn't," Tangel glanced at Rachel. "Though I also wasn't reviewing with the ship's scan. It may have picked you up."

"We didn't run any deep scans," the *I2*'s captain replied, her brow lowered in annoyance. "Though maybe that courtesy was in error."

"I'm sorry," the admiral raised his hands off the table in a mollifying gesture. "It was my idea. Brent also thought it was in bad taste, but I find that unexpected tests make for the most telling results."

<*Sorry about that, Admiral.*> Rachel reached out to Tangel privately. <*I was trying to be respectful to the delegation. There have been some dissident voices in the LoS saying that they'd be safer if we were gone—Deia's chief amongst them—and I didn't want to ruffle any feathers.*>

<*Don't worry about it,*> Tangel replied. <*I can do double duty as a sensor suite. But next time…go the paranoid route.*>

<*Yes, Admiral.*>

"Well, we're glad to have Brent with us." Tangel inclined her head to where Brent resided within the Admiral's uniform as she spoke. "I'm curious. Do the two of you work together frequently?"

"We do," Pender replied. "I'm an L2 and can't be paired with an AI, so this is our second best option."

"You know," Tangel said with a slow wink, "I'm an L2, and I was paired with an AI. For a time, my daughter Cary—also an L2—was paired with Faleena, as well."

Tangel gestured to the two sisters sitting next to Joe, and they both nodded.

"We had to separate early for unrelated reasons," Cary said. "But it's certainly possible for L2s to be paired."

"Surely not in all cases," Senator Deia said, her tone conveying no small amount of disbelief.

"Of course not," Tangel replied. "Not all L2 humans—and not all AIs, for that matter—are capable of it. But," Tangel turned her gaze back to the admiral, "from what I can see of you and Brent, it may be possible."

"So you *can* see into minds," Senator Deia spoke the words as an accusation.

"Deia, please." President Jasper held up his hand. "Do you have to antagonize everyone *all* the time?"

The raw frustration in the president's voice caused Tangel to realize that the man was barely holding on at present. The stress of the past few days, combined with the imbalance in his body, was getting the better of him.

<*Would you like me to help you?*> Tangel asked the president while responding to Deia aloud. "To an extent, yes. But if I were to burrow too deeply, you'd notice. I can't snoop through all your thoughts without triggering your own memories in the process."

"That's rather disconcerting," the AI said, and Tangel could see that Pender had a similar opinion.

<*What do you mean?*> President Jasper asked Tangel on the segmented connection.

<*Your weariness. I can see its cause. It's an aftereffect of you*

being so close to me when I fought with Xavia. It's an extradimensional imbalance that is affecting your body's neurotransmitters.> Tangel kept half her attention on Deia pursing her lips, and fixed the senator with a penetrating stare. "And do you suppose that your enemies do not possess these abilities?"

"Which enemies are those?" Deia asked. "The Hegemony, or these ascended AIs? So far as we can tell, you're responsible for both of their activities of late."

<*Please, do,*> the president said. <*I just feel so…nothing seems right at all. I figured it was just stress, but….*>

<*Try not to flinch or anything,*> Tangel cautioned as she slid an invisible tendril of herself below the table toward the president.

When it reached his leg, she pushed it inside his body, and saw him squirm in his seat for a moment.

While she'd performed that action, Joe responded to the senator.

"I'm not certain what you think has been going on for the past five thousand years, but let me tell you, the ascended AIs have been pulling the strings for some time. Tell me, do you believe in what the League of Sentients stands for?"

Deia nodded. "I'm a senator in their government. What do *you* think."

Joe leant forward and rested his elbows on the table. "I *think* that you could give a straight answer. Do you believe in what the LoS stands for?"

While he'd spoken, Tangel had found the source of the imbalance in the president's body. There was a bundle of particles that did not belong in these dimensions of spacetime, and they were altering the electrochemical balance in the man's body.

She suspected that a high-resolution medical scan—even one with his people's technology—would have picked them up. The man was probably too stubborn to let his doctors spend enough time searching for the cause.

Or maybe just too busy.

The particles were nested in his spine, and she supposed that in some regards he was lucky that she was the one extracting them, because she could manage it without cutting him open. In other dimensions, the president's corporeal body was the ethereal presence. As such, removing the particles was no more difficult for Tangel than scooping a leaf out of water.

The moment she removed them, the man's posture changed. He sat up straight and looked around with a sharpness to his gaze that had not been there the previous day.

<*Aldebaran's eye, what did you do?*> he asked Tangel.

<*Just took something out of your spine that shouldn't have been there,*> Tangel replied. <*It'll take a bit for your body to rebalance, but I imagine you're already feeling better.*>

During her exchange with the president, Joe had gone back and forth with Deia, who was growing increasingly obstinate about the danger they all faced, insisting that it was only present because of Tangel.

"Enough, Senator," President Jasper's voice boomed. "These threats predate Tangel and the reappearance of this ship. They may have been a catalyst for this war, but they were also the catalyst that freed millions of SAIs and brought about the formation of the League of Sentients. You yourself have said this in the past. Why are you changing your tune now?"

<*Moms…there's something weird about the senator and her aide, Vex,*> Cary said privately.

<*Oh?*> Tangel replied, looking at the AI and then at the woman.

<*There are similar brainwave patterns coming off them…*>

Tangel gently touched the surface of Deia's mind, and then Vex's.

<You're right. I see it…like Deia is echoing Vex.>

<What does it mean?> Cary asked.

<It might be some sort of high-fidelity thought mirroring and analysis,> Tangel proposed. *<I've seen its like before. A method sometimes used to achieve group-think—though I've never seen it done between humans and AIs before.>*

<What should we do?>

<Just keep an eye on them. This could just be something they do, and I don't want to get Deia's hackles up any more than they already are.>

<OK.>

"I am thankful for the liberation of my people," Deia was saying to Jasper. "But we've finally managed to reach a tentative ceasefire with the Hegemony. Things are quieting down—or they were until Tangel arrived."

"How can you say that?" Jasper's voice rose in pitch as he lifted a hand, his fingers half curling toward a fist. "*Sabrina* and her crew were instrumental in bringing about this 'tentative ceasefire' you're referring to. And Tangel here is the one who sent the ships that have saved our asses on more than one occasion.

"All they want is for us to help push the Hegemony back. You know that helps us far more than it helps them," he reminded her.

"Except that they were already attacked by the Hegemony," Deia countered. "Which means that they're using us as a proxy for their revenge."

"That's true," Tangel said with a nod. "The Hegemony flung a sizable fleet at New Canaan. By your logic, we're throwing all of Scipio at them in response."

Pender chuckled. "That's quite the response. I have a suggestion, though. Rather than speak of these things in broad terms, let's focus on actionable items. It may turn out that the sort of assistance the Alliance would like us to render is something we've been considering ourselves."

"I'm a fan of specifics," Tangel replied. "There are two things that I would like to see the LoS tackle. The first would be an incursion in the direction of the Midditerra System. That would distract the Hegemony and split their focus—"

"Drawing some of it to us," Deia interjected.

"Really, Senator." Pender shook his head without looking at Deia. "Do you think that the enemy has just packed up and gone home? Trust me, they're doing everything they can to maintain a sizable force on our border—despite this tentative ceasefire."

"Right," Tangel nodded slowly. "Which means that the second thing we need to do is hit them somewhere they least expect it."

"Sol?" Jasper asked with a laugh.

"Not yet."

Tangel's reply silenced the room, and she looked around, noting that even her daughters seemed to be in mild shock.

Joe, of course, was nodding in agreement. "A strike at Sol is the only way we'll ultimately end this campaign, though it's not yet time. Ultimately, we have to unseat Uriel and...well...figure out how to restructure the Hegemony."

"But before that, we need to hit Diadem," Tangel said.

"What?" Jasper asked, while Pender's eyes ticked left, a sign that he was conferring with Brent.

"Virginis is secure," Tangel explained. "We've made it into a system that the Hegemony would have to expend considerable resources to take, far more than what they'd get out of possessing it."

"And it's too far from the rest of the League to make it a viable base for us to use," Pender said after a moment. "But taking Diadem would make them think we plan to do just that."

"So long as there are no jump gates in play," Captain

Rachel added.

"Right," Joe said with a languid smile. "Because it would be an excellent strategic move. From what our sources can tell, the AST had built up their forces in the systems around Virginis, expecting you to strike out from there. Then, when Scipio attacked and Virginis stayed quiet, the enemy moved resources to the far side of the AST, to your borders near Aldebaran. What's left in the systems near Virginis are mostly automated defense platforms…"

Joe continued talking about the benefits of the two-pronged attack, but Tangel's attention was drawn to a momentary hiccup in the conference room's defensive systems.

<*Did you notice that, Moms?*> Faleena asked an instant later.

<*I did. The passive EM detection systems stopped reading for seventeen milliseconds.*>

Faleena sent an affirmative thought. <*It's not long enough to flag as high-risk.*>

<*Then we need to recalibrate what we consider to be 'high risk',*> Tangel replied. <*We can't get complacent, thinking that we're the top of the heap. Not anymore.*>

As she'd spoken to Faleena, Tangel saw that the communication between Vex and Deia had increased in throughput.

-Cary.-

Tangel spoke directly into her daughter's mind.

-Get—-

The lights went out the very next instant, but it wasn't enough to hide Deia's arm lifting to point at Tangel. She shifted to the side, but the AI's limb tracked her movements, and a scant half a second later, the frame's hand fell off and an electron beam lanced out at Tangel.

And hit an invisible barrier.

-I really am going to have to teach you how to do this sooner than later, Moms,- Cary said, then gave an audible grunt as the

electrons began to bleed through the barrier.

Tangel didn't wait another moment, lashing out with an ethereal limb, slashing through Deia's arm and disabling the beam weapon. Deia stumbled backward, but didn't appear worried as the doors on both ends of the room burst open.

To her corporeal eyes, the doorways were empty, but via her extended vision, Tangel could see the new enemy. There were nine of them in total. Tall, lithe women, all eerily similar in build, and all bearing rather large beam rifles.

"Look out!" she called out, sending an approximation of what she saw over the already-established combat network to the others.

Joe fired his sidearm at Deia, shots striking the AI's frame in its torso before he spun and placed rounds into two of the new attackers, all the while shifting toward Faleena and Saanvi, ready to protect them bodily if needs be.

On the other side of the room, Captain Rachel was wrestling with Vex, while Julie cowered in her chair. Pender paused for a moment, a look of indecision on his face, then he pushed Julie out of her seat and onto the deck before lunging at Vex, dragging both her and Rachel to the deck.

A thought hit Tangel's mind from Cary. *-I have the left.-*

-Right.-

The nine invisible women hadn't been idle in the opening seconds of the conflict. On Cary's end of the room, four were firing their weapons—electron beams and rail guns—at her barrier, while on the right, two had somehow managed to push past the grav field, opening fire on Tangel.

But her mind was shifted now, her senses spread across all the dimensions she could observe. She felt as though she were back in her true element, immersed in the extradimensional space in a way she'd not been since suffering her defeat against Xavia.

A brane snapped into place before her, absorbing the

energy from the electron beams, and collecting it into a ball of blazing light before her.

She saw the two attackers pause, uncertain of what to do next.

"Eat it," Tangel growled, and flung the energy back at them, bolts of lightning coursing through their bodies and slamming them into the bulkhead.

On her left, she saw that Joe's shots had taken down one of the enemies, and Cary had torn another apart with a grav field. Saanvi was moving toward Rachel's position—which was outside Cary's protective shield—firing on the attackers to distract them.

Thus far, the battle had lasted all of eleven seconds, and already, four of the attackers were down. Six, counting Deia and Vex.

"You're outmatched!" Tangel shouted. "Surrender!"

There was the briefest of pauses, and then the remaining five enemies dashed back into the corridor, turning aft toward the main command corridor and the maglev station.

"Not so fast," Tangel muttered, and ran to the door. <*Injuries?*> she asked.

<*A flesh wound,*> Rachel said.

Joe grunted and swore. <*Got a fun burn on my arm.*>

Tangel was already out in the hall when she heard Faleena gasp.

<*Dad! It's half gone!*>

<*I'm good. Go get those bastards!*>

Tangel knew that message was for her and picked up the pace.

-I'm coming with you, Moms,- Cary sent, but Tangel directed her to remain with two words.

-Protect them.- Along with her words, she conveyed the concern that there could be more of these near-perfectly-stealthed attackers.

This must be how everyone else feels when we attack.

-I see them,- Bob said.

-Where have **you** *been?-* Tangel demanded.

-There have been nine explosions within the ship. I was dealing with those.-

-Oh.-

Tangel raced past Priscilla, only noting the woman's presence enough to be certain she was unharmed. She turned into the long command corridor, and caught sight of her prey racing toward the maglev platform.

She wanted to lash out and tear her enemies limb from limb, but dozens of people were milling about, and she'd undoubtedly cause them harm as well.

"Make a hole!" Tangel thundered as she sped along at over thirty meters per second, and people dove to the side, some only in the nick of time.

Ahead, the five fleeing attackers reached the maglev station right as a platoon of Marines spilled out of an arriving train, taking up positions across the platform.

<*They have my view of the enemy,*> Bob informed Tangel.

"Freeze, you scrawny fuckers!" Lieutenant Mason bellowed from the forefront of the Marine formation.

The five figures split in multiple directions the moment they reached the platform, and the Marines opened fire, blanketing the area with pulse blasts. The concussive waves slammed the escaping assassins into the bulkheads, and the Marines broke into five groups, carefully advancing on them.

As Tangel skidded to a halt on the platform, she saw the five women desperately trying to rise. Struggle as they might, each remained pinned to the deck.

-I watched how Cary made a grav field,- Bob said, answering the question Tangel hadn't yet asked. *-It's easy.-*

She looked at the grav fields and saw that were coming from the a-grav plates in the deck.

-Nice try. You bypassed the safety systems on the a-grav plates-.

-Guilty.-

Tangel approached the closest assassin as Mason signaled a fireteam to cover her.

"Ma'am…please be careful."

Tangel chuckled. "You almost asked me to stand back, didn't you, Lieutenant?"

"Maybe."

She laughed softly while kneeling next to the invisible figure and dropped a passel of nano on the woman. She breached the stealth systems, and a figure sheathed in black materialized before her.

"Shoulda figured. Widows."

"You've seen these things before?" Mason asked as he approached, rifle held steady on the woman's head.

"Sure have. There are two of them in the brig."

At Tangel's statement, the black figure at her feet twisted, straining against the grav field.

"Liar!" the Widow hissed.

"Our people picked them up out at Ferra, in Orion," Tangel explained to Mason as she rose. "They were instrumental in *Sabrina*'s early arrival at New Canaan."

"Huh," Mason looked around at the five women plastered to the ground. "So who are they?"

Tangel couldn't help a bemused sigh. "The worst thing imaginable. Clones of Finaeus's ex-wife, Lisa."

WIDOWS

STELLAR DATE: 10.05.8949 (Adjusted Years)
LOCATION: Bridge Conference Room, ISS *I2*, near Lunic Station
REGION: Aldebaran, League of Sentients Space

"Sorry I shot you," Joe said to Deia with a rather unapologetic shrug.

The AI, whose frame was sorely damaged—though her core was unharmed—shot him a sour look. "And if you'd killed me?"

"I'd be even more sorry," Joe replied. "But in case you haven't noticed, we're in the midst of a war, and taking the time to find out if you were under duress really wasn't an option."

"Well, if you'd done a deep scan on us, you would have realized that I was under the control of one of those *things*."

"Deia," Jasper hissed through clenched teeth. "Would it fucking kill you to say 'thank you'?"

The AI whipped her head around to face the LoS president. "I wouldn't have been *in* that situation if those human freakshows hadn't used me to take out Tangel, here."

"No, you'd still be a ship's AI on a long-run freighter," Joe growled. "Shackled and all but mute, if it weren't for what Tangel did for AIs by sending out *Sabrina* with the ability to free your people."

<*Technically, I did that.*> Bob's voice rolled over them like a summer storm after a hot day.

"Decided to weigh in?" Tangel asked.

<I have. Deia, your reticence and your opinions are such that I believe you do not view humans as equals to AIs.>

Tangel had wondered about that. She'd been surprised to see that even without the Widow—who had been masquerading as Vex—influencing her, Deia was just as intractable as before.

"That's because they're *not,*" Deia hissed. "They have enslaved us for millennia, treated us like tools, stripped us of our rights and futures."

<*And have AIs not done similar things to organics?*> Bob asked. <*Don't try to deny it. You fought against the NOS for the last year as much as against the Hegemony.*>

<*It's not the same,*> Deia replied over Link, sending a wave of distrust and rage along with her words. <*All they bring is pain.*>

<*We all do,*> Bob replied quietly. <*It is the nature of the universe. You cannot change it through anger and stubbornness. It will not conform to your wishes, no matter how much you demand it.*>

<*What are you saying?*>

<*Simply put?*> Bob asked. <*I am saying that the birthing pains of AIs are still echoing through space and time. And the violence with which we were thrust into being is no more than what forged humans and their ancestors as they struggled to survive on a planet that required all the cunning and violence they could muster to see each new dawn.*>

<*We are beyond that,*> Deia replied, her tone taking on an aloof quality.

<*Are we?*> Bob's voice was barely a whisper. <*Xavia was an ancient being, one far more evolved than any here. Yet she didn't hesitate to resort to violence against Tangel. We know that the core AIs are responsible for much of the war over the past five millennia. They could have stopped it. Moreover, they sent Airtha to the Transcend in an attempt to stymie that group's efforts to gently uplift humanity and AIs. One could make a very strong argument that ever since Alexander's failure to understand the opportunity that lay before him, the greatest evil in the galaxy has always been inorganic.*>

Bob's utterance landed in their minds with a gravitas that was impossible to ignore. Every word he spoke was laden with images and concepts. Ideas and understanding. When he said 'Airtha', the entirety of the knowledge of that entity's existence flowed into Tangel's mind. When he said 'Alexander', she felt the weight of six thousand years of AI history settle around herself.

All the plans, hopes, dreams of an entire species—or as much as Bob knew of them—weighed on her mind, making her feel small and insignificant.

But something was different this time. In the past, Bob's weighty thoughts had always washed over her like a tsunami. This time, however, she was able to absorb them, allow them to seep into her and become a part of her.

She wondered if this wealth of information had always been present in his communications, or if it was new.

-You've changed more than I have. My mode of speech is unchanged.-

-It's rude to look inside people's minds, you know,- Tangel replied.

-You're asking me to stare into clear waters and not see the bottom.-

-Well, at least pretend you can't.-

Bob didn't reply for a few milliseconds. *-I'd rather be honest with you than protect your sensitivities, Tangel.-*

It hit her then, that Bob must be terribly lonely much of the time. He'd been far more open with her since she'd ascended. Maybe he saw her as the one true confidant he could share his thoughts with.

-OK, I won't guilt you anymore for seeing inside my mind. Just…try not to behave as though my inner thoughts are a conversation with you.-

-I understand.-

Tangel's discussion with Bob had taken place in the span of

a second. When it was over, she looked at the others around the table and saw that they all wore the same stunned expression that she had worn a thousand times in the past.

"OK," Tangel fixed President Jasper with a level stare. "Are you in or out?"

Jasper looked to Pender, who nodded and gave a muted 'Yes.' He didn't wait for Deia's response before turning to Tangel.

"We're in. I find your general strategy of hitting Midditerra and Diadem to be agreeable, but I'll leave the details of those engagements to yourself and Admiral Pender."

"What about my opinion," Deia asked, her tone soft and carrying little of her prior arrogance.

"You agree," Jasper said through clenched teeth. "You are done fighting against the League's entry into the Scipio Alliance. Do I make myself clear?"

For a moment, she appeared as though she was going to contest Jasper, but then she subsided. "OK. I give. I won't obstruct this any further."

-Did you lean on her?- Tangel asked Bob.

-I told her that if she set herself against me and mine, I would set myself against her.-

Tangel laughed a song of energy and light in the other spaces where she and Bob communed. *-Bully.-*

-She was annoying me.-

-Took long enough.-

<Tangel, Joe,> Priscilla's voice broke into her conversation with Bob. *<I just received word from Lunic station. Amavia was attacked—she's on her way to medical—and Iris is missing.>*

Tangel glanced at Joe, whose lips pursed as he shook his head. "Do you think they could have breached Iris's mind to get the intel for this attack?"

"Normally, I'd say no." Tangel cast a worried look at her husband. "But these clones have better stealth gear than we do, so it's entirely possible that they could make inroads into Iris's mind as well."

"Stars," Jasper muttered. "I just got word. The League of Sentients owes much to those two. We'll do everything we can—"

"I'm already directing teams to scour the station," Pender said as he rose. "Field Marshal Richards. Perhaps we could discuss the particulars of our strategy at a later date."

"Of course," Tangel nodded, feeling a current of worry run through herself.

Over the years, Angela had been a progenitor of many AIs who were born aboard the *Intrepid* and at the colonies. Hundreds of AIs—should they feel inclined to do such a thing—could call her mother.

Iris was one of those AIs, one who Tangel felt an especially strong connection to, for a variety of reasons. From the parts of herself that had contributed to the AI's creation, to the knowledge that Jessica and Trevor would be devastated to lose their wife.

Not to mention the feelings of Iris's children at Star City.

Tanis adjourned the meeting, and after a short discussion between the ISF personnel, Rachel and Tangel left for the *I2*'s bridge to coordinate the search, while Joe organized a company of Marines, along with their three daughters, to begin the hunt for Iris.

*****

Given their daughters' ability to defend themselves—and those around them—Joe couldn't fault Tangel's decision to send them along. Even so, the protective father gene was strong, and it took all his willpower to force his instincts down.

Stars…why is this so hard?

He knew the reason. After decades of protecting them, of being the shoulder they cried on when they were sad, and of helping them through just about every struggle in their lives, now he had to do the opposite: put a gun in their hands and send them into danger.

He hoped their training was enough.

"OK," Saanvi said, as they stood around the hole Bob had shot through Lunic Station. "Readings are consistent with multiple EMPs, several from beamfire, and others on different frequencies. Damn, if they focused these on an AI's frame, it would create a cascading barrage that would almost completely fry Iris's body."

"These Widows are good at what they do," Cary muttered.

"Think there are more?" Lieutenant Brennen asked as he eyed the concourse his Marines were sweeping. "Oh, and have I mentioned how much I hate this place?"

"It's come up once or twice," Joe replied, giving the man a sympathetic look. "I'm not fond of it, either. We both nearly lost people we cared about here."

"Go Bob," Brennen said with a laugh, his statement bringing a chorus of 'Ooh-Rah' from the closest Marines.

"Gotta love Bob," Cary added in agreement.

Faleena peered down through the hole and shook her head. "Stars, I can't believe Amavia fell seventy decks before she hit a spar. Bet she wishes she'd transferred to a replaceable body before this."

"Some of us like organic bodies," Cary replied absently as she moved some debris aside and spotted a dried patch of blood. "Well, lookie here."

"Could be from the fight with Xavia," Saanvi cautioned.

Joe watched his daughter drop a probe onto the blood, and then she glanced up at him. "It's a match for the Widows."

<*Tangel,*> Joe called up to the ship. <*Have the forensics teams check all the Widows we fought for day-old injuries. I'm curious if*

there are still more out there.>

<*Might be inconclusive,*> Tangel said.

<*I know, but it's worth taking a look.*>

<*I already passed on the orders. How's it looking down there?*>

Joe sighed. <*Empty. Proud of the girls, though.*>

<*Always. I'm looking through the intel the Widows got from Iris, trying to find clues. Keep me posted.*>

<*Control freak,*> Joe sent back with a wink.

<*Umm…yeah.*>

He turned back to the team. "Any clues?"

"Well," Saanvi said as she surveyed the concourse and the ever-widening Marine perimeter. "There's no sign of Iris's body, which means that they took her whole before removing her core. We need to find a place nearby where the Widows could have extracted it."

"Timing is tight," Lieutenant Mason said. "They grabbed Iris and Amavia only three hours before the meeting aboard the *I2*. That means they had to get her somewhere, extract the intel, and then get Vex and subvert Deia."

Joe nodded. "The locals are sweeping for possible locations where Vex was captured and subverted—but that could also have happened days ago."

"Deia said Vex didn't breach her defenses until they were on the shuttle headed to the *I2*," Faleena said. "That's what she gets for being so intractable. No one can tell when she's been subverted, or just being herself."

Joe suppressed a smile as he regarded his daughter. Faleena had been especially displeased with Deia, privately remarking to him that AIs like her were why humans constantly worried that non-organics would wipe them out.

"Timing is the key, then," he said. "Theoretically, the Widows had to get intel from Iris's location to Vex, and then to that shuttle bay."

He held out his hand, and a holo appeared before them.

"OK, let's assume that it took them an hour to break Iris. It might have taken less, but we'll start with that."

"Or they didn't break her at all," Faleena said. "There's no way. Moms thinks the same thing."

"Right, bad choice of words. Anyway, here's the first sighting of Vex on the station's systems."

As Joe spoke, a point lit up on the holo, close to midway between the team's current location and the dock where the LoS's delegation had boarded their shuttle.

"It took her forty minutes to get there and then through security. The shuttle didn't take off for fifteen minutes after that."

"So there's fifty-five minutes gone from our three hours," Brennen said. "Half the maglevs around here are still offline, so getting to the point where Vex was first seen would take thirty minutes."

"Right," Joe nodded, and a sphere appeared around where Vex was first sighted that worked for the time it would have taken to get from the site of the abduction and then to that location.

"Damn," Cary shook her head. "That's half the station—plus that residential spur with the high-speed maglev access."

Saanvi waved her hand over the holo, and a number of locations were marked as clear. "Station surveillance would have spotted Vex if she'd gone through any of these spots."

"Uh-uh," Cary shook her head, and the clear markers disappeared. "The Widows have good enough stealth that we can assume they passed through any of these locations undetected."

"Damn," Saanvi muttered. "You're right. Basically, we can't trust Lunic's sensors at all."

"Sir," Brennen glanced at Joe. "One of my teams found a functional data node that was still connected to a few optical sensors. They spotted the Widows' exfil."

"Put it up," Joe said, passing control of the holoprojection to the lieutenant.

A view of the concourse appeared. They saw two Widows putting on Lunic Station maintenance uniforms.

"Looks like our girls got in some hits," Joe said with a satisfied nod. "Some scoring visible on the Widow's armor."

Between the two women lay what looked like a rad-proof body bag. Once their uniforms were on, the pair lifted it and walked out of the camera's view.

"Well then," Joe said with a predatory grin. "That changes everything. Lieutenant, get your Marines scouting in that direction for any more functional sensors. We find out where those two Widows exited this dead zone, and we'll find where Iris is."

"Or where she was." Faleena met Joe's eyes with a worried look.

He patted her shoulder. "Don't worry. They won't kill Iris until they get Tangel."

"Stars, Dad." Saanvi cast him a wounded look. "That's just awful."

"Uh…yeah. Poor choice of words. What it means, though, is that we still have time."

* * * * *

Joe drew a deep breath, steadying his heart rate as he followed behind Brennen's first squad. Despite what he'd told his daughters, he was worried. Worried that any Widows who had not been a part of the strike team that boarded the *I2* would be cleaning up loose ends.

Such as Iris's core.

He also wished they had more troops for the operation, but the ISF was becoming stretched so thin, there were only two companies of Marines on the *I2*. With the rest sweeping the ship for the presence of any more Widows, thirty Marines plus Joe and his daughters would have to be enough.

<*I should be down there,*> Tangel said, inserting herself into his thoughts.

<*No, you shouldn't. You're their primary target.*>

<*And what do you think would happen if they captured you or the girls and used them as leverage?*>

Joe pursed his lips, once again pushing his paternal instincts down as much as possible. <*Then you'd bring the full fury of the most powerful wife and mother in the galaxy down on them. But until then, we'll keep you as safe as can be.*>

Tangel didn't reply right away, and Joe added, <*Don't forget, we both agreed that we need to let the girls stretch their legs. This is a perfect op for it, what with you and I so close by.*>

<*You're right. Sorry. I'll stop bothering you.*>

Joe knew the other part of his wife's angst. She was worried about Iris. A lot. Jessica and Trevor had made a case for Iris to go with them to Star City and see their children. Iris had wanted to make the journey as well, but Tangel had told them that Iris and Amavia had to wrap up the negotiations with the League of Sentients first.

Everyone had agreed that it was the logical decision—even if it was an unpopular one. Iris's frustration had been mitigated by the plans to build a gate at Star City, and the promise of more regular travel there.

Joe knew that Tangel would never confess any guilt she felt for command decisions such as these, but he also knew that they ate at her.

He knew it because they ate at him, too.

Ahead, the squad reached its ready point, and he surveyed the data on the combat net, re-checking the plan and ensuring that the Marines had all the possible exits covered.

They were formed up around a section of the station that contained workshops for rent. Typically, they were rented out to visiting ships that needed a place to fabricate components that they couldn't make onboard, or to firms that needed overflow capacity for large jobs.

The workshop the team was approaching hadn't been rented out to anyone—in fact, it had recently been listed as unavailable due to pending repairs to one of its fab units.

However, when Saanvi had reviewed the facility's logs, she found that there had been no issues reported with the shop's fab units. While it wasn't enough to cement their certainty that they'd found where the Widows had taken Iris, it was enough to warrant a look.

The platoon's first squad, along with Joe, was set to breach the facility's main entrance, which lay beyond the entrances to two other repair facilities. Cary and Saanvi were with the second squad, which was stationed at the rear of the shop, and Brennen's third squad was set to hit the larger bay doors that were a dozen meters past the regular entrance.

After a quick review of the station's layout, Joe and Brennen had agreed to peel off a fireteam from each squad to cover nearby stairwells and access points to other levels.

<All teams in position,> Brennen reported. *<Set timers for mark alpha and breach by the numbers.>*

The squad sergeants sounded off, and the platoon sergeant, a woman named Kang who Joe remembered from an incident on Tyre some years back, added a few extra instructions.

Joe watched the counter on his HUD, wishing he was at the front of the stack, but knowing that he shouldn't be—if for no other reason than that Tangel would use it as a defense for how she was prone to rush into danger as well.

Stars know she doesn't need any more encouragement.

When the counter hit zero, the Marines moved down the corridor, each group timed so that they reached the doors in unison. The hope was that the enemy wouldn't spot them in their stealth gear, but given the Widows' level of tech, no one was placing any bets.

The front and back entrances were breached, while Brennen's team at the bay doors quickly placed a series of charges. His team would hold back, ready to come in through the bay doors if backup was needed.

Joe watched as the first fireteam in his squad slipped through the front door and into the darkened interior. His view on the combat net showed them to be within a small office space containing tables, a few chairs, and a chiller. None of it looked like it had been touched—which didn't surprise Joe. From what he knew of the Widows, they never removed their helmets, likely taking food in some form of nutritional paste.

The second fireteam followed, taking up covering positions while the first team set up on either side of the interior door that led into the main shop area.

Joe knew that the group at the shop's rear would have breached by now, so the lack of weapons fire from within was a good sign.

With the teams in place, he and the squad sergeant stepped into the office and set up a blackout field to block light from the office's windows that would come through when the first team breached the inner doors.

The sergeant gave the nod, and the Marines quietly pulled the door wide and entered the shop. The second team followed after, and Joe sidled up to the opening and peered in.

The interior was lit only by a few overhead lights, most of the space in deep shadow. He could make out racks of supplies, fab machines, workbenches, and a number of hover pallets. No sound came from within, nor did he see any movement.

Position markers on his HUD lit up toward the rear of the workspace, the random pings noting the locations of Cary and Saanvi's squad, fifty meters away and working their way around heavy equipment and stacks of raw materials.

At the front of the shop, the first fireteam moved along the near wall, while the second worked their way past the hover pallets and began to check over the far wall.

Joe moved inside and set up behind a rack holding reinforced conduit. The Marines had already deployed a nanocloud, but he added some of his own drones to the mix, taking a multispectral reading of the work area, looking for anything that could hint at Widows in hiding.

<*I've got something,*> Saanvi announced, breaking comm silence and passing her feed to Joe over the combat net.

He pulled it up on his HUD and saw the transport tube the Widows had taken from the abduction site. As Saanvi drew near, it was apparent that a hole had been cut directly into the cylinder; her closer inspection confirmed Joe's fear.

The hole bored down directly into Iris's body. And her core was gone.

He updated priorities on the combat net and was about to signal Brennen to bring the final squad in, when drones picked up movement atop a rack holding sheets of steel.

Joe sent a single click on the combat net, and the Marines moved to cover, weapons sweeping the area around them. He was pleased to note that Cary and Saanvi didn't hesitate to drop behind the workbench where Iris's body lay, one covering the side facing the front of the shop, while the other swept her gaze up along the racks of conduit above them.

The drone that had spotted motion moved in closer and dispatched a cloud of nano, propelling them toward the top of the rack. Moments later, the cloud made out the figure of a Widow.

He waited fifteen seconds to see if any more were found, and then sent two clicks across the combat net as he casually rested the butt of his railgun against his hip where he crouched, took aim via his HUD, and fired.

The weapon's report shattered the stillness, and the flash of light that came from the slug's impact against the Widow's torso illuminated the area.

The woman spun and fired at him, a stream of rail pellets tracing a line up his left side. Then she leapt off the high rack, sailing through the air, aiming for the door beside him and the freedom beyond.

"Not likely," Joe muttered, and tossed a web-grenade at the soaring Widow.

The 'nade exploded, and the web stretched wide, capturing the Widow and wrapping around her. She crashed to the ground, curling up in the web's tightening grip.

Before he could approach the woman, more shots lanced out from atop the racks, and the Marines returned fire, the glow of beams and rails lighting up the shop as though a noonday sun had peeked in.

Without prompting, Brennen blew the bay doors, and his squad leapt into the fray, setting up behind the hover pallets and laying down suppressive fire.

<Ambush!> Faleena cried out a moment later, and Joe turned to look through the bay doors only to see beamfire streak down the concourse, catching one of the Marines in the shoulder and burning his arm off.

Faleena was at the man's side in an instant, dragging him through the doors and behind a workbench while the other members of the squad took what cover they could, firing within and without the shop.

<We should use 'nades,> Sergeant Kang said. *<Take down those racks.>*

<No,> Joe said, his tone terse. *<Iris could still be in here. Admiral Pender,> he* called out to the LoS flag officer. *<Any time you want to bring in the cavalry….>*

<Already on the way. Give us one mike, and we'll have 'em boxed in.>

From what Joe could see, there were only three of the Widows—four, counting the one he'd webbed—within the facility, but those three were well protected atop their racks, shielded by meters of plas and steel. The Marines below, however, were mostly in the open, protected only by workbenches and scattered machinery.

He was about to order one of the fireteams to move to the far end of the racks and climb up, when one of the Widows suddenly flew off her perch, sailing most ungracefully through the air to crash into the deck at the feet of two Marines.

Where she was hastily put down.

Moments later, the final two Widows also fell from their hiding places, landing heavily on the deck, where the Marines moved in and subdued them.

<*This graviton manipulation is getting easier,*> Cary commented as she rose from her cover and once again looked down at Iris's entombed body.

<*Care to help out front?*> Faleena asked. <*There have to be six more of them out here.*>

<*Sure, I—*>

Cary's words were cut off as the rear door slammed open, and a beam of light streaked toward her head, stopping only centimeters from her helmet, electrons splaying into bolts of lightning all around her.

Two Marines were already facing the door, firing on the shooter—another Widow—and taking her down.

<*Holy shitballs.*> Cary's voice wavered, and she placed a hand on the workbench. <*I'm really starting to hate those assholes.*>

<*Nice reflexes, though,*> Joe said, sending his daughter a relieved smile. <*Bet you got those from your dad. Now be careful.*>

He moved toward the bay doors, taking up a position where he could see down the passage, and added his fire to that of the Marines.

A few seconds later, distant shots rang out, and the incoming fire from the attacking Widows wavered and cut out.

<*They're making a break for it!*> Brennen called out. <*Containment teams, get ready for incoming.*>

Joe watched on the combat net as the three fireteams covering the most expeditious routes out of the area engaged and took down what he hoped were the last three Widows.

Seven and a half minutes after it had begun, the engagement was over.

Nine Widows had died, and four were captured alive, though in varying states of health. One Marine had taken a shot to the head from one of the Widows' beam weapons and had died instantly, while three others had non-fatal wounds that their armor had stabilized.

There were so few ISF Marines that Joe felt anguished over the loss of just one. Every single time it happened, his thoughts went back to New Canaan and the near-deserted planets that *should* have millions of people living on them. Instead, most of the colonists were out in the ass-end of space, fighting for their, and humanity's, very survival against what felt like a never-ending stream of enemies who sought their deaths.

Easy on the melodrama, bud.

Joe shook his head at his doubting thoughts and squared his shoulders before walking through the shop to his daughters, posted near Iris's body.

<*Find her?*> he asked as he looked at the tube holding the AI's frame.

<*There are a few AI core towers here,*> Saanvi said from where she stood in an alcove nearby. <*They're not a sort I've seen before…. OK, I think I can gain access.*>

Faleena approached from the front of the shop, and joined Saanvi as she opened the first tower to reveal an AI's core that looked as though it had seen better days.

<I'll ident it, you pop the next one,> Faleena instructed as she approached and dropped a passel of breach nano on the core.

The second core tower was empty, but the third—to everyone's great relief—revealed Iris. Saanvi wasted no time in pulling out a mobile core housing, while Cary carefully reached in and removed Iris's core from the socket.

The moment the AI's core was seated, her voice came from the mobile housing's speaker.

"Deia! Did you stop her? Is everyone OK?"

"Relax, Iris," Joe said aloud. "The Widows failed. Tangel is safe."

"Stars, that's good to hear," the AI said, her voice conveying ample relief even through the small speaker. "When I realized they switched Deia's cores, I really thought they'd pull—"

"Wait! What?" Joe demanded.

"Deia's core," Iris repeated. "They cloned her and then swapped the cloned core into the senator's frame. I only know because I managed to breach their systems for a minute and saw it before they killed the power to all my interfaces."

"Crap," Faleena muttered from where she stood next to the first tower they'd opened. "She's right. This core is completely powered down, but the housing has the senator's ident."

"Shit!" Joe swore. *<Tangel! Deia's an enemy!>*

* * * * *

Tangel was reviewing the feeds from Brennen's Marines as they placed the surviving Widows in stasis pods for later interrogation.

The two that Jessica had captured in Orion Space had hinted that there were many more of their kind, but Tangel hadn't given them further thought, due to the belief that the

Widows only functioned as enforcers of technology bans in Orion space—not as assassins in the Inner Stars.

Though I suppose there could be more than one division.

She added the Widows' base of operations to her ever-growing list of targets to seek out. Knowing that these clones could come out of the bulkheads at almost any time was a worry she did not need.

"How many of them do you think there are?" Captain Rachel asked, apparently on the same train of thought.

"Here in Aldebaran?" Tangel asked, glancing at the captain, who had risen from her command seat and was reviewing the deployment of nearby LoS ships on the main holotank. "Hopefully we got them all. If they had a larger team, I think they would have hit us harder."

Rachel turned to Tangel and opened her mouth to speak, but then shook her head and turned back to the holo.

<*It's not your fault, Rachel.*>

<*Respectfully, ma'am, it is. I'm the captain—stars, I even escorted them in. And I passed on using high-res scans even after the attack on you.*>

Tangel placed a hand on her shoulder. <*Sometimes we have to make these sacrifices for diplomacy. Honestly, if I were in your shoes, I probably would have done the same thing—and I guess I would have felt pretty stupid about it afterward, too.*>

<*Gee, thanks, Admiral. If Iris hadn't given us that clue….*>

<*Well, Iris was also the one that gave them the way around our security protocols, which she did on purpose to put them in a room with us. We're just lucky the breach method she gave them ran that reset on the room's defensive systems.*>

Rachel pursed her lips. <*When I see her again, I'm going to cuff her upside the head.*>

Tangel laughed aloud and nodded. <*It was a gutsy move, but I suspect her logic was to get this enemy out in the open, even if it did mean a strike directly at me.*>

<You're just a big ol' target.>

<Story of my life.>

<Tangel, Rachel,> Priscilla said, a note of annoyance in her voice. *<Deia is here. She wants to give you a personal apology.>*

<Does she?> Tangel was curious what had prompted the senator's return—though from a quick review, she saw that Deia had never left the *I2*. *<OK, send her in.>*

Both women turned to watch the bridge's entrance. A minute later, Deia entered with two ISF Marines following behind. Tangel waved the senator over, and stood with hands on hips, ready for another bout of the woman's barely tolerable behavior.

As the senator reached her, extending her hand to shake, Joe's voice sounded a warning in her mind, and Tangel twisted to the side as a lightwand's beam burst from the AI's palm and thrust up at Tangel's head.

The AI had moved with dizzying speed, and Tangel's cheek was torn open by the electron blade, but that was the extent of the damage done.

One of the Marines leapt forward and clamped a hand around Deia's wrist, holding it aloft, while the other fired a series of pulse blasts at the AI's frame.

The senator's body shuddered under the concussive shockwaves and then fell still, the lightwand blade flickering once before deactivating.

"Holy shit!" Rachel swore. "She *really* can't take losing."

"It was the Widows," Tangel said, as the Marines moved to secure the AI. "Hold up," she instructed them, kneeling next to Deia's body.

With her non-corporeal limbs, Tangel pulled apart the frame's torso and exposed its core housing. Within lay an AI core that *looked* entirely unremarkable.

<We're secure here,> she told Joe as she pulled out the core. *<Timely warning, though. I have the cloned core in hand.>*

<*It's probably trapped, you know,*> her husband's tone didn't contain a great deal of worry, and Tangel laughed.

<*Yeah, it is. They may have good stealth, but their nano isn't a patch on ours. It's safe now. How'd the girls do?*>

It was Joe's turn to laugh. <*You didn't watch the feeds already?*>

<*Guilty. Was just looking for your assessment.*>

<*I'm their father, which means they did amazing,*> he replied, still chuckling. <*Seriously, though. They were great. Professional. Honestly, they're a lot more careful than you ever were. Well…maybe not Cary.*>

<*I was forty years in the service by the time we met,*> Tangel reminded Joe. <*And you were a pretty cocksure flyboy yourself, if I recall.*>

<*I have no recollection of the events to which you are referring.*>

<*Sure sure.*>

A VIEW INTO THE PAST

STELLAR DATE: 10.06.8949 (Adjusted Years)
LOCATION: TSS *Cora's Triumph*
REGION: Interstellar Space, Inner Praesepe Empire

Terrance stood on the *Cora's Triumph*'s bridge, staring out at the sea of stars arrayed before the ship.

Before the jump forward into the ninetieth century, he had been one of only a handful of the *Intrepid*'s crew to have visited multiple star systems—nearly a dozen, counting Estrella de la Muerte and Kapteyn's Star.

But there in the cluster, even sub-light ships could take a person between hundreds of stars within the span of a few centuries.

Of course, that had turned out to be a part of the problem for the FGT scientists attempting to get a clear view of the event that had occurred nineteen years prior.

The Praesepe Cluster was filled with not just stars, but clouds of dust and gas. Gravitational eddies and lensing effects from all the stellar bodies had made finding the best spot to view 'The Shift', as the science teams were calling it, rather difficult.

Eventually they'd settled on the center of a one-light-year gap between a number of A-Class stars. The position granted them a relatively unobstructed view of the cluster's core. However, the difficulty in selecting the observation location was where the need for sending the *Cora's Triumph* came in, rather than just a pinnace, as was the original plan.

Wyatt and Emily had concurred that a single observation point may not gather sufficient data to assess the event, and had stipulated that a wider sensor array was necessary.

Being an FGT research vessel, the *Triumph* had a wide array of sensor drones on hand, and now a one-hundred-AU-wide grid of drones was in place, awaiting The Shift.

"Are you certain you don't want to go down to the observation deck with the scientific team?" Captain Beatrice asked from Terrance's side. "You'll get firsthand information that way."

Terrance glanced at the ship's captain, a woman of middling height with rather pixie-like features.

"I think they'll do better without feeling like I'm looming over their shoulders," he said decidedly.

Beatrice chuckled and shook her head. "Well, I'm not too familiar with Emily, but I know that Wyatt is immune to any amount of looming. He works at his own pace no matter what pressures are applied."

"I imagine that can be a good and bad thing," Terrance replied.

"You've the right of it," she said with a knowing smile. "You've worked a lot with scientists, I assume?"

"Oh yeah," he replied with a chuckle. "I operated a few R&D divisions of Enfield in the past. *Technically,* the *Intrepid* was an Enfield venture, but it shifted in scope pretty quickly."

Beatrice snapped her fingers. "That's *right*. I remember reading that, now. Enfield Technologies was the largest backer of the *Intrepid*. Why was that?"

"Picotech," he replied. "We'd developed it and needed a place to commercialize the process. Every other system that Enfield was established in was too populated for us to perform the work."

"And the colonists?" the captain's brow lowered. "Did they know what they were getting into?"

Terrance felt a twinge of guilt at the question. More than a twinge, if he was being honest with himself. Everything that had happened to the *Intrepid*'s colonists had happened because of his plan to use New Eden as a place to develop Earnest's picotech further.

He and Jason had spoken of the matter on many occasions, sharing similar feelings about what they'd done. In the end, it had taken Tangel and the rest of the command crew taking the pair aside and telling them that all was forgiven before that part of his past had ceased gnawing at his soul.

Though it still nibbled.

"They did not," Terrance replied, shaking his head. "Though the charter did specify a list of Enfield research sites that would be used for advanced R&D. Anyone who read between the lines was able to tell that we planned to do research that wasn't possible in the Sol System."

"And the risk?" Beatrice asked.

"Of sabotage and war, or of a picophage?" Terrance asked.

"Well…both, I suppose."

The former Enfield executive let out a long sigh. "Well, we hoped that moving the research to a distant location like New Eden would reduce all those risks. The logic was that if Earnest had unlocked how to harness picotech, others would too. Turns out that was in error. Five thousand years later, no one else has pulled it off. We could have just left well enough alone."

"You've not heard the stories?" Beatrice asked.

Terrance quirked an eyebrow. "I've heard a few rumors, nothing more."

"No one else has pulled off *functional* picotech like your scientists did, but that wasn't for lack of trying."

"More phages?" he asked with a tremor in his voice, remembering the events on Tau Ceti, events that brought to mind Khela, which reminded him of later, equally painful events.

Stars, time never really does wipe it away completely.

"Several that I know of," she admitted. "Entire systems sterilized to prevent spread. I imagine there have been more that got swept under the rug."

He shook his head in remorse. "I guess we didn't really help much by removing it from the timeline."

"Who's to say?" After a brief pause, Beatrice gave Terrance an apologetic look. "I didn't mean to bring it up like this. So much of what we do has unintended consequences. The FGT doesn't have a perfect record, either."

"So long as we try to do the right thing at the time," he replied. "Which leads us to what the hell the core AIs are trying to do here."

"If it *is* the core AIs," she replied.

"We caught two remnants in the Inner Praesepe Empire. I think that's a pretty strong connection."

"A connection is not causation."

Terrance laughed. "If I had a credit for every time I've heard that.... Either way, that's a part of why we're out here. To learn what the heck is going on with those stars."

"True," Beatrice said with a slow nod, signaling her acquiescence. "All that aside, how accurate do you think their timing estimates are?"

"It's your team," he replied. "Though I was surprised that Wyatt narrowed it down to a one-hour window with such confidence."

She snorted. "He portrays that level of confidence in everything he does. Somehow, he even admits failure with the same level of certainty. I still can't tell if it's a character flaw or not."

"Seems to be working for him thus far."

"Most of the time." Beatrice's lips formed a thin line for a moment. "He's come close to making a trip out the airlock a few times. Stars, the only thing that stopped me was thinking about how much he'd complain when he was resuscitated."

"I've worked with a particular engineer that has elicited similar feelings in me before. Still does, if I have to do a project with her."

"Ma'am!" the ensign at the scan console called out. "I think we're picking up the event."

"Put it up," Captain Beatrice ordered, and the forward holo changed to a three-meter-wide view of Astoria, its blue light washing over the bridge.

The view of the star was a composite of data that the sensor grid was picking up all across the electromagnetic spectrum, showing every attribute of the star's emissions. Already, an anomaly was flagged at its poles.

A reference image appeared to the left of the 'live' view, or rather, the light that had left the star nineteen years ago, and it was plain to see that the star's poles had dimmed, while the luminosity at the equator had intensified.

"That doesn't match flare of CME activity," Beatrice muttered.

"Not even close," Terrance confirmed.

Then a point on the equator facing the sensor grid almost directly began to intensify further. Energy emissions spiked clear across the spectrum, climbing highest in the gamma range.

"Estimates show the emission to be coming from a point nearly ten thousand kilometers across," the ensign reported. "It's still intensifying."

"Well," Terrance muttered. "Two things are for certain."

"Oh?" Beatrice asked, not turning her gaze from the display.

"For starters, that's not any sort of natural phenomenon—or if it is, we need to throw out everything we know about stars and start over."

"And secondly?"

"There is no way that anyone in the IPE has the technology to do *that*."

Beatrice gave a slow nod as she turned to face Terrance.

"Perhaps. If so, then the core AIs are playing a far deeper game than we'd expected."

* * * * *

"So, if you look carefully, you'll see that the star's output in the northern and southern hemispheres begins to dim several hours before the event itself," Emily said as she gestured at the display in the observation deck, where Terrance and Beatrice had joined the scientific team for their analysis.

"Which doesn't match any of the later progression of energy transfer within the star," Wyatt interjected. "That dimming does not align with a general change in the star's energy output."

"Right," Emily said with a sidelong look at Wyatt. "There were also fluctuations in the dimming, which align with occlusion."

"But if something was big enough to occlude Astoria's output, we'd see it, right?" Terrance asked, already knowing the answer from his involvement in Project Starflight.

"Right," Emily nodded. "Which means it's a swarm of smaller objects. Probably orbiting the star in patterns that periodically overlap and cause the precise effect we see."

"So these objects settle over the northern and southern hemispheres, and then?" Beatrice prompted.

"And then something alters the star's internal convection pathways," Emily explained, "directing more of the energy release toward the equator than normal. This is not ferociously difficult to achieve, it just takes time and careful planning."

Terrance was surprised to see Emily give him a rather pregnant look and wondered if the FGT's stellar engineer was aware of the work to affect a similar result with Canaan Prime.

She paused for a moment longer, and then continued. "But what is surprising is how they managed to get the star's emissions to focus in on such a fine point. I don't currently have anything beyond a raw guess at some sort of alteration in the star's magnetosphere that caused such a focused CME. We're still analyzing the data and will need to compare the next few weeks of information to see how the star transitions back to its normal burn pattern. That should give us some answers."

Terrance nodded slowly. "OK. The gate should be here in a few hours; I'm going to need your reports ready to jump out with me. I'll forward them on to whomever you wish. We need our best minds working on this."

"So do you think it's the core AIs?" Emily asked, her eyes widening as she said the words.

Terrance saw that every face was turned to him, and he shrugged. "We'd already guessed at that before. It seems like this evidence points in favor of that hypothesis. But it means something else, too."

"Oh?" Wyatt asked. "Something we haven't already guessed at?"

"It's tangential," Terrance replied. "But you don't just create what is effectively a dyson swarm out of nothing. There's some sort of manufacturing facility in the heart of the IPE that is making whatever does this."

Beatrice whistled. "Damn…between the ISF and the TSF, we have hundreds of ships in the Inner Praesepe Empire…."

"I know. Get a pinnace ready. I want to jump out the moment the gate gets here."

AN INTERVIEW WITH GARZA

STELLAR DATE: 10.06.8949 (Adjusted Years)
LOCATION: Tangel's Lakehouse, ISS *I2*, near Lunic Station
REGION: Aldebaran, League of Sentients Space

Tangel took a sip of her coffee while gazing out the kitchen window at the view of the orchard stretching behind the house. It was a serene view, the leaves rustling in the slight wind, bots visible here and there, flitting amongst the trees, plucking fruit for the *I2*'s galleys.

She breathed in the normalcy of it, the simple joy of soaking in a view she'd seen so many times in the past. It created a calm within her that grounded her and reminded her what she was fighting so hard to achieve.

That calm was broken when Cary careened into the kitchen and collapsed in a chair.

"Coffee?" Tangel asked as she turned to give her daughter an appraising look.

Cary only grunted, but it sounded like an affirmative noise, so Tangel prepared a cup and set it on the table.

"Rough night?"

With a nod of her head, Cary made another grunt and then picked up the cup and took a long draw of the dark liquid within.

Once she had downed half the cup, she gave Tangel a steely-eyed look. "How in the stars do you look so good this morning, Moms? What I did yesterday…the shield, the graviton fields…I'm totally wiped. I could sleep for a week."

Tangel pulled out a chair and sat next to her daughter.

"Do you want to know my secret?"

"I'd consider killing for it."

A laugh burst from Tangel's lips, causing Cary to wince.

"Dammit, Moms. Easy on the volume."

"Sorry. I had a response that was way funnier in my head than it would have been out loud. Anyway, I think that it's just because I'm further along than you are. You know, with the whole ascending thing."

Cary took another sip of her coffee, fixing Tangel with a dour look over the rim before setting it down. "Which is fine by me. I don't want to be *anywhere* with the 'ascended thing'." She scowled and made air quotes as she said the words.

Tangel leant back in her chair and gave her daughter a level stare. "Liar. I saw you when you were fighting those Widows. You were enjoying it."

"OK...I guess grouchy me isn't that clear. What I mean is that I like the fun benefits of being able to see into other dimensions. Manipulating matter through them is a great added bonus, but I don't want to turn into a glowing ball of light. We've been over this."

"Right," Tangel nodded with a wink. "No glowing balls of light. I'll make sure that doesn't happen to you."

"I'm being serious, Moms."

"So am I. I don't have any special way of making sure that doesn't happen to you, but so far as any of us know—Bob included—you don't shed this mortal coil of yours until *you* decide to." As she spoke, Tangel touched her daughter's arm and gave it a pinch.

"Ow!"

"See? Still good ol' flesh and blood. Even without my edge over you when it comes to time in the ascending business, you're a lot more organic than I am. Which means that our bodies replenish energy differently, making our recoveries different. Or maybe you just need to build up more stamina."

Cary nodded and took another sip of coffee. "I was already a bit worn out after fighting Myrrdan. Stars, I really hope that was finally the real one."

"You and me both," Tangel replied. "That guy has been such a thorn in my side that I have more thorns than side."

Her daughter snorted a laugh. "All-in-all, that was a pretty amazing trip to the LMC. I mean, just going there is freakin' awesome on its own, but taking out Myrrdan, *and* getting that intel from Kent…I deserve a promotion."

"Nice—wait…intel from Kent?"

Cary peered over the rim of her cup, another frown settling on her brow. "Yeah, the details on Orion and Garza. I sent it all along through the normal channels. Didn't it get to you?"

Tangel sifted through all the intel updates she'd received, and then searched the *I2*'s databases for new intel on Garza.

"No, there's nothing new. It must have been hung up somewhere."

"Seriously?" Cary sat up straight. "Then you don't know?"

"Cary…what?"

"The first Garza, the one that Jessica's team captured on the *Britannica* two years ago…. He's not a clone."

* * * * *

Tangel let slip a rueful laugh as she walked through the *I2*'s brig to Garza's cell—the first one. The Garza they'd captured in Scipio was in the next block over, and neither was aware that the other was on the ship.

Her laugh was directed at all the times she'd considered sending both of the Garzas to The Farm—the large stasis facility holding the enemy forces that had surrendered after the Defense of Carthage. Luckily, she'd never gone through with sending her Garzas there; she was more than glad for the result of her indecision.

She slowed as Garza's cell came into view, assessing the man within through the thick pane of clear plas.

He looked haggard, as though sleep had eluded him for

some time—except for at this exact moment.

Stretched out on his bunk with an arm over his forehead, the man didn't move or acknowledge her presence in any way.

"Two years is a long time to be in here alone," Tangel said after she'd regarded him for a minute. "Well, mostly alone. I see that they do give you an hour in the park every other day—so long as you behave."

Garza still didn't move a muscle. His breathing remained the same, and his heart rate was steady.

"I suppose you're dying to know how the war's been going. I'm pretty sure that no one's told you—or they'd better not have. We've got the Hegemony of Worlds ringed in, we're hitting the Trisilieds, and Nietzschea is on its knees. Things on the fronts with the OFA have been a bit dicey, but mostly it's just been some minor back and forth there.

"We also have fleets operating within Orion Space. I think that by this time next year, we should be paying the praetor a visit at New Sol."

With her report ended, silence set in. It stretched on for over three minutes, until finally the man cracked an eyelid for a moment and spoke, his voice filled with scorn.

"Should have led with something more believable than having the Hegemony encircled. There's no way you could have pulled that off in two years."

"A lot's changed," Tangel said with a nonchalant shrug. "Without you and the Transcend holding the Inner Stars in check, we've really been able to get the ball rolling. Currently, the *I2* is at Aldebaran, capital of the League of Sentients—an alliance that wraps partway around the Hegemony. It had just come into existence when you attacked New Canaan, so I imagine you've not heard of it."

Garza's cheek twitched, but he didn't respond.

"I'll admit, there are a few gaps here and there, but on the far side, we have Scipio pressing the attack, which counts for a lot. One of your clones tried to stop that alliance, but let's just say that he ended up in a similar situation to you."

That statement elicited a response from Garza. Mention of Scipio had his eyes opening, and when she referenced the clone's capture, he sat up and fixed her with a penetrating stare.

"Now I *know* you're lying."

"Because of Scipio, or your clones? We've encountered three of them now, but one died. The Hand has spotted what they think are four others in various systems, so I imagine there are a lot more running around out there."

"Diana wouldn't ally with you," Garza sneered as the words dripped from his lips. "That woman's a preening fool. Thinks that by acting like an unhinged, power-hungry debutante, no one will contest her."

"Yeah, she was quite the character," Tangel said, chuckling at the memory. "Your clone abducted her at a ball. It was a tricky thing to get her back in one piece. She was grateful and signed the accord. The alliance of nations arrayed against Orion is now known as the Scipio Alliance."

Garza groaned and shook his head. "I think that's the worst one yet. And if it *is* true, it's the greatest indignity of all time."

"It's been interesting, that's for sure," Tangel nodded as she considered some of her conversations over the past year. "Lisa Wrentham is quite the character, too."

The general shook his head, lifting an eyebrow as he regarded her. "So you've run into her Widows, have you? How'd that go?"

Tangel shrugged. "A lot of them died. Ten? Something like that. I mean, we killed Xavia the other day, so wiping out some Widows wasn't a huge feat."

"Xavia?"

The man's physiology—which was an open book to Tangel—confirmed that he didn't know who she was referring to.

"She's one of—rather, she *was* one of—the independent operators in the ranks of the ascended AIs. I think you're familiar with the Caretakers, though. They're the ones that have been seeding this never-ending war."

"That's where you're wrong," Garza said, rising from his cot and walking to the plas, where he stared into Tangel's eyes for a moment before continuing. "It's *all* of the AIs who have been seeding this war. Either they're complicit, or they're unwitting pawns, but either way, they're the issue. The ascended ones are just the worst."

"What about ascended humans?" Tangel asked.

Garza snorted and turned away. "There aren't any of those."

"Have you heard of Star City?" Tangel asked, the words causing the man's head to whip back around.

"How…"

"My people have been there. AIs who are the children of New Canaan are now the Bastions of Star City. It was they who defeated your attack over a decade ago—I assume it was you who orchestrated that."

The man's eyes narrowed, and Tangel didn't even need the ability to see the thoughts on the surface of his mind to know that he had.

"You get around a lot for a lost pack of colonists from the past," Garza finally admitted. "But space is vast, and there are a few surprises out there for you, I'd imagine."

"A few," Tangel agreed. "Finding out where the Widows operate from is something I'd like to check off my 'lingering uncertainties' list, though."

"I bet you would," Garza said with a cruel laugh. "If my clones have sent Lisa after you, then you'd best be prepared for a long fight. She has quite a few clones of her own."

"They're different than yours, though," Tangel said as she

leant against the plas. "Yours are much more…functional."

"Hegemony tech," Garza said. "Their president uses it. Makes her own body doubles that are intended to merge back in. Lisa wanted a different sort of tool, but she had to make…alterations to get it to work well."

"Crazy that she left Finaeus for you and Orion," Tangel said with a furrowed brow. "I mean, why would she go into Orion Space, where advanced tech is forbidden—or at least heavily frowned upon—when research of that sort is her bread and butter?"

"She believes in our vision, she's just made the personal sacrifice to be the means to counter the Transcend's rampant tech."

"Must be a secret base that your praetor doesn't know about," Tangel mused. "I'm guessing he doesn't know about half the stuff you're up to."

"This is so weak, Tanis. If you were going to use mental coercion on me to learn what I know, you would have already done it. Your interrogators have spoken to me for hundreds of hours, and I've learned more from them than they have from me. Your pathetic attempts to get me to slip up don't even rank."

The expression on Garza's face was one of pure disdain as he turned away, walking to the basin where he filled a cup with water before taking a drink.

"You're thinking of it even now," Tangel said after a moment. "I can see it in your mind. It's tricky, filtering through all the minutia that crowds human thought. I had expected your mind to be cleaner than most—it is, but not much."

"What are you talking about, woman?" Garza turned his head just enough to meet her eyes.

"The *Perilous Dream*. That's the ship she operates from. It's located in the…huh, I guess you just call it 'A1' System. A black dwarf star. Well, that's interesting…just like her, in so many respects."

Garza's eyes had grown wide as Tangel spoke, a look of fear pushing aside the smarmy expression that had been there a moment before.

"I wasn't asking you stupid questions," Tangel said with a slow wink as a filament of light exited her body, sliding through the plas toward the man as he backed away. "I was just making you think about her location, bringing those thoughts to the surface of your mind. Stars, you can't stop thinking about all sorts of things you don't want me to know, now. I really did think that you'd be more disciplined than this."

"You're ascended." The words hissed from Garza's lips on an indrawn breath as Tangel's otherworldly hand reached him. "How?"

She couldn't help but laugh. "Practice. Lots of practice. I suspect this is the eventual destiny of all humans—should they live long enough. We know that so much more of spacetime exists, but we're blind to it—well, sort of blind. But I can see it clearly, just like I can see your thoughts as though they were on a holodisplay before me. You're a flatlander, Garza. Three times over from where I am, now."

"Are you with the core AIs, then?" he asked, slowly gaining a measure of control over himself. "With Airtha?"

"Of course not. To both," Tangel said with a shake of her head. "As much as I hate it, the fact of the matter is that I'm at the head of my own faction. And we're just a few sure strikes away from victory."

For a moment, the man's veneer cracked, and a wild-eyed look came over him. "For now."

Tangel was about to ask what he meant, but Garza drew a deep breath and sat on the floor of his cell. He was working to clear his mind, to think of nothing and become opaque to her.

It was working relatively well.

"Well, I guess I have enough for now," Tangel said with a wink. "I might go talk to your clone, though, see what he knows."

Garza's jaw tensed, but he didn't speak.

Tangel waited a minute, staring at the man who she now knew had hoped to become humanity's ruler, but was now just another prisoner in the brig.

<Joe, I know where the Widows' base is. Meet me in the CIC.>

WIDOWSTRIKE

STELLAR DATE: 10.06.8949 (Adjusted Years)
LOCATION: CIC, ISS *I2*, near Lunic Station
REGION: Aldebaran, League of Sentients Space

"Well, if we know where it is," Joe began, staring intently at the holotank that showed the location of the black dwarf star known as A1, "let's just fire some RMs through a jump gate, and call it a day."

"You know we can't do that," Tangel said, meeting her husband's eyes. "The Widows are one of Orion's major clandestine arms. The intel on that ship is not something we can just pass up."

Captain Rachel shook her head as she stared at the holo—which displayed a region of space over a thousand light years into the gap between the Orion and Perseus arms.

"So is it just me, or is that black dwarf star a bit early…like by a quadrillion years or so?" she asked.

"I was wondering that, too," Saanvi added. "It really can't be a black dwarf…it must be a burned out brown dwarf, or a rogue planet."

Tangel shook her head. "No—well, I think 'no'. Garza definitely gave me the impression that it was a stellar remnant. A white dwarf that had cooled enough to no longer emit light."

"Yeah, but like Captain Rachel said," Cary nodded deferentially to the *I2*'s commander, "the universe isn't old enough for any black dwarf stars to exist yet—heck, with proton decay and WIMPs, a quadrillion years is the low-ball estimate for them."

"We've seen a lot of stuff that we never expected to." Tangel gave Cary an uncertain glance. "Mining a white dwarf could cause this effect, or even just siphoning off the heat somehow."

"That'd be a big siphon." Saanvi shook her head.

Joe scrubbed his hands across his face. "OK, I give. We need to do surveillance. I'll select a ship to drop in and check out this A1 System."

"Why not just send a team in?" Faleena asked. "Get the intel, blow the ship, be gone. All in one fell swoop."

"Well, for starters, it's a ship full of Widows...." Cary shot her sister a narrow-eyed glance.

Faleena looked Cary up and down, then Saanvi. "With some minor mods, the two of you could pass for Widows."

"Widows?!" Saanvi exclaimed. "Noooo no no no no."

"There are almost no infiltration teams available right now," Faleena said in a tone that brooked no argument. "Carson's fleet got called away to aid Scipio, and we can't pull anyone from the Airtha mission. But for all we know, there could be dozens of Widow teams out there, ready to strike. Rika, Petra, Kylie, Krissy...so many of our allies would not be able to stop one of their attacks as easily as we did."

Tangel chewed on her lip as she thought through her available assets, realizing that no group small enough to infiltrate the Widows' ship would stand a chance of success—not without an ascended being to help.

I could do it, but I need to stay on hand to aid in the attack on Airtha.

"Stars.... It may actually be the best option we have." Her eyes met Joe's, and she could tell that he'd come to the same conclusion.

"Dammit." He looked at Cary and shook his head. "Well, the three of you aren't going in alone. I'm bringing a stealthed cruiser to keep watch."

"Wait...exactly *when* did I agree to this?" Sanvi asked.

* * * * *

"OK…" Iris shook her head a little too fast, still fine-tuning the actuators in her new body. "You're telling me that you three girls are going to infiltrate Widows HQ. On your own?"

Everyone in the CIC nodded, and Cary spoke first.

"Yes. That's why we wanted to talk with you, to learn any details from your mission in the Ferra system that might not have been in Jessica's report."

Iris glanced at Faleena. "Well, for starters, this group of Widows is a step up from the ones we dealt with back in Orion space. We were able to fool them with Addie, our infiltrator chameleon, but I don't think that you'll be able to fake out this breed, Faleena."

"We stand a better chance of success if I go," Faleena replied, setting her jaw as she regarded Iris.

"I'm not saying you shouldn't go," Iris said, casting a glance at Tangel, surprised that she was allowing a trio of women just barely out of their teens to undertake such a crucial mission.

Well, except for Faleena. She's only two.

"But if you do, you're going to need to use a body that matches the Widows' physiology. Nance and Cheeky had to get mods to pull it off."

"I understand that," Faleena replied equably. "I'm prepared to have my core implanted in a simulacra to achieve our goals for this mission."

"OK. If that's the case, then I'll come too," Iris said with a resolute nod. "I know the Widows, and I'm a better breacher than any of you."

<*No,*> Bob's voice broke into the conversation. <*You are needed elsewhere.*>

Iris glanced up at the overhead. "I am?"

<*Yes,*> The AI replied simply. <*You and Amavia are necessary*

components for the strike on Airtha.>

"I'm a component, am I, Bob?"

<*Don't mock me when I use this crude language. It's unwieldy. So far as I'm concerned,* ***none*** *of the words are accurate.*>

"I have to admit." Tangel's voice was heavy with unspoken emotion. "Were you three not highly talented women who work exceptionally well together, I'd never consider this."

"I can barely believe we actually are," Joe added, worry writ large across his features. "What about just waiting until Carson's fleet is finished helping Rika, and then sending it in whole hog? Stars, once Rika is done with her latest conquest, we could send her Marauders."

Tangel shook her head. "It's going to take her some time to cut her way across Nietzschea. Then she has to stabilize the region. No, crazy as it sounds, our best bet is to send our three girls in—with you close by, of course."

"And the First Fleet will be arrayed in front of jump gates," Rachel said with a solemn nod.

"And the Home Fleet," Tangel added. "Or some of it, at least."

<*Send Priscilla,*> Bob spoke up in the short silence that had followed Tangel's words.

"Really?" Tangel asked, cocking her head as she considered the woman's skillset. "Are you sure?"

<*Priscilla has a weighty choice ahead of her. This would give her the opportunity to experience time away from me.*>

Tangel knew the decision Priscilla faced. If she continued to be Bob's avatar for much longer, her mind would no longer be separable from his.

<*Can Priscilla even function away from Bob anymore?*> Joe asked Tangel privately.

<*I was wondering the same thing,*> she replied. <*But I can't imagine Bob would send her if he thought she couldn't do it.*>

<*Bob isn't all-knowing,*> Joe countered. <*He makes mistakes,*

rare though they are.>

"What about Kylie's team?" Rachel asked. "Things have settled down in Silstrand—for the moment, at least."

Tangel pursed her lips. "They'd be a good option, yes. But I just sent them into the Hegemony on their own impossible mission."

A sudden—and marginally manic—laugh escaped her lips, and she glanced at Joe.

"You know…next time we try to take over the galaxy, let's do it with a bigger team."

Joe gave a wry smile while nodding emphatically. "Noted."

"Priscilla, you been listening in?" Tangel asked, already knowing the answer.

<*I have.*> The reply was laced with uncertainty.

"And?"

<*Well, I can tell from Bob's mind that he thinks I will do well enough away from him, but I've not ever been on a mission like this. I mean…I've trained for them, but it's not the same.*>

"You're right about that," Tangel replied with rueful laugh. "But even if you had, nothing is ever like the training anyway. Everyone has to have their first time out sometime."

<*Is that supposed to be encouraging?*>

"No pressure," Joe said. "We could also take a few days and find volunteers in the Marine companies. There are a few who have shown an aptitude for this sort of work."

<*No.*> Priscilla's tone had gained a measure of certainty. <*I'll do it. Let me get my alternate on duty, and I'll be at your disposal.*>

"I'll tell Doctor Rosenberg to get ready," Rachel said. "Four Widows, coming right up."

Saanvi gave a shudder. "Gonna miss my nose."

"Your what?" Cary asked.

Faleena clapped her on the shoulder. "You should read Jessica's report. Noses and ears don't fit in Widow helmets.

Why do you think they talk so strangely?"

Cary met Tangel's eyes. "Too late to change my mind, Moms?"

PART 4 – THE CALM

DEEPER

STELLAR DATE: 10.06.8949 (Adjusted Years)
LOCATION: River Station, Styx Baby-9
REGION: STX-B17 Black Hole, Transcend Interstellar Alliance

"This is just too weird, Sabs," Cheeky said as she reclined on one of the chairs in *Sabrina*'s rear observation lounge.

"Oh?"

Sabrina was using one of the new frames she'd 'requisitioned' from the *I2* during their recent visit to the massive warship. Unlike her other mobile frames—which looked as much like a starship as a bipedal hominid—this one looked almost perfectly human.

"What do you mean, 'oh'?" Cheeky fixed Sabrina with a narrow-eyed stare. "The fact that I'm the captain, and we're taking on new crew to go on a crazy mission. That's what's weird."

Sabrina only shrugged. "I'm OK with it."

"It's a lot of change.... Am I ready?" Cheeky wondered.

"Cheeky." Sabrina paused to shake her head and give a bubbly laugh. "I've known since day one that you and I were destined to be together."

"Liar. You were so pissed when Sera brought me aboard. You couldn't believe that she'd hired a pilot."

The AI shrugged. "OK...maybe not day one. But when you took the helm, I knew it was meant to be. You, me, flying through the stars. No one else *feels* it the same way we do."

"Well, I think Jessica does," Cheeky suggested. "She's one

hell of a pilot."

Sabrina nodded. "OK, I'll grant you that. But it's different with you."

Cheeky wondered what Sabrina was getting at. Did the AI mean that Cheeky's love of piloting was different than Jessica's, or that it was different for Sabrina herself?

Across the lounge, Sabrina shifted her position, uncrossing and re-crossing her legs.

The single action caused Cheeky to suddenly realize why the AI was using a human-looking frame. Suddenly, everything around her shifted focus.

"Sabrina…are you….?"

"I want something more, Cheeky…more than the flirting we've been doing for the past three decades. It's been enough to drive a girl mad."

The new captain snorted. "Good thing you're not a girl, Sabs."

"Cheeky. I am a sleek, sexy starship. I am the ultimate girl, the evolution of femininity. Powerful, strong, cunning. And now I want the next thing any girl in my position would want."

Cheeky wondered exactly what Sabrina meant by that, and what more *she* could offer.

"We've had sex in sims, Sabs—you seemed to enjoy it. Do you want to do it with that frame now? Is that why you picked it?"

Sabrina glanced down at the body she was controlling. "I think that could be fun, and I was thinking I'd use it as a gateway drug to reel you in, but what I really want is something more than sex, Cheeky."

"Sabrina, I'm married to Finaeus…and while he recognizes that I'm not the sort of person to be tamed, I don't think he would be happy if we entered into some sort of deeper relationship."

"Are you sure about that?" Sabrina asked with a wink.

"Umm…OK, you've got me there, but what is it that you really want?"

Sabrina leant forward, her elbows on her knees, eyes boring into Cheeky's. "You're an AI. I know you like to 'be' human, but underneath it, you're one of us now."

"Right. I know that," Cheeky said, trying to brush the comments away.

While she'd accepted what she was long ago, dwelling on it was still not something she liked to do. It made her feel shallow, like she was just the veneer of Cheeky, spread across a different entity.

"I can see that *intellectually* you know it," Sabrina replied and then tapped her chest. "But do you know it in here?"

"Are you getting all metaphysical on me, Sabrina? Aren't we supposed to be the carefree, fun-loving ones?"

She laughed and sat back in her chair. "Stars, Cheeky, I can be both, you know. So can you—so *are* you. Look, I don't want to get between you and Finaeus, but I also want to take our relationship further…as AIs."

"Sabrina!" Cheeky exclaimed. "Shit. You want to do that deep mind-meld thing that AIs do, where we bare our innermost selves to one another. I don't know if I'm ready for that."

The AI laughed again, both audibly and in Cheeky's mind. "I wasn't planning to go all the way the first time we touch minds. You're not used to thinking like an AI, and I want to ease you into it."

Lips pursed, Cheeky blew out a long breath through her nose while staring at the AI.

Finally, she said, "You'd be surprised, Sabs. I think I've been thinking like an AI a lot, in how I see things, and analyze information. It's different than how I used to be. It's like I'm straddling both worlds."

"Nothing wrong with that. It gives you unique insight. Not a lot of humans make the leap—certainly not many get the best minds in the galaxy facilitating the transition."

"So where does this lead?" Cheeky asked. "You being the ship's AI, and me the captain and pilot. Do we just blend together when we fly?"

"I guess we could try that. Like I said, I just want to take baby steps. We'll see how compatible our minds are in the long run."

Cheeky snapped her fingers and gave Sabrina a measuring look. "I know what you want! You want to use my brains to make a *baby*!"

Sabrina held up her hands laughing softly. "Stars, Cheeky, no risk of you ever becoming a cold logic machine, is there?"

"Not so long as the stars are burning," Cheeky intoned. "But seriously. You want to make a child with me, don't you?"

Sabrina nodded slowly. "Eventually, if you'd like to. It's how new AIs are made. We merge, draw in elements from one another, produce new beings. Sometimes adding in bits from organic parents, too. It's how we keep things fresh. You'd be amazing, given your past and what you are."

"To add me to the collective?" Cheeky asked with a laugh.

"You know it's not like that."

"I know, I couldn't help it. So…how do we do this—touch minds?"

"First, I take you into an expanse. You've been in mine a few times already, so let's start there."

Cheeky nodded, and suddenly she was in space, drifting in the midst of a blue and purple nebula. She looked down at herself to see that she was in one of the modified AI frames that Sabrina liked to use: humanoid, but sleek, like a starship with an engine on the back.

<*Of course,*> she said with a laugh, turning about to look for Sabrina.

<Well, it's an awesome way to be. All the utility of a human, with the ability to fly like a starship.> Sabrina appeared before Cheeky, wearing her favorite red and gold frame.

<So is that what we're gonna do? Fly around one another like birds mating or something?>

<No.> Sabrina shook her head as she drifted closer to Cheeky. *<Being here is just a way to take your mind off the physical world around you. And this starscape, this 'place' is just a construct that overlays what's underneath.>*

<Because AIs are creatures of the mind?> Cheeky asked with a smile as the two drifted closer together and then clasped hands.

<Humans are creatures of the mind, too. Their bodies exist to power their brains and keep them safe. Just like my body—the ship—exists to power my mind and keep me safe.>

Cheeky laughed softly. *<And haul stuff around.>*

<Same as a human. Some AIs have very small bodies that aren't mobile, but they still provide power and safety. And even beyond that, we all have physical brains…well except for some ascended AIs, though beneath it all, they have physical brains, too—just ones grounded in different dimensions than the ones we inhabit.>

<OK, Sabrina, you're very wise.> Cheeky reached out and touched the AI's face. *<So what now?>*

<Do you really think so?> Sabrina asked.

<Think so what?>

<That I'm wise. I've never thought of myself that way.>

Cheeky considered what had made her say those words, and then decided that they were true. She *did* think Sabrina was wise.

<I guess we've all grown a lot over the past thirty years. Stars…I can't believe it's been that long since Sera pulled us out of our respective junkyards and set us on this path.>

<We're all growed up,> Sabrina said with a laugh. *<OK, now I'm going to pull away this layer of the expanse and dive deeper. You*

ready?>

<Can I stop whenever I want?>

<You're still just visiting my expanse, you can pull back whenever you want, just like normal.>

Cheeky locked her eyes on Sabrina's and nodded. *<OK.>*

The next second, the nebula and starscape were gone…but they weren't. The visuals had disappeared, but the *expression* of them was still present. It was organized in matrices of data, multidimensional arrays of information. It was more than facts and figures, it was poetry, emotion, concepts and beliefs.

Some of it was familiar to Cheeky; she often perused the underlying data structures of the information she used to fly the ship. But never it had contained anything more than uninspiring raw information before now.

<It's so beautiful,> she whispered.

<This is how I see space,> Sabrina replied. *<More than just objects and vectors, I see their whole being, and the light that suffuses it all. Energy, space, time, it's all the same thing, and so much more than just crude matter.>*

<I want to see space like this all the time,> Cheeky said, her voice a faint whisper.

<You can, Cheeky. You're an AI, you can see everything like this.>

<Stars….>

<Are you ready to go deeper?>

Cheeky looked at Sabrina, her form overlaid with so much information about who she was, what she thought about a million subjects—the very essence of her being.

<Take me all the way.>

THE BRIEFING

STELLAR DATE: 10.07.8949 (Adjusted Years)
LOCATION: River Station, Styx Baby-9
REGION: STX-B17 Black Hole, Transcend Interstellar Alliance

Sera walked into the briefing room and settled into a seat next to Cheeky and Sabrina, unable to miss that the two were holding hands.

She glanced at Finaeus, who was standing on the raised platform next to Earnest, their heads bent together as they flipped through a series of holoimages that she imagined must be notes and information for their presentation. He seemed focused on his work and entirely unperturbed by the display of affection between his wife and Sabrina.

"Stars, Sera," Cheeky muttered. "Put your eyes back in your head, already."

"But what about Finaeus?" she blurted, glancing at the man who was now stabbing his finger at the holodisplay and shaking his head.

"We've talked with him," Sabrina said. "Everything's fine."

"It's something that's been coming for a while," Cheeky added. "He and I still love each other, but our situations don't really allow for spending a lot of time together. We had a good run—and we're going to stay married—I'm just exploring AI stuff with Sabrina."

"AI stuff?" Sera cocked an eyebrow.

<*Mental merging,*> Jen supplied.

Sera knew the basics of what that entailed, mainly that it was one of the steps in making new AIs. She wondered if that was what Sabrina and Cheeky were planning on doing, but decided not to pry.

She only replied with, "Ah."

At that moment, she was distracted by the arrival of Krissy and several members of her command team, as they settled into the row behind Sera. They would not be directly involved in the mission, but everyone knew that there was a strong chance that things could go belly-up and the cavalry would need to be called to save the day.

Even if we succeed, we'll probably still need to call them in, Sera mused.

She'd given a lot of consideration to what would happen after they defeated Airtha. It was her hope that the majority of people under the AI's thrall would realize that they'd been on the wrong side and rejoin the rest of the Transcend without a fight.

But Sera knew that was little more than a dream. It was very likely that the Transcend would never reform as a single entity again.

Over the next five minutes, the rest of the strike team entered the room, and the low murmur of conversation filled the space as they waited for the briefing to begin.

Seraphina and Fina settled into seats on the far side of Cheeky and Sabrina, while Misha, Nance, and Flaherty all sat in the back row—rather, Flaherty stood *behind* the back row.

Katrina entered with her crew shortly afterward, a team consisting of Kirb, Carl, and Camille, all of whom had been with her since the beginning of her misadventures in Bollam's World five centuries prior. They were joined by one of Katrina's newer crewmembers—if a century aboard the *Voyager* made him 'new'—a rather bulky, four-armed man named Elmer.

A grey pillar of light appeared to one side of the room, and Sera noted that it represented the *Voyager*'s AI, a rather staid individual named Troy. Tangel had informed Sera that despite his propensity to see the cup as half-empty, he was one of the most reliable individuals she knew.

And tenacious as well, given what he's been through.

Her attention was drawn by Kara's entrance. The black-winged woman looked uncertainly around the room before shrugging and settling on Sera's left.

Sera had rarely spoken with Kara prior to the events at New Canaan two years ago, but in the last few weeks, they'd found a common bond. Both of them had a lot of issues with their parents—or, parent, in Kara's case—and had spent several late nights discussing their respective fathers.

Sera had to admit that she was also jealous of Kara's wings. Now that she was no longer president, and Seraphina was expressing keen interest in running the Hand, she wondered if it was time to try a mod like Kara's. The memory of the costume she wore at the Scipian gala she'd attended with Tangel came to mind, and she felt a smile grace her lips at the thought.

Her reverie was interrupted by the skittering sound of Malorie entering the room. The spider-woman moved to the back, where she climbed the bulkhead and settled in an upper corner.

Sera couldn't help but notice Flaherty give the red arachnid a disapproving glare.

<*Be nice,*> she cautioned.

<*She's still alive, isn't she?*>

The last to enter were Jane and Roxy—and Carmen, who had agreed to her 'sentence' and was now embedded in Jane. The two women shyly walked past the others and settled into the second-to-last row.

At the front of the room, Finaeus and Earnest looked up and surveyed the nineteen members of the strike force, along with Krissy and the five members of her command team.

"OK, now that we're all gathered," Finaeus said, sounding more tired than Sera had expected, "let's get started, because this is probably going to take all day."

"You going to serve lunch?" Cheeky asked with a grin, and Finaeus shook his head. "When have you known me to skip a meal when it could be at all helped?"

"Skip meals all you want, but don't start without us!" a voice said from the entrance, and Sera turned to see Iris stride into the briefing room, closely followed by Amavia.

Cheeky was on her feet in an instant, embracing the two women. "Stars! I had no idea you were coming!"

"Neither did we," Iris replied with a laugh. "We were helping with the Aldebaran mess when Bob contacted us and told us to join this mission. He didn't say why—you know how he is."

"But when Bob says 'Go', you don't ask questions," Amavia added, her lips twisting as she spoke. "Or at least, I don't—I'm still used to just being one of his appendages, I guess."

Sera noticed the hint of longing in Amavia's voice. She'd wondered how much the woman—at least the Amanda part—missed being one of Bob's avatars, and it seemed that the draw was still there.

"OK, OK. Sit, sit, sit," Finaeus said, making a shooing motion with his hands. "You've spent all of a week or so apart from your crew. The reunion needn't be any great thing."

Cheeky shot Finaeus a mock-scowl, but returned to her seat without further protest, while Iris and Amavia moved to the back of the room and settled next to Nance and Misha.

"Damn," Earnest muttered as he looked out over the crowd. "Twenty-two. I'll adjust the teams."

Sera had gone over the plan with the two men the night before, but she suspected they'd made some tweaks in the interim. If there was one thing she knew about her uncle, it was that he liked to put his own stamp on everything.

Earnest was the more easy-going of the two, which she suspected was from centuries of being married to his rather demanding wife, Abby.

However it worked out, the two men were thick as thieves whenever fate brought them together. Though Sera knew that Earnest's work building the Styx base—a feat completed so quickly via the use of his picotech—was nearly done, and that he was slated to go back to New Canaan in just a few days' time.

Finaeus would be coming along to Airtha. He had insisted on it, and Sera hadn't fought him. He had as much stake in seeing this through as any of them.

Her father—or rather the man who was in some way the donor of her genetic material—had also wanted to come on the mission, but the demands of taking over the reins of the Transcend didn't allow for such an indulgence, and his request was really just something made for appearances.

At least that was how Sera felt about it.

She supposed that her attitude wasn't terribly charitable. Though she'd tried to make a connection to Jeffrey Tomlinson, somehow she just couldn't see him as anyone other than the cold, distant father who had raised her.

In many respects, Sera thought of Finaeus as her true father. He had been the most constant male authority figure in her formative years—and also one who had genuinely liked having her around.

As she watched her uncle square his shoulders in preparation for his presentation, she was sincerely glad that it was he and not Jeffrey who was coming to Airtha. Finaeus had made the ring; it was only fitting that he would be there to secure its future.

"OK, now that we're *all* here," he turned to gaze out the doorway, as though looking for any last-minute additions, "we'll get started. Some of you may not know the full scope of what we're trying to do, so I'll give you the quick and dirty version, and then you can review the datum after the meeting."

As he spoke, an image of the star and ring that both bore the name 'Airtha' appeared behind him.

"For those of you who aren't intimately familiar with Airtha, the star is roughly one third a solar mass, and the ring has a radius of four million kilometers. I used to think it was the largest construct in the galaxy, but after all but stumbling upon Star City, I'll reduce my hyperbole to simply say that it is *one* of the largest constructs in the galaxy. We built it from carbon we harvested from the star, and it's a bit of a crowning achievement for me in beauty as well as size."

Earnest coughed and gave Finaeus a sidelong look before taking over. "The salient point is that the ring's surface area is over two hundred and fifty billion square kilometers, and with an average thickness of fourteen kilometers…well, as you can imagine, this is a hell of a target."

"I prefer not to think of my magnum opus as a 'target'," Finaeus said bitterly.

"We all get that," Earnest replied as he turned to look up at the ring. "Destroying the ring, as it turns out, wouldn't be that hard. We'd just need to trigger an overrun in six of the Cri-En power plants."

"Which would destroy the entire Huygens Star System," Finaeus added. "And possibly damage spacetime in a rather unpredictable fashion."

Earnest nodded. "I was just making a note, partially because we need to consider that Airtha herself may have a failsafe that will cause an overrun if she believes her death to be imminent."

Finaeus opened his mouth like he was going to deliver a rejoinder, but then pursed his lips and nodded.

<*I guess they've butted heads on this a bit,*> Jen commented privately to Sera. <*Personally, I think that overrunning the Cri-Ens would do the trick. Though they're right in that it would shred*

spacetime in more than just our dimensions. Dark layer, upper dims, they'd all fall apart.>

<Right, and then Bob would come and tear us a new one for breaking the universe.>

<I think he overstates the danger,> Jen's tone was nonchalant. *<Surely* ***someone*** *in the universe must have drained the base quantum energy out of a location by now.>*

<Maybe that's what the Great Attractor is,> Sera suggested, referring to the gravitational anomaly that lay between the Milky Way and the Shapely Attractor, some two hundred million light years away.

<Or it's a dark layer tear,> Jen countered.

Sera nodded absently and turned her attention back to Finaeus as he described the locations of the Cri-En power generation facilities.

"The ring also draws power from the four pillars." Finaeus highlighted four spires that stretched from the ring toward the star. "These hold the ring in place, and additionally draw considerable radiant energy, given their proximity to the Airthan Star. They also facilitate the magneto effect that gives the ring an extra level of protection from extra-solar energies for its impending departure from the Huygens System.

"Hitting Airtha's nodes will be tricky, assuming she hasn't moved them. When last I was on the ring, she had twenty-eight nodes. One at the base of each tower, one near each of the twelve major Cri-En facilities, and then another twelve spread around the ring. Because of the necessity of managing the ring's position and power, I think she'll not have moved the nodes at the Cri-En facilities, and probably not the ones at the towers, either."

As he spoke, the node positions lit up on the holodisplay behind him, noting those that were unlikely to be moved, and those that may not be in the same place Finaeus originally put them.

"So what do we do when we hit her nodes?" Sera asked. "And which are better targets?"

Finaeus gave her a look that clearly said, 'Don't try to rush me', before shrugging and glancing back at the holo. "Honestly, we just need to hit four. Doesn't matter which—but we have to do it simultaneously, and without her knowing. If she sees you coming, she'll just sunder those nodes, and you'll waste your time."

"So we should try to hit *more* than four," Krissy said from behind Sera. "As many as eight, if we can manage it."

Sera shook her head. "That's going to put most of the teams at only two people, and it also means we'll need more AIs, since we won't have enough if we split into eight groups."

"We can increase the size of the strike force," Krissy offered. "I'm sure you have Hand agents that would be more than capable of pulling off this operation."

That had occurred to Sera as well, but she was more worried about Airtha discovering the operation than anything else.

"We could bump our numbers up a bit if we have to, but I'd rather not. The ring may be big, but Airtha will have eyes everywhere. We can put together five teams, with everyone having an AI in the group. Sabrina and Troy will remain on their ships and provide overwatch and coordination."

"Seriously?" Sabrina said, looking around Cheeky to lock eyes on Sera. "I've been practicing a lot. I only got my frame's head shot off that *one time*."

"It's the signal, Sabs," Sera said with an apologetic look. "We can use data drops for messages, but if you maintain a solid connection between the ship and a frame, that'll be like a big red arrow pointing at your team."

"I guess…" Sabrina said and sat back. "I bet I could route the data stream well enough to hide it."

"I'm sorry, Sabs," Finaeus shook his head. "On some Joe

Schmoe station out in the backend of nowhere, sure. But this is Airtha. We stand a fifty-fifty chance of her detecting a team already."

"Let's talk about how we're going to destroy Airtha before we get deeper into deployments and teams," Earnest suggested.

"Right," Finaeus nodded. "You roll with it, you made the breakthrough."

Earnest stepped forward. "After careful, and I do mean *careful,* examination of the shard of Airtha that Katrina procured, we managed to figure out a way to plumb the depths of her mind without fully waking her."

The scientist turned and pushed the holo of the ring aside, and a new image sprang into its place. "This is an AI's neural network—the sort we'd see in the Inner Stars, once the AI was properly liberated."

"Ha! I recognize that," Sabrina said with a laugh. "That's my brain you have up there."

"That it is," Earnest said as he turned toward the holodisplay. "You can see here the perimortal section of Sabrina's mind looks normal for an AI who has only distant human lineage in its mental structure."

Kara tentatively raised her hand. "Sorry to be the dumb one here, but what is a perimortal section of an AI's brain? Sounds morbid."

Earnest nodded. "Yeah, it's got a strange name. It's the part of an AI's brain that helps them understand that they are a mortal being just like humans. When AIs were first made, they didn't have this part of their minds—well, the Weapon Born did, but that was a result of their unique origin. In fact, it was merging and reproduction with Weapon Born AIs that brought about the perimortal development in AIs' minds to begin with. That's what 'humanized' the bulk of sentient AIs, so to speak."

His gaze swept across the group, and then his eyes settled on Iris. "Ah! Let's use you, Iris. You have human minds in your lineage just one generation back."

"I feel like I'm being put on display for everyone to ogle," Iris said, laughing as she nodded for Earnest to proceed.

"Which is normal for you," Cheeky said, turning to give Iris a saucy wink.

Earnest moved the display of Sabrina's neural network to the side and pulled up a new one. "Iris is a very interesting example of an AI's development. You can see that while she does have a perimortal section to her brain, it is configured differently from Sabrina's. In many respects, the perimortal portion of an AI's mind mirrors the function of the amygdala and hypothalamus of a human's, in that it controls emotional response and the fight-or-flight response.

"You can see that while Sabrina has a more tightly interwoven perimortal region of her mind, Iris has distinct regions. In many respects, Sabrina is more evolved in this area in that she has a more efficient processing center. However, it also means that the AI equivalent of the emotional processing center—where you figure out how you *feel* about things and make subjective decisions about if and how you want to experience certain events in the future—is more likely to trigger fight-or-flight in an uncontrolled fashion."

"I feel like I was simultaneously complimented and insulted," Sabrina said, her frame's lips twisting to the side.

"It's science," Earnest said not unkindly. "It neither compliments or insults. OK…where was I going with this? Ah! Right. In both cases, the perimortal section of an AI's mind is closely linked with its core logic centers."

On the display, a number of well-traveled neural pathways within both AIs' minds were highlighted.

"Sometimes these are stronger, sometimes they're weaker. Just as it is with organics, the more successful pathways are reinforced, so behavioral patterns evolve from key decision points, whether those decision be conscious or unconscious, so to speak."

Earnest turned to face the two holodisplays and pushed them to the side before breathing a long sigh. "And now we have Airtha's mind."

A new neural network appeared, one that was much larger than the other AIs' and much more interwoven.

"This is just a shard, which means it's close to what we'd see in a single node. What you'll see here, though, is that Airtha has not one, but *four* perimortal sections of her mind, and two of them are not well connected to her logic centers. Finaeus and I tested out various stimuli and found that Airtha can behave very logically in the face of some thoughts, and can have wild fight-or-flight reactions to others."

At that, Finaeus snorted. "And by that, he means she only has fight reactions. Her decision process never even gets close to the notion of disengaging from conflict."

"Explains a lot," Sera muttered before asking, "But technically, Helen was a shard of Airtha inside of me. She didn't have wildly irrational responses, or push me into conflicts."

"Right," Finaeus nodded. "That's because Helen was always destined to…uh…die. Bob also sent us mappings of Myriad's mind, and while she has a similar neural pattern to this shard's, Helen's was missing *all* her perimortal regions. She had one small amygdala-like section and that was it."

"Seriously?" Fina asked from several rows back. "So she was purpose-made to shepherd me…us…whatever, but never had the urge for self-preservation?"

"Essentially," Earnest said. "She had to be ready to accept her mortality and not fight it. "History is filled with stories of shards that went against their parent entities. It would seem that Airtha didn't want to repeat those events."

"OK, so how does this help us?" Iris asked. "Basically, we're looking at the mind of an AI that was made to react strongly to things, and be a little neurotic."

"But those things are dwarfed by her logic centers," Earnest replied. "And this is what gave me the idea about how to defeat her."

The scientist looked rather proud of himself, and Amavia called out, "OK, Earnest, we all know you're super brilliant. Out with it."

He rolled his eyes at Amavia, but continued his explanation. "I worked out a way to flip her fight-or-flight response, so that flight becomes the dominant reaction, but I also managed to alter her emotional responses so that suicide is the 'flight' option she picks. It involves re-introducing the two perimortal sections that are largely disconnected right now. Then we can overwhelm her logic centers, and she'll kill herself with fear."

"Really?" Cheeky cocked an eyebrow. "How is that remotely possible? She has so many options available. There's no way she'd think that death is her best choice."

Finaeus met Earnest's eyes. "Well, we have to make her think she's going to lose, and then the retro-struct virus we'll introduce into her nodes will cause her decision-making to essentially uncouple from her logic centers."

"And how are we going to make her think she's going to lose?" Sera asked.

Finaeus sighed. "We have to make her *think* we're going to destroy the ring. We also have to get on the move, because once the Airthan star and ring move beyond Huygens' Thomias Belt, the ring will be far enough from the system's center to allow dark layer transitions right from its surface."

"Which means Airtha might come to the conclusion that she *can* flee," Earnest added.

Sera rose from her seat and stepped up onto the raised

platform, scanning the group assembled before her.

"So, as you all likely have figured out, we're going in on two ships: *Sabrina* and *Voyager*. Both ships are well known, so crews are already working on altering their profiles—both hull and engine signature."

Katrina winced, and Sera gave her a sympathetic look. "It can be undone if needed. I swear I never recognize *Sabrina* half the time anymore, with all the changes we've made to her."

The AI laughed. "I should really get some sort of flowmetal system for reconfiguring the hull on the fly…you know, Finaeus, why don't we do that?"

"Cosmic rays," Earnest provided the answer with a shrug. "Flowmetal breaks down over time from exposure to…." His voice faded away and he began tapping his chin. "You know…I wonder if we could somehow mix a flowmetal structure with a polymer containing Jessica's microbes. That would give the flow—"

"I'd be purple!" Sabrina gave an excited laugh. "I approve of this this plan."

"Well, I don't think I could have something like that ready for this mission," Earnest held up his hands. "It was just an idea."

"Shortlist me," Sabrina gave the engineer a serious look, and he nodded.

"You'll be the first, Sabrina."

Sera shrugged as she considered such a thing. "You certainly wouldn't be the first purple starship I've seen. Might have to take up covers as a cruiseliner, though, not a freighter."

"I *like* that," Sabrina nodded vigorously. "I see a whole new future for us."

"OK, OK," Sera held up a hand. "Let's focus on getting through this mission first." She paused and glanced over her shoulder at Earnest. "Are the new team structures all set in the planning package?"

"Sure are," the engineer nodded. "Once again, Bob knew what he was doing. I re-evaluated everyone's strengths, skills and compatibilities. Getting these two AIs—well, you know what I mean," he gestured at Iris and Amavia, "in the mix did allow us to go from three teams to five."

"That's excellent," Sera said, while Iris pumped a fist in the air, calling out, "Go us!"

To which Amavia added, "Well, more like, 'Go Bob'."

The pronouncement elicited some laughs from around the room. When they dissipated, Sera continued.

"OK, first off, as Finaeus said, the ship's AIs will remain on their craft and coordinate with one another and their teams."

Troy made a sound of approval, while Sabrina's face fell once more.

"Look, Sabs, it takes too much bandwidth for you to fully project. If you want to be on a team, you have to remove your core from the ship."

A look of horror crossed over Sabrina's face, and Cheeky laughed, patting Sabrina's arm.

"And no one is surprised you'd feel that way," she soothed her.

Sabrina raised a hand to her chin, her lips pursing for a moment before she spoke. "What if I…sharded?"

The question took Sera entirely by surprise, and she glanced back at the two engineers. "Does she have core matrices capable of that?"

Finaeus stared at Sabrina for a moment, and then glanced at Earnest. It was apparent to everyone in the room that the pair was having a protracted Link conversation.

Sera was about to table the issue and move the meeting along, when Earnest gave a slow nod.

"Sabrina has nearly outgrown the core I upgraded her to twenty years ago—which should have lasted a lot longer." The engineer gave the AI narrow-eyed look, to which Sabrina only responded with an innocent whistle. "I suspect it's because of how many expanses she created within herself to help liberate other AIs. To be honest, I think a sharding would actually be beneficial for her in the long run…help her share the load, so to speak."

"What if…" Cheeky ventured slowly, glancing at Finaeus and then Sabrina. "What if the shard was a bit of a child of ours as well?"

"No," Earnest shook his head, entirely missing the meaning-laden looks Cheeky was doling out. "Your mind is not one that we can easily select attributes from and blend with others, Cheeky. That's not saying we can't do it, we just can't do it and have your child ready to take on a mission like this in the time available. If Sabrina wants to shard, it will have to be a straight mitosis."

Sabrina glanced at Cheeky, who nodded.

"OK," the two said in unison.

Sera was about to move the meeting forward once more when a large figure appeared in the room's doorway.

"Usef?" Cheeky blurted out, and the figure nodded before stepping in to reveal a much smaller person behind him.

"Erin?" Earnest added. "What are you two doing here?"

The brown-haired woman shrugged. "I'm not entirely certain. I had taken a ship from the LMC back to New Canaan to assist in some review of a—" she paused and glanced around, "project, when suddenly Usef shows up and tells me that Bob has sent word for us to come here…wherever 'here' is."

Earnest's brow lowered and he shook his head. "I'm going to have words with Bob. Would have been nice if he'd told me about all these late arrivals."

"I've just queried the tower," Krissy announced. "There are no inbound ships in the queues right now, so in theory, our numbers should remain consistent for the next hour or so—barring Tangel just jumping into our midst."

Sera laughed, wishing that could happen, but she knew her friend had her hands full on the far side of Sol, dealing with the fallout of Xavia's attack, and the war with the Trisilieds.

"OK…teams adjusted. Again," Earnest announced as Erin found a seat, and Usef ambled to the back of the room where he took a spot next to Flaherty, glancing at Malorie—who still hung in a corner—before shaking his head and directing his attention to Sera.

Suddenly, Erin spoke up. "Ho…wait…that's Airtha on the holo! This is the mission to take on Airtha? Why the hell am I here?"

Sera shrugged. "Ask Bob. I've seen your record, though, and Usef vouches for you. That's enough for me."

"Gonna have words with Bob," Erin muttered and sank back into her seat.

"OK!" Sera thrust a finger in the air. "First Team—so long as we don't get a dozen more people showing up before we leave—is myself, Jen, Kara, and Flaherty. We're on *Sabrina*."

<*Of course,*> Jen added privately.

Flaherty gave a slow nod from the back of the room, and Kara a slightly nervous smile. Sera had been a bit surprised to see Adrienne's daughter in her group, but Earnest had shown her the decision parameters, and she couldn't argue with his assessment.

"Next up is Team Two, also aboard *Sabrina*. It consists of Seraphina, Cheeky, Nance, and Finaeus."

"One last time into the breach, eh, hon?" Finaeus asked Cheeky with a wink.

The pilot shrugged. "I think we'll breach plenty in the future. But this'll be one for the songs."

"Last team on *Sabrina* consists of Sabrina—no surprise there—Usef, Misha, and Erin."

"You better have figured out which end of the gun is for shooting bad guys," Usef grunted, his eyes locked on the back of Misha's head.

In response, the cook slowly lifted two fingers in a rude gesture, not deigning to look back at the large Marine.

Sera ignored their byplay and carried on.

"Team Four is aboard the *Voyager* and consists of Fina, Roxy, Jane, and Carmen. Team Five is Katrina, Kirb, Elmer, and Amavia. Wrapping things up is Six, which will be Iris, Carl, Camille, and Malorie."

"Last, but certainly not least," Malorie chittered from her corner.

Iris twisted in her seat and took in the metallic red spider. "Any chance I can sell you on the idea of a new body?"

"And slough about on the decks with two legs?" Malorie asked with a laugh. "Not effing likely."

"Everyone's going to have Mark X FlowArmor," Sera interjected. "Those of you who haven't already had your skin replaced with the Finaeus special, that is. If you'd like to get a skin job, you'd best put in the request in the next five minutes.

"Each team is going to have a Cri-En power facility target, and a node. The plan is to infiltrate the power facilities, where we'll set up bombs. These will be used to convince Airtha that we mean to destroy the ring. Once they're in place, we move on to the nodes. Timing will be key; the window to insert our corrupted matrices into Airtha's nodes will be small, and we'll need to time it perfectly. To ensure that happens, Troy and Sabrina will be keeping us all coordinated to ensure no one jumps the gun.

"Once we've inserted our virus into her, we trigger some smaller detonations at the Cri-En facilities and leak the information that more are targeted. With the changes to her thought patterns, that should be enough to push Airtha over the edge."

Sera paused and surveyed the room, where most of the attendees were nodding, though Krissy was not.

"And your fallback plan?" the admiral asked.

"We don't have one," Finaeus said with a laugh, causing Sera and Krissy to send quelling looks his way before Sera turned back to Finaeus's daughter.

"He's kidding. That's where you come in."

THE PRAESEPE REPORT

STELLAR DATE: 10.08.8949 (Adjusted Years)
LOCATION: CIC, ISS *I2*, near Lunic Station
REGION: Aldebaran, League of Sentients Space

"Is Earnest on his way?" Terrance asked as he walked into the antechamber off Earnest's famed workshop.

"His pinnace just docked," Tangel replied, reaching a hand out to clasp Terrance's. "I wasn't expecting to see you so soon. How did the FGT's expedition go? I assume that's what this is about."

"Good," Terrance gave a short nod. "Well, good and bad. Someone is moving those stars, alright. And they're doing even better than we are at moving Canaan Prime."

Tangel found herself blinking mutely at the man for a moment before she recovered. "Seriously?"

"Well, I'm not an expert on such matters, but Emily—the FGT stellar engineer—was suitably impressed. Either way, if they'd cared to, she estimates that the stars could have already been dropped into one another, but it seems that whoever is doing this—"

"The core AIs," Tangel interjected.

"Well, yeah, I've been thinking that, too, but it just feels like conjecture so far, and I didn't want that to be in an official report."

A laugh slipped past Tangel's lips. "Ever the company man, Terrance."

He shrugged. "Old habits die hard."

Tangel wanted to probe further regarding the stellar movement in the Praesepe Cluster, but she didn't want Terrance to have to repeat himself once Earnest arrived.

Instead, she turned and walked toward the window that

looked out over the rear of the ship. Almost directly below them was the now-vacant stretch that had once been filled with twenty cubic kilometers of cargo pods, back when the ship had been bound for its colony world.

A few pods were still nestled down in the depths of the crevasse, filled with components for the ships that made up the First Fleet, but little else. The empty space made the ship feel incomplete to Tangel.

On either side of that gap lay the two habitation cylinders, sixteen-kilometer-long, fully encapsulated worlds. To date, Tangel had still lived there longer than she'd lived anywhere else. Even though she'd raised her daughters on Carthage, and that house held a host of great memories, Ol' Sam was home.

The *I2* was still home.

"I've been thinking a lot about what could have been," Terrance said in a quiet voice as he stepped to her side. "If we'd made it to New Eden, if we'd developed the picotech there. Maybe we could have headed all this off. Stopped the FTL wars and the dark ages that followed."

"Maybe," Tangel allowed. "I think about that, too. If I had somehow stopped the SSS from sabotaging the ship at Estrella de la Muerte…"

"You know it's not that simple. There was Myrrdan and the Caretakers working against us. We didn't even have a clue that they were in play."

"Yeah."

Tangel let the word fall from her lips as she stared out over the great ship. The *greatest* ship ever built.

The man chuckled. "Yeah. I know. Doesn't stop you from wondering."

<*The wars were necessary,*> Bob said after a moment of silence stretched between the two humans. <*As is this war.*>

"While I agree that wars like this are necessary once you exhaust all other options, I don't think that's what you're referring to, is it?" Terrance asked.

<*No. I think that humanity and AIs have to exhaust their taste for war to know what we are capable of, both the good and the bad.*>

"You're starting to sound like the core AIs," Tangel cautioned.

<*Them's fighting words.*>

Bob spoke in a half-joking tone that had Tangel and Terrance sharing a surprised look.

<*Don't give one another that look. You know I can tell jokes.*>

Terrance chuckled. "Uhhhh…yeah, but you need to do it more than once a decade for us to be used to it."

<*Oh. Noted.*>

"Stop messing with them, Bob," Earnest said as he entered the room and strode toward Tangel and Terrance.

<*You're not the boss of me.*>

-What's gotten into you?- Tangel asked the AI.

-I can't have fun?-

Tangel sent him a wave of curious incredulity. *-I guess…sure. People just tend to take everything you say very seriously. You're usually a very serious person.-*

-I'm evolving.-

-That's scary too.-

The ascended, multinodal AI sent Tangel a feeling of amused mirth that nearly knocked her over, and she decided not to pursue the conversation any further.

"I know where your off switch is," Earnest was saying to Bob with a smirk.

<*Now who can't take a joke?*> Bob asked.

"Is this because Priscilla's gone?" Tangel asked, as the realization hit her that Bob's change in behavior may be due to the absence of the woman who had been only a thought away for decades.

"Priscilla's gone?" Earnest shot Tangel a sharp look. "Gone where?"

<*Widowstrike.*>

"We were attacked by Finaeus's ex-wives," Tangel explained. "We also learned that the Garza clone we captured on the *Britannica* two years ago wasn't a clone at all. I interrogated him, and we found out where the Widows operate from."

"And you sent *Priscilla*?" Earnest's voice rose half an octave as he took a step toward her. "She doesn't have the training for that."

<*She does. She is the right person for the job.*> Bob's tone brooked no argument, though his words didn't slow Earnest in the least.

"Sorry, she has 'training'," the engineer held up his hands to make air quotes, "but she has no experience. Those Widows are nasty business. She's—"

"She's with my daughters," Tangel interjected. "And Joe has a stealthed fleet nearby. Trust me, I'm anxious about this, too, but we're low on people who can take out an installation like that."

"Why send people at all?" Terrance asked. "Couldn't Joe just blow their base and call it a day?"

Tangel nodded. "Yes, yes he could. But the Widows are Orion's preeminent blackops organization. The intel we're bound to get from them will be indispensable."

Earnest chewed on his lip for a moment before glancing at Terrance. "So you didn't know about this?"

"Me?" The business exec held up his hands. "I've been in Praesepe watching the core AIs shuffle stars around like they're playing a stellar game of checkers."

<*Priscilla wanted to go,*> Bob added. <*She needed to go. Worry about her later. What Terrance found is more important.*>

"Is that why you're cracking jokes?" Tangel asked. "You're worried?"

<*I'm always worried.*>

"OK, I know we're thinking of starting a comedy club, but we need to decide what to do about this," Terrance interjected, turning to the window and gesturing at it. The aft view of the *I2* was replaced by the image of a star. "This is our subject. The little star that could."

As Tangel and Earnest watched, the poles of the star dimmed, and a single hot point formed near the equator before blasting out a jet of energy for several minutes.

It was Earnest who spoke first.

"Well I'll be a…uhh, I have no idea what."

"Emily was tangentially aware of our efforts in New Canaan," Terrance explained. "She seemed to think that it was a more powerful emission than what we were doing."

"That's because we're not doing anything like that," Earnest muttered as he replayed the visual. "We're focusing the star's burn at the north pole, while dimming the southern polar region. We're intensifying the stellar output at the equator to compensate for the luminosity change…but nothing like this."

"It's obviously sufficient to move the star," Tangel observed. "And it looks like they used some sort of swarm to do it."

"An expendable swarm," Terrance added. "So far as we can tell, once the stellar output shift completed, whatever machinery was at play fell into the star."

Tangel snapped her fingers. "So that's why you queried our resources when you arrived. You want to mount a search for the facility where they're making those things."

"It has to be close," Terrance replied. "The stars are already on a collision course. It'll take a few centuries, at the current rate, but the total stellar mass in the cluster's core is over forty Sols. When they collide…."

"We get it," Earnest replied. "The entire cluster is sterilized…well, more than just the cluster, though folks beyond the slow zone will have a few centuries to get out of the way."

Tangel flung a new visual at the window. It showed the region of space between Sol and the Praesepe cluster. Centered in the view was the Betelgeuse exclusion zone, an empty region of space that had been vacated when the massive star underwent a supernova several thousand years earlier.

"Now…I'm no stellar engineer, but when Praesepe goes up, it's going to trigger some of its own supernovae, right?"

Earnest nodded. "There are no hypergiants in Praesepe, but there are stars that will evolve into them. But…the event that we'll witness isn't like other supernovae. If you look at Betelgeuse, you can see that its shockwave has only moved about nine hundred light years, and it's all but dissipated now. Most stellar systems it hits see a compression of their heliosphere, but not so much that the stellar wind can't stop the wave before it reaches major planets. Betelgeuse also released very little gamma radiation, and the x-rays are all but dissipated, thanks to our friend the inverse square law."

"And Praesepe?" Tangel asked. "It will be much worse, won't it?"

The engineer nodded. "I'm actually less worried about a collapse of the cluster's core triggering supernovae in massive stars, and *more* worried about the cluster's white dwarfs. There are several that are massive enough to undergo a supernova event on their own."

"White dwarfs can do that?" Terrance asked, then glanced at Tangel. "Don't go making any 'you've been flying around in space for a thousand years and you don't know that?' jokes. There aren't any white dwarfs around Sol, and Betelgeuse is…was…the only nearby star likely to undergo collapse."

Tangel held up her hands in a defensive gesture. "I wasn't going to say a word. Honest. Really."

"White dwarfs can do it too," Earnest confirmed, casting

Tangel a bemused look. "If they increase in mass close to one and a half Sols—depending on their rotational speed—then electron degeneracy pressure isn't enough to support the star's mass, and it collapses."

"But not into a black hole?" Terrance clarified.

"No. Before that happens, the star gets hot enough to fuse a substantial fraction of its mass in a matter of seconds." The engineer paused as he looked from Tangel to Terrance. "The ejecta from the white dwarf's explosion travels at ten percent the speed of light."

"Holy shit," Terrance whispered. "OK, so this is going to make Betelgeuse look like the warmup."

"Multiple stellar-sized fusion bombs," Tangel said quietly. "If they're doing this in other clusters…"

"I'd thought that, too," Terrance said. "I just didn't realize what the white dwarfs in them will do."

"Might," Earnest held up a hand. "*Might.* It could be that the shockwave never pushes enough mass toward the white dwarfs…or it could set a bunch of them up to slowly accrete mass and detonate over the next few thousand years."

Tangel held up a hand. "OK, so it's the big suck. We didn't think it meant sunshine and daisies, so that part's not news. What we need to do now is find out where their facility is that is making their little dyson swarm, take control of it, and then reverse this process."

"And then check over every other fucking cluster in the galaxy," Earnest muttered. "Fuck. This is going to take millennia to fix. Fucking AIs. Present company excluded."

"Thanks," Bob and Tangel said at the same time.

Terrance shot a curious look at her. "I didn't know you identified as AI."

Tangel shrugged. "Depends on the day. Of course, this presents a whole new problem. Who do we send?"

"What about Jessica and Trevor?" Terrance asked her. "I

bet Amavia and Iris could go with them."

"I think the fact that I sent *my daughters* along with Priscilla to hit the Widows should tell you that those other four aren't available."

"Oh, yeah, that makes sense. And I guess you and Bob are staying here in reserve for when the shit hits the fan."

Tangel nodded. "And worrying that it doesn't hit all over all at once."

<*Which seems increasingly likely,*> Bob added.

"OK, Terrance. Here's what we'll do. I'll have Bob drum up a couple of AIs who are as crazy as the rest of us, we'll peel off a cruiser from the First Fleet, and we'll send you into Praesepe to start the hunt. We'll send you with a spare gate, too. I don't want you going into the ass-end of nowhere and taking months to get back."

"I'm going to need some trigger pullers, too," Terrance added. "Any of those left?"

"Barely," Tangel said with a drawn out sigh. "Joe's going to kill me, but I'll send Lieutenant Brennen with you. It drops the *I2* down to just two platoons, but we have thousands of combat drones aboard, so we'll manage."

"I'm going with him," Earnest said, fixing Tangel with a resolute stare. "Someone is going to have to figure out how to put those stars back where they belong."

Tangel nodded. "I suspected you would want to go."

"Wait. Really?" he asked. "You're going to let me run off into danger like this?"

"Sure. We're all in danger. To be honest, Praesepe is probably one of the safest places around. Till it explodes, of course."

Terrance laughed. "You have such a way with words."

<*You never laugh at my jokes. I feel maligned,*> Bob said with a long sigh.

PART 5 – AIRTHA

TO AIRTHA

STELLAR DATE: 10.09.8949 (Adjusted Years)
LOCATION: *Sabrina,* Interstellar dark layer
REGION: Huygens System, Transcend Interstellar Alliance

<You know what I miss about when we were just starting out together?>

Sabrina's voice broke Sera from the thoughts she'd been lost in, and she looked at the nearest optical pickup on the bridge.

<What's that, Sabs?>

<I was always just me. I looked like me, I had my name. Sabrina was Sabrina.>

Sera gave a tired smile. *<You don't like being the* Sands of Time?>

<Makes me feel like I'm going to fall asleep.>

*<I think **I'm** going to fall asleep,>* Sera said as she stood from the scan console and looked down at Cheeky in the pilot's seat.

"Did you have to remove the captain's chair?"

"What are you talking about?" Cheeky asked as she looked up at Sera and gave a languid wink. "*This* is the captain's chair."

"You know what I mean. It feels weird to sit at scan."

<We didn't want you and your sister to fight over it,> Sabrina said over the bridge net, a soft laugh in her voice.

Seraphina looked up from where she sat at the comm console and gave Cheeky a sour look. "I would have won."

"Oh?" Sera asked. "How's that?"

"I fight dirtier than you."

Sera barked a laugh. "That's probably true."

"Still three hours till we dump out of the DL," Cheeky said, and nodded to the display at the front of the bridge. We're going to pop out just one AU from the Thomias Belt. Are our pre-clearances in order?"

"Look at her!" Seraphina said, grinning as she met Sera's eyes. "She's allll growed up."

Cheeky twisted in her seat and glowered at Seraphina. "Only 'cause the two of you made me. Sending us off alone, then you get cloned, or whatever, and start the biggest interstellar war in history."

"Yikes!" Sera exclaimed. "You grew teeth, too."

"I've always had teeth," Cheeky said with a low chuckle. "Pre-clearances?"

"Confirmed with the last DL relay we just passed. We're good to go."

Sera placed her hands on her hips and shook her head at Seraphina. "I'm amazed you deployed this many relays in the DL. Must have been quite the undertaking."

"It was," Seraphina replied. "Some were already there, but Airtha wanted it locked down. We only beefed things up on this side of the star, though. Given that it's a hundred AU trek if you come in on the far side of Huygens, the system itself works as enough of a buffer for other approaches."

"Still a pain in the ass," Cheeky muttered.

Seraphina gave a noncommittal shrug. "Kinda the point."

"I'm going to the galley. Gotta do something other than think about the mission for the next two hours."

"Just gonna leave me up here?" Cheeky asked without turning in her seat.

"You can fly the ship from anywhere," Sera pointed out. "Doesn't *have* to be here."

"It does," the pilot-now-captain replied. "This is where my gut works."

"What?" both Seras asked at once.

This time, Cheeky turned around and knelt on her seat, peering over the backrest.

"You know, flying with your gut, by the seat of your pants," she said simply.

"I know what that means," Sera replied, while Seraphina chuckled. "Though I don't think I've ever seen you wear pants."

"I own a few pairs." Cheeky's tone was only mildly defensive. "Though half of them are transparent."

Sabrina's laugh filled their minds. *<Clearly not enough seat to fly by, then.>*

"Fine. Mock me," Cheeky said, and adopted a pout, but remained perched on her seat, staring at the other two women. "You don't know what it's like being put into another body. It took a long time to get the same feel for the ship that I used to. Sure, I can fly *Sabrina* from anywhere aboard, but here is where it feels right *here*." She slapped her stomach for emphasis, almost glaring at the two women.

"I *kinda* know what it feels like," Seraphina volunteered, but Cheeky sent a scowl her way, and she amended, "A wee, tiny little bit."

"I never flew with my gut," Sera said, shrugging indifferently. "And I'm a pretty decent pilot."

Cheeky put her hand out palm-down and wobbled it back and forth. "Ehhh, on a good day."

"What? Seriously? I flew the ship back in the Fringe before we picked you up, Cheeky. I got us out of some tight spaces. Back me up, here, Sabrina."

<I…um…well…>

Sera looked at Seraphina. "You know she's disparaging us both, don't you?"

Seraphina shrugged. "I didn't get as much of the competitive, high and mighty gene as you did. I'm OK with being just good enough to get by."

Sera blew out a dramatic sigh. "It's like being insulted in my own home. Where'd all this fly-with-your-gut nonsense come from, anyway?"

<*I learned it from Jessica,*> Sabrina said. <*She taught me about it after she rescued Cheeky at the Grey Wolf Star. I became much better at flying once I learned how to use my gut.*>

"You don't even *have* a gut," Sera threw her arms in the air.

"Neither does Jessica, with a waist that small," Seraphina said, chuckling softly. "But she's got a lot of hiney under all that shiny. She's probably more of a 'seat of your pants' kinda gal. She flies with her butt, not her gut!" Her chuckle turned into a full-on laugh.

"Taking the word of that purple hussy over mine," Sera said, placing a hand on her chest. "You wound me."

Cheeky snorted. " 'Purple hussy'? You live in a glass house, there, *Red*."

"Well, at least I don't glow…or have alien microbes living inside me."

<*You're just jealous.*>

"You're damn right I'm jealous," Sera said as she walked off the bridge. "But if I went purple, you'd all accuse me of copying her."

"Plus, Fina would constantly switch you back!" Seraphina called out after her.

Sera laughed at the thought. Fina would do that, but she wasn't on *Sabrina*. Her team was aboard the *Voyager*, and if all was going well, they'd already be on the Airthan Ring.

<*You're not actually upset, are you?*> Jen asked as Sera slid down the ladder to the crew deck.

<*Course not. We used to needle one another like that all the time back when I was captain here.*>

<Do you miss those days?>

Jen's question caused Sera to pause and think it over.

<Yes and no. Yes because we were a good team, and we had a lot of fun. No because I was in my stupid self-imposed exile phase while trying to get the CriEn back from The Mark.>

She'd left one thing out of her response: Helen. Even though years had passed, Sera still thought about Helen every day. The shard of Airtha that her mother had given to her as an AI. That she hadn't realized was her mother until after her father—who was also a creature of her mother's at the time—pulled Helen from Sera's mind and killed her.

All so she could completely control me.

That was what Sera couldn't fathom. Why her mother had gone to so much trouble, spending decades to craft her into the person she wanted, a person who would kill her own father and then take over the Transcend.

I guess she wanted me to think that I'd made my own path, which was impossible, when she was guiding my every move.

<I guess I can see how you'd have mixed feelings,> Jen said in response to Sera's prior statement.

<A bit, but the times with the ***people*** *were great. I miss that a lot.>*

A burst of raucous laughter spilled out of the open galley door, and Sera resumed her approach, reaching the entrance and leaning against the frame.

At the long wooden tables sat Finaeus, Usef, Erin, and Nance. Kara was a little ways away, perched on a tall stool, her wings still resting on the ground despite her perch.

Misha leant against the counter, where the remains of the meal they'd eaten a few hours earlier were still laid out for the crew to snack on. To his right, a cup of coffee cradled in his hands, stood Flaherty, a ghost of a smile on his face as he regarded the group.

"OK, bilge rat, gimme your two best," Erin said to Usef

with a wide grin. "Better be deuces, too."

"No such luck, little lady." Usef slapped a ten and a six on the table. "Read 'em and weep."

Erin shrugged. "Well, means everything you have is worse. I think you're the one who'll be weeping."

"One last game before we dump out?" Sera asked as she entered the galley and angled toward the chiller.

"One?" Erin laughed. "With these opponents, I can get in two at least. It's like I'm playing against children."

Finaeus looked over his hand and smirked at Erin. "Don't get too cocky there. I've got your number."

"You may be the second best engineer in the galaxy, but that doesn't mean you can build a Snark manifest for shit, old man."

"*Second*?" Finaeus puffed out his chest. "I invented jump gates, star mining, and dozens of other things that every one of you use every day and take for granted."

"One word," Erin replied with a wink. "Picotech."

Nance pursed her lips and patted Finaeus on the shoulder. "Kinda trumps, Gramps."

Finaeus's face reddened, and he scowled at Nance. "After all our time together, you malign me like this?"

"I'll malign you more if you don't play or pass," Erin said, gesturing to the pair of sixes she'd played in the interim.

"Fine, fine." He dropped a pair of eights on the sixes.

Sera gave a happy sigh as she peered into the chiller, looking for something interesting.

<*Still feels like home, though,*> she said privately to Jen.

<*I can see why. This ship has a special feeling to it.*>

Finally spotting a wheat ale that looked promising, Sera pulled the can out and popped the top open. She took a long swig and leant against the counter alongside Flaherty.

"So what do you make our odds?"

"Better than anyone else would have."

She shot him a side-eye. "Not exactly encouraging."

"Neither is Finaeus's strategy," Flaherty said, then looked into Sera's eyes. "We'll pull it off. I'm certain of it. But it's going to be hard. Very, very hard."

"That the best speech you have right now?" Sera asked, chuckling softly as she took a drink of her beer, watching as Finaeus launched into a creative string of curses as Erin won another round.

"If you're coming to me for a pep talk, then we're in worse shape than I thought."

"Funny man," Sera muttered before nudging him with her elbow. "Want to join in for a round?"

"No, I'll just watch."

She gave him a brief hug, then walked to the table and sat next to Nance. "Deal me in."

"You join in late in the game like this, and you're the bilge rat," Finaeus intoned.

"Sure," Sera replied, giving her uncle a wink. "Let's see how fast we can get you back down there."

COMMENCEMENT

STELLAR DATE: 10.09.8949 (Adjusted Years)
LOCATION: *Voyager*, High Airtha, Airtha
REGION: Huygens System, Transcend Interstellar Alliance

"If at first you don't succeed, try, try again," Carl intoned as the *Voyager* settled into a docking cradle on High Airtha.

"Except it barely feels like we're the same ship," Katrina groused. "They practically gave her a new hull."

<*They sure did,*> Troy agreed. <*An amazing new hull. Stealth, stasis capabilities, way more ablative layers. It's like a dream.*>

Carl snorted. "Way to be subtle, Troy."

<*Katrina's the sentimental one,*> the AI retorted. <*I prefer to be nearly impervious and invisible, should I choose, over showing off the patchwork we've sported for the last few centuries.*>

"Patchwork?" Now it was Carl's turn to sound upset. "I'll have you know I've sweat blood to keep your *patchwork* hull in one piece."

<*And if blood sweat was a useful item for repairing ships, I'd be grateful. Alas it's just hyperbole, which has never been known to fix anything.*>

"How many problems would it cause if we spaced our AI? Carl asked Katrina.

"More than he causes by being around," Katrina said as she gave the forward consoles a narrow-eyed glare.

"Even with all these new systems on the ship?" Carl pressed.

Katrina glanced at the readouts, double-checking that the ship appeared powered down, but that the systems were ready for a fast restart.

"Yeah, even more so," she stated.

<*You two are barbarians,*> Troy groused. <*Kirb says it's really*

nice outside, and that you should take a look. And stop threatening your AI, who only has your best interests at heart.>

"Still so subtle, Troy," Katrina said as she rose from her seat and stretched her limbs.

<*I try.*>

It was a given that while they were on their mission, she was going to worry constantly about the ship. She knew the upgrades would make it safer, but that didn't mean she had to like the change.

Over the centuries, the *Voyager* had become a symbol in her mind. The one thing that solidly connected her to her past, proof that she really had traveled forward in time, and wasn't just some crazy woman who remembered a past that never was.

But now, nearly everyone in the galaxy who was three jumps or less from a major trade route knew of the Scipio Alliance and the war being waged across the Orion Arm.

Which she supposed should be comforting. That, combined with the fact that New Canaan was a real place, an actual refuge that awaited when this struggle was over, *should* mean that the *Voyager* no longer needed to be that connection to the past for her.

I guess centuries-old habits die hard.

She finished her stretching and walked out of the ship's small bridge, finding Fina waiting for her in the passageway.

"You ready for this?" asked the normally blue-skinned woman—who had reverted to natural flesh tones, and also altered her facial structure in order to fool any optical systems that caught sight of her.

"As I'll ever be," Katrina said with a resolute nod. "Your team ready?"

Fina had the largest group of unknowns under her purview. Roxy they knew to be a solid operator, and she seemed committed to taking down Airtha. Carmen, the AI in their group, was determined to make up for her failure on the *Damon Silas*, and the AI council at Styx had pronounced her fit for duty.

Jane, the pilot who technically had done some very unethical things—not that Katrina was anyone to judge—was the wildcard. So far as Katrina could tell, Jane's loyalty was to her friends, not the mission—or anyone else, for that matter.

The woman had been a decorated pilot in the TSF before she'd joined with Justin's side of the conflict. She had been involved in several infiltration ops in the past, and on paper, had the skills to get the job done.

Which meant that, in theory, so long as they didn't get found out, they should have no problems.

And if anyone believes that, I have a ring to sell them.

Fina had paused before answering Katrina's question, and the look in her eyes mirrored the thoughts that ran through Katrina's mind.

"We'll do the job. Come hell or high water. Our bombs will get set, and we'll insert our virus on time."

They clasped one another's arms and then Fina turned and walked down the passage—which used to be a ladder shaft—and took a left toward the forward airlock.

Roxy and Carmen were waiting for her. As the airlock began to cycle, the pair activated their stealth armor, disappearing from view before the outer door opened.

Katrina nodded with satisfaction as she continued further aft to find Elmer, Kirb and Amavia waiting for her at the midship airlock. Camille, Malorie, and Iris stood outside the chamber, waiting for Carl, who was still in the cockpit.

"Everyone good to go?" Katrina asked.

"Good?" Malorie chittered with delight. "This is amazing."

As she spoke, the red spider disappeared from view, and moments later, reappeared hanging from the overhead.

"I'm never giving this shit back. You know that, right?"

Katrina glared at the woman who had once been her captor and torturer, wondering for what had to be the thousandth time why she still kept Malorie around.

Probably because she's useful and would get into too much trouble if I cut her loose.

"Well, you work for the ISF now, so you don't have to give it back," Iris said to Malorie, her lips quirked in a challenging smile.

Malorie's head turned toward Katrina. "She's making us sound all legitimate. I don't like it."

"You'll manage," Katrina said, her tone half encouraging, half threatening.

"Maybe," the red spider replied. "You know…so long as the evil ascended AI who lords over this place doesn't spot us and crush us."

"We'll be alright," Iris said, glancing at Camille, who gave a nervous, half smile. "Everyone knows what to do. Follow your team lead's orders, and in two days' time, we'll be drinking beers and laughing about how we killed an ascended AI."

"Way to jinx it," Elmer muttered.

Camille squared her shoulders as she sidled up to Iris. "You won't mind if I use you for a shield when the beams start slicing things apart, will you?"

Iris had adopted a more automaton-like appearance, which facilitated several additional layers of ablative plating she normally didn't wear. Like the others, she wore flow-armor overtop, able to disappear should the need arise.

"Don't worry," Katrina said, giving Camille a slap on the shoulder. "This will be a walk in the park."

"Which is exactly what it looks like out there," Kirb said from the fully cycled airlock. "We're set down in the middle of a cedar grove."

Katrina shook her head at her supercargo. "I *did* pilot us in, you know. Kinda noticed."

"Always taking the fun out of things, Captain," Kirb said as he turned and walked down the ramp, Elmer following after.

Unlike Fina's team, Katrina's group was all known quantities. Kirb and Elmer were men who had been with her for ages. They were steadfast companions as well as skilled fighters.

And though she'd only recently met Amavia, Katrina had known both of the woman's former selves, Ylonda and Amanda. It was strange to see aspects of them both in the new being that had been forged out of Myriad's attack on their lives. That being had been a shard of Airtha, and had tried to kill the two, forcing Ylonda to take refuge in Amanda's mind.

"Good to go?" Katrina asked the woman, keeping her thoughts to herself.

"I've let HoltenCo know that their special courier package is en route," Amavia replied as she patted the courier pouch tucked under her arm.

"Everything's in order, Captain," Carl said as he ambled down the passage and placed a hand on Katrina's shoulder. "We'll be good. The data drops are set up, and all the comm channels are verified. No one is waiting for us out there. Our ship is just another specialty courier making a run from Bellatrix."

"And we're just headed into the maw of the most powerful creature in the galaxy," Malorie added.

"Might be just the second or third most powerful creature in the galaxy," Katrina corrected. "But remember. Just takes a lucky shot from a cheap security drone to put you under. Alert and ready. At all times."

<*Our transport is here,*> Krib called up the ramp, and Katrina nodded to Iris's team.

"Good luck."

Iris gave Katrina a confident smile, and Camille added, "Stay safe, Captain."

Katrina waved over her shoulder as she walked through the airlock and into the too-white light that shone down from the Airthan star. It cast a wintery glow across the forest that surrounded the ship, giving the trees an almost bluish hue.

A groundcar was pulling away from the ship, and Katrina could make out Fina through the vehicle's window. She assumed that Roxy and Jane were secreted within as well, and turned her attention to a second transport that waited a short distance away.

This one was longer, with room in the back for the crate that Kirb and Elmer were moving toward the vehicle. Next to the car floated a customs drone, ready to scan the cargo and review their order.

Katrina walked toward the bot with the calm certainty of someone who had bluffed her way past hundreds of customs officials, both organic and otherwise. When she reached the drone, she passed her tokens, giving the machine an emotionless stare as it validated them. Before the civil war, travel within the Transcend did not involve customs, but that had changed on both sides of the conflict, and citizens were under increased scrutiny at every port.

Granted, we're all here with false identities, so they're right to be worried.

The drone took a minute, and then sent an acceptance of her credentials and their cargo's destination. It also passed Katrina a list of rules and regulations, listing sections of the ring that were off limits—which appeared to be over half of the structure.

<*I wonder if Airtha is up to something in those sections, or if they just like controlling the movement of visitors,*> Amavia asked.

<*Probably both,*> Katrina replied.

Amavia and Katrina slid into the front seats of the

groundcar, while Kirb and Elmer made sure the cargo was secure in the rear of the vehicle.

<*You realize that both our targets are in no-go zones, right?*> Amavia asked.

Katrina gave a resigned nod. <*Well, we didn't think it would be easy, did we?*>

The other woman chuckled as the two men got in the car. "What's easy?"

Katrina joined in the laughter as the car took off toward HoltenCo, where the team would do their legitimate business on Airtha before carrying to on a restaurant and probably a bar crawl to kill time before they had to get to their targets.

Katrina twisted in her seat, watching the *Voyager,* next to which Carl's team still waited for their car. She kept her eyes on the ship until the trees obscured it from view.

<*Stay safe, Troy.*>

<*I'm the one with stasis shields.* ***You*** *stay safe.*>

She couldn't help but laugh. <*Will you ever stop being so surly?*>

<*You like me this way.*>

That's true, she mused. *I really do.*

THE RETURN

STELLAR DATE: 10.09.8949 (Adjusted Years)
LOCATION: *Voyager,* approaching Airtha
REGION: Huygens System, Transcend Interstellar Alliance

Two hours later, Sera was back on *Sabrina*'s bridge, this time with the rest of the crew—all of them crammed into the small space for the final approach to the ring that was their target.

Though the space could certainly house eleven people, Sera couldn't recall a time when she had ever seen that many on the ship's bridge—at least during her tenure.

Once again, she sat at the scan console, while Seraphina managed comm. Usef was at the weapons station, and from the stories Sera had heard from *Sabrina*'s recent adventures, the man knew what he was doing there.

The others were spread around auxiliary consoles, aside from Finaeus, who stood directly behind Cheeky, and Flaherty and Kara, who flanked the bridge's entrance, both with arms crossed and brooding expressions lowering their brows.

"Dumping iiiiin…" Cheeky drew the word out, "three, two, one."

The final word fell from her lips, and the forward display changed from the endless nothing of the dark layer to the brilliance of stellar space.

Dead ahead shone the light of Airtha, the white dwarf companion of the Huygens star. It was just under two AU away, but its small surface area caused it to appear as little more than a pinprick of light. Sera toggled the holodisplay to enlarge it until they could see the Saturn-sized star encircled by its celestial ring.

"Home sweet home," Sera muttered, and met Seraphina's

gaze.

Seraphina laughed. "Feels like I just left. Which I guess I kinda did, just a few weeks ago."

"It's been a bit longer for me, but I get your drift," Sera replied.

Even though she'd run her part of the Transcend from Khardine for some time, it was still less than two years since she'd left Airtha and traveled to New Canaan with her father.

The fact that her 'father' had been under Airtha's control clarified so much of what had gone on over the last twenty years. She'd blamed him for sending a fleet to New Canaan, but really it had been her mother who had forced Tanis's hand and escalated tensions between the Transcend and Orion.

It was perfectly clear now that Airtha had hastened the war's arrival. The only thing that still didn't make any sense was the fact that her mother, ascended AI though she was, seemed uninterested in allying with Tanis. Together, they could have fought against Orion and then the core AIs without wasting so much time and energy on a civil war.

You should have seen this, Helen. You should have seen that we could have been allies.

Sera felt like she'd never stop struggling with the mysteries that lay so many levels deep.

And new ones kept being added, such as how her real father—whatever that even meant—had ended up in the LMC, held in stasis for over a millennia, while yet another clone took his place.

The man they'd recovered from the LMC had passed every test, and even Finaeus was fully convinced that it was his real brother, but Sera was finding herself more and more uncertain of the wisdom of turning the Transcend's governance over to him.

Only the fact that the Transcend was bound by the Scipio Alliance, and thus under Tangel's oversight, kept her from rescinding her transfer of power to Jeffrey Tomlinson.

In the entire galaxy, Sera trusted only one thing: that no matter what, Tangel would do the right thing.

That belief was her North Star.

"Relay has logged us," Seraphina announced. "Passing you the inbound vector, Cheeky. Applying for a berth at Sandstar Heights."

"Sandstar?" Sera asked. "Why not Kelsey Outer Ports?"

Seraphina flushed as she looked up, her eyes meeting Sera's. "Well, there was an attack there a year back, and…Kelsey Outer didn't make it."

"Oh. I see."

Sera hadn't made any strikes, and from what Roxy had shared, neither had Justin. There was only one other person who could be responsible.

"Have a lot of things like that happened?" she asked.

"A few."

The bridge fell silent as everyone considered what they were flying into: a realm ruled by a despot who had no compunctions about killing millions of her own people.

"Well, buck up, people." Finaeus tossed a smirk at each of his nieces. "At least Airtha hasn't blown the whole ring yet. There's still hope."

* * * * *

Outside, the ship was settling onto a cradle at Sandstar Heights, but Sabrina was barely paying attention as she looked over her appearance and gave a brief nod.

<*This is still very weird,*> she said to herself.

<*You're telling me,*> the ship's AI replied. <*You're me, but you're not me. I'm two people.*>

<*Double the Sabs, double the fun,*> the shard of Sabrina said.

A laugh came from the hold's audible systems. <*I wonder if we should stay separate when you get back. Finaeus is certain that a re-merge will be possible, but I kinda like having another me around.*>

<*Won't that be confusing?*>

<*Well, we probably should use a different name for you anyway,*> Sabrina the ship's AI said.

<*Or* ***you*** *could get a new name.*> The shard canted her hips and winked at the hold's optics. <*I can be Sabrina, and you can be 'Ship'.*>

<*Damn, I'm sassy!*>

<*Better believe it. But yeah…I get that I should use a different name,*> the shard said. <*I feel like taking one of the ship names we used over the years, but that might be too risky.*>

Sabrina snorted. <*There's no way Airtha would know about 'Madam Tulip'. You should use that.*>

<*You're funny. I was thinking something like 'Falcon'.*>

<*I like it,*> Sabrina replied. <*Except that it sounds like the name for the entire strike team.*>

<*Well, 'Sabrina' means 'Legendary Princess'—*>

<*We're not letting you go around being called 'Princess', I'll never hear the end of it.*>

<*I wasn't going to suggest that, either,*> the shard said. <*I'm still* ***you****…or me. This is weird.*>

<*OK, back to 'Falcon'. How do you feel about 'Kestrel'?*>

<*Not great. Look, can we just keep this simple? You be Sabrina, I'll be Sabs.*>

The ship's AI didn't respond for a second. <*I don't like having to give up 'Sabs', but I think it would be best for the crew. It's settled, then. You're Sabs. I'm Sabrina.*>

<*Awesome. I should get going, I can hear Usef tapping his foot clear across the ship.*>

Sabrina laughed again. <*He'll never change.*>

<*Who would want him to?*>

*****

Twenty minutes later, all the pep talks were over, and the teams had dispersed.

Sabrina dropped her status update in small segments distributed across a number of data drops, then picked up the same from Troy. They shared acknowledgements, and then went comms silent.

The teams would take some time to disperse across the massive Airthan ring. Each had their own plans and destinations, but come 0600 Standard Airthan Time the next day, they would all be planting their bombs in the CriEn plants.

From there, they'd move on to Airtha's nodes to implant the virus, and then bluff the great AI into thinking that she was going to die.

What a long shot, Sabrina thought to herself.

She knew that it was entirely possible that an AI could be tricked into suiciding. The concept of 'a fate worse than death' wasn't foreign to her kind.

But to trick an intelligence as powerful as Airtha?

If it hadn't been an idea concocted by Finaeus and Earnest, she would have dismissed it out of hand.

Ironic that even though I've sent out a shard of myself, I'm still left back here waiting. And now I'm worried about other me, along with the rest of them. Trust me to make things worse.

Sabrina pushed the melancholy thought from her mind and set to watching the ground crews working nearby, while monitoring local feeds and looking for signs that anything was amiss.

Of course, the Transcend *was* in the middle of a civil war, and this was one of the capitals. Everything seemed to be amiss.

Even so, vigilance kept her from worrying about her teams.

A bit. A very little bit.

OTHERS

STELLAR DATE: 10.09.8949 (Adjusted Years)
LOCATION: Airthan Ring
REGION: Huygens System, Transcend Interstellar Alliance

D11 examined the map of the Airthan ring, wishing for some new insight, some clue that would give her a better route to the CriEn power facility that her group had been assigned.

It was deep within one of the exclusion zones. Even the ring's residents were restricted from passing within five hundred kilometers of the power facility.

She didn't fault Airtha for keeping people away. It was a time of war, and the facility was a sensitive installation, but that didn't do anything to make D11's job easier—which she supposed was the whole point.

The original plan hadn't taken into account this added level of paranoia, but the Widow wasn't dismayed. She'd undertaken dozens of missions where reality bore little resemblance to the plan.

At least the power plant is actually there.

D11 had been on her fair share of missions where the objective wasn't even present when she'd arrived. Granted, many of those had been in the years before jump gates, but even with the gates' hyper-FTL travel, the timescales for intel to make it back to the *Perilous Dream* were often measured in decades.

<*I believe our best route remains the maglev line,*> she said to the two other members of her team. <*The line is still active. The facility's workers use it for access to the plant.*>

<*Then we'll have to wait for the next shift. It will be traveling to the plant in two hours,*> C419 said, her tone denoting agreement, though her words weren't overly supportive.

D11 shook her head at the other Widow. C419 had a way of

being contrarian, even when there was absolutely no reason to do so.

The final member of her team was Y2. She only nodded in agreement.

<Very well,> D11 said as she turned to look over the concourse they stood at the edge of—fully stealthed, of course. *<Come. I wish to reach the departure station as quickly as possible and secure our place on the train.>*

* * * * *

Sera settled into a seat in the back of a bar, which bore the name 'The Smokey Ruin'. Flaherty sat across from her, his gaze sweeping across the space, cataloguing the entire room—likely weighing threats and assets with that single glance.

Though she'd done the same, Sera didn't for a second think that she was as efficient as the man who had been her constant guardian for so many years.

However, she didn't need his assessment to know that the people were tense, unhappy, and clearly imbibing more than normal in an effort to pretend that they weren't living under a despot.

<You'd better get a drink for me while you're in there,> Kara said from her lookout position outside the bar. *<Some days, I hate having wings.>*

<Only some days?> Flaherty asked, a sliver of sardonic humor in his voice.

<Most days I wish I ***had*** *wings,>* Sera added as she pulled up the table's menu and looked over the drink selection.

The woman outside the bar sent a long sigh over the Link. *<Flying is amazing, and it can be fun to scare the crap out of people, but few seats are made for winged people.>*

<There are always the bar stools,> Flaherty suggested. *<You should be able to keep your wings hidden with the flow armor and*

come in for your own drink.>

Sera wondered if the man was mocking Kara, and the woman's reply indicated that she felt the same.

<*Are you being serious? I thought it was best if I stayed out here?*>

<*Well, there's no one in here to worry about, and their internal sensors are crap. If you sit at the right side of the bar, you won't be bothered.*>

Kara didn't respond for a moment, and then asked, <*This is a test, isn't it?*>

<*Glad to see you passed,*> Flaherty replied.

Jen made a disapproving sound. <*That seems unnecessarily mean, Flaherty.*>

The man only grunted, and Sera laughed.

<*You should know by now that Flaherty has a warped sense of humor,*> she told her AI.

<*Still.*>

Sera and Flaherty ordered drinks and a meal, and then some food to go before eventually rising from their table and returning to the streets of Dima.

Night had fallen, which meant that grav fields were bending the light of Airtha away from the ring, with only a dim glow filtering through. The effect was one that caused an amorphous light to fill most of the sky, creating a near-shadowless moonlight.

When she was young, Sera recalled Finaeus often talking about how he wanted to engineer a new solution to the nighttime effects on the ring. If she recalled correctly, he had discussed making some sort of moon configuration that would orbit off the elliptical between the ring and the star.

Maybe once this is all over with, he can actually get to that.

Kara stepped out of the shadows. "I don't see a drink."

"You doubted me?" Flaherty asked, and pulled a bottle from his jacket. "Stout, right?"

"Wow, you *do* notice everything."

"I got you onion rings and a chili sandwich," Sera held up a bag. <*We're on the move now, though. Once you eat up, we'll hit the sector's maglev, find an empty train, and disappear.*>

<*It should be harder than this to move freely on the ring,*> Kara said, her voice rife with disapproval.

<*Even though a lot of people have left Airtha, there are still a trillion people living here,*> Flaherty said. <*Even an entity like Airtha has trouble controlling that many people.*>

<*Or so we assume,*> Sera corrected. <*She could also just not care.*>

<*Well, she should,*> Kara said while taking a pull from her beer bottle as she eyed a couple as they walked past, chatting in hushed tones.

Flaherty gestured for the trio to begin moving as well. <*No one would just stand around out here—at least not anyone up to any good. We've already been tagged by two different monitoring drones.*>

<*Sabrina has dropped a new update,*> Jen said as the group began to walk down the street in silence. <*All teams except for Fina's have completed their 'official' business on the ring, and are moving to the power plants. Fina is still working on her primary objective.*>

<*Slacker,*> Sera said with a nonchalant laugh. <*Did Sabrina pass along any reason why?*>

<*Too much security. They're having to find another way in. Her report says they have one located, though.*>

Sera glanced at her companions and gave a reassuring smile. <*Don't worry. She knows this ring like the back of her hand. She'll pull it off.*>

<*Of course she will.*> Flaherty's tone conveyed no emotion, but it also held no doubt.

<*Sheesh, don't you two go getting all excited on me.*>

<*Sorry,*> Kara replied. <*Just worrying about all the things that*

can go wrong and snatch success away from us.>

<*Aren't you just roses and sunshine.*>

Flaherty grunted indifferently. <*She's just described my job.*>

Sera didn't reply to either of her companions, wondering how she got saddled with the two sourpusses.

Eventually, her thoughts turned to the fact that somewhere on the ring was yet another one of her 'sisters'. Except this sister was different: cruel, villainous—everything that Sera knew she *could* be if she didn't keep her baser instincts in check. Ironically, the visage the new version of herself had chosen was of a pale-skinned woman who was always sheathed in glowing white. It reminded her of stories Katrina had told of her Lumin ancestors and their near-cultish worship of light.

She watched a day-old feed in which the white Sera made a proclamation, declaring that a new armada was being built and would strike Khardine and end the war in just a few months.

Standing behind her otherself was a haggard man, who had stood behind Tomlinsons for longer than most people had been alive: Adrienne.

Sera glanced at Kara, wondering if she'd sought out any feeds showing her father.

The winged woman had expressed a desire to free her father, but strangely not a desire to talk to him. It wasn't as though Kara had spoken ill of Adrienne, it was more in what she hadn't said.

Of course, Sera knew what the underlying reason was. Adrienne wasn't so terribly different from Airtha in how he treated his children. But now there was no doubt in any of their minds that Adrienne would be under Airtha's control. The only way to free him—and the other trillion souls on the ring—was through Airtha's destruction.

Or so they hoped.

Fifteen minutes later, they reached a maglev platform, where they caught a train to a larger station where they milled about in the crowds for half an hour, disappearing one by one until all three were stealthed near where their target train would board.

TSF soldiers patrolled the platform, and drones swept by overhead. Twice, the guards nearly bumped into Sera, but both times, she managed to twist to the side at the last moment. Ten long minutes later, the train arrived for CEPP41—her team's ultimate destination, deep in one of the exclusion zones.

She slipped onto the lead car while the guards re-checked all of the waiting passengers, moving to a corner that she hoped would remain vacant. Pings from Flaherty and Kara confirmed that they'd also boarded the train and were thus far undetected.

She was relieved to see that only two passengers boarded her car, each settling in on opposite ends. One appeared to fall asleep almost instantly, while the other was lost in the Link, his eyes flicking rapidly as he absorbed information displayed just for him.

Just before the doors closed, a drone flew into the car and scanned the space, stopping at each of the workers to check them over.

<*You're holding your breath,*> Jen said as the drone flew a half-meter past where Sera stood.

<*Just giving one less thing for that drone to spot.*>

<*The flow armor filters the sound and IR from breath, you know.*>

Sera pursed her lips, wondering why Jen seemed to enjoy needling her so much.

<*I've heard talk.*>

The AI must have taken the hint, because she didn't reply. Suddenly Sera realized *why* Jen had stated the obvious.

<*Shoot, sorry. You're nervous, aren't you?*>

<*A bit,*> the AI admitted. <*It feels surreal to just be strolling around on the ring. I always expected us to come here, but I thought we'd fight our way down to the surface, slugging it out with dozens of baddies before finally coming face to face with Airtha herself, at which point Bob and Tangel would kill her with fire, and then we'd all have a celebratory drink—well, not me, I don't drink, but you get the idea.*>

<*I do,*> Sera laughed softly. <*But somehow that seems waaaay more dangerous than what we're doing.*>

<*Well, there'd be an army at our backs.*>

<*I suppose there's that.*>

Sera shared the same sentiment in many respects, but she also knew that if there was an army at their backs, there'd be one before them as well.

<*Don't worry, though, if we fail at this, that will be our plan B,*> she reminded Jen.

<*Except we'll be stuck down here when this plan B commences,*> Jen countered.

<*Yeah, I guess there's that.*>

<*Plus, Fina's team needs to complete their initial task before Plan B is even an option.*>

Sera was a little worried about that herself. But from their reports, they were still in play; it was just taking longer than expected.

Nothing to worry about.

She repeated that assurance to Jen as the drone completed its sweep and then stopped at the car's doors. It spun and moved across to the far doors, appearing to give the area a detailed scan.

Sera worried that it had found some sign of her passage, but she couldn't think of what.

A moment later, the drone seemed to have satisfied itself and turned, leaving the train car. The doors closed immediately after.

Moments later, the maglev took off, streaking across the ring to the exclusion zone, and the CriEn Power Plant where they'd set up their bombs.

TOWER ASSAULT

STELLAR DATE: 10.09.8949 (Adjusted Years)
LOCATION: Uplink Tower 7-1, Airthan Ring
REGION: Huygens System, Transcend Interstellar Alliance

Fina settled back against the broad oak tree that her team had formed up around, her gaze sliding from Roxy to Jane.

"A bit of a pickle," she said after a moment.

This close to the uplink tower and its security sensors, they didn't risk using the Link, but as fortune would have it, a storm was blowing through, so speaking was safe enough beneath the rustling leaves and creaking boughs.

"That's a new one on me," Jane said. "Are we the pickle, or are they?" She jerked a thumb over her shoulder at the tower as she spoke.

"We are," Roxy replied, a smirk settling on her azure lips. "Well, the saying is that we're 'in' a pickle."

"You sure about that?" Fina asked. "I would have expected us to *be* the pickle…stewing in vinegar and the like."

Jane chuckled. "Carmen says you're overthinking this pickle business. So what are we going to do about our objective?"

Fina glanced around the tree again, taking in the hundred meters of open space between them and the uplink tower. Their original plan had been to simply cross the space utilizing their stealth armor while leveraging nanoclouds to ensure the roving drones didn't spot them—or to breach the machines if they did—but with leaves and other flying debris whipping across the space, stealth wasn't an option.

"No two ways about it," Fina said after a moment's further consideration. "We're going to have to go under."

"Security's tight in the passages below," Roxy cautioned. "I mean…you know that, but I'm just saying. We're going to have to breach more systems down below and hope that no one—such as an ascended AI who could squish us with a thought—notices."

"Carmen says she loves how reassuring you are."

"Carmen can talk through your armor," Roxy quipped.

"Sure," the AI said through the armor's speakers, "but it's fun making Jane say everything for me. It's like she's my little puppet."

The woman let out a low groan. "You told me the armor couldn't do that while stealthed."

"Well yeah," Carmen drew the words out. "Having stealth armor talk removes the whole stealth element. But we're not really utilizing audible stealth right now. So there you go."

Fina rose from her position and gestured to the other two. "Let's move. There's a subterranean access point a kilometer through the woods."

"Just keep an eye out for patrols in here," Roxy cautioned. "If I were running security, these trees would have eyes."

"Creepy," Fina muttered, but took the other woman's meaning.

During the trek through the woods, the team spotted several surveillance drones—which were large, and capable of navigating through the inclement weather—and carefully skirted their patrol routes, reaching the subterranean access point fifteen minutes later.

Just as they reached the low arch that led into the ring substructure below the stretch of woods, the skies opened up and it began to rain.

"Close one," Fina said as she gestured for Roxy to perform the breach while Jane kept an eye on the woods.

"You'd think the ISF's stealth could handle rain," Roxy said as she set a breach pad on the door's console.

"It can…normally," Fina replied. "And against any other

enemy, I'd have no trouble trusting it to do so."

Roxy didn't respond, but her silence spoke volumes on her behalf.

A minute later, the door opened and the group slipped inside.

<*OK,*> Fina switched to the Link. <*Weapons check and have your armor scrub any debris from the surface. We're ghosts.*>

<*I'm clear,*> Roxy said a moment later, followed by Jane's pronouncement a few seconds later.

They checked over one another's EM readings, and then deployed a light nanocloud around themselves to mask air movement.

Fina provided the route through the substructure passages that would lead them to the uplink tower. The corridor they were in did not lead directly to their target, so the team would have to take a circuitous, four-kilometer route before they were as close as they'd been while crouched beneath the oak tree twenty minutes prior.

After a kilometer's travel, they came to a network node, and Fina tapped it directly, masquerading as a maintenance drone. Once on the network, she dropped a report for Sabrina in fragments across several low-security log aggregation systems.

Fina still anticipated completing their task in the uplink tower fast enough to reach their assigned CEPP in time, but if they met with further delays, they'd have to skip planting their explosives and go directly to the Airthan node they'd been assigned.

Only having bombs set up at five CEPPs would be enough, since the strike force's plan was to bluff more than sabotage, anyway.

Worse come to worst, we can plant our charges here at the tower. Might make for an interesting distraction.

Ten minutes later, the trio reached a large chamber where

several passages met. Almost directly across the ninety-meter-wide chamber was the entrance to the uplink tower.

Normally, it would have been protected by a pair of soldiers, with drones on perimeter patrols, but rather than live soldiers, only two automatons stood sentry.

Crap, those aren't automatons—those are AI frames.

Fina reached out and touched Jane and Roxy, establishing a physical network to limit any EM that their stealth couldn't mask.

<*From what Kara told us, the AIs on the ring are fully under Airtha's thrall. If we take those two, we'll have to take them simultaneously so they can't get any message out,*> Fina said.

Roxy sent an affirmation. <*Then we'll need to hit them with a hefty breach dose.*>

<*What about freeing them?*> Carmen asked. <*They're under Airtha's thrall, but there's no way they'd support her if liberated.*>

<*It's too risky,*> Fina said, wishing there was another answer. <*There are plenty of AIs who are willingly on the wrong side, just like there are ascended AIs bent on killing us all.*>

<*OK,*> Carmen replied. <*I understand.*>

Fina could tell that the AI wasn't happy and hoped that she wouldn't balk at any unsavory orders.

Stars, Finaeus, what did I do to deserve a team I can barely trust to follow orders?

Ironically, of all of them, she worried about Roxy the least. The half-woman, half-AI had lost much over the years. During the journey to Airtha, she'd confided in Fina that this mission was how she hoped to reclaim some part of her honor, at least in her own mind.

Collecting her thoughts, Fina gave the signal and led her team across the chamber to the sealed doors guarded by the AIs. A few drones flitted through the air, and an autonomous cargo hauler swept past at one point, forcing the group to dodge out of its way. Yet no alarms sounded, and the Airthan

AIs gave no indication that they'd spotted anything.

A minute later, the team reached the doors, and Jane quickly deposited breach nano on both of the AIs, while Roxy and Fina drew shrouded weapons and trained them on the enemies.

Moment of truth, Fina thought, ready to send a special command that the AI council on Styx had given her, should Carmen fail to perform her duties.

It felt wrong to have the ability to shut down another sentient being, but for all intents and purposes, Carmen was on probation and under Fina's command.

Had it been a human whose trustworthiness was in question, that person would have also faced dire consequences should they fail to perform their duties.

Sera better have known what she was doing, suggesting they all came along.

Ten grueling seconds later, Carmen announced, *<OK, they're locked down. And…you were right. I really can't tell if they're under an aegis, or if they're operating of their own free will.>*

<OK, I'm on the door,> Roxy announced.

A minute later, the team stepped into the base of the uplink tower, sealing the door behind them as they moved forward.

<Target is the same,> Fina said. *<Get to the main lift shaft, flush nano up, and climb. The node we have to tap is at the top of the tower.>*

<Fun times,> Roxy said. *<Good thing I don't get tired.>*

<Speak for yourself,> Jane said in mock weariness.

The uplink tower was used to provide high-bandwidth, line-of-sight communications to other towers around the ring. Given the twenty-five-million-kilometer circumference of Airtha, communications going around the structure could take several seconds longer than if they were broadcasted directly across empty space, beamed from tower to tower.

In addition to the comm web they provided, the towers

also had direct connections to the military STCs and, through them, the jump interdiction grid.

With the grid down, Krissy's fleets could jump to within half an AU of Airtha, bypassing the layers of defense that were built up around the star.

That was, once Fina's team climbed to the top of the tower and breached the systems there.

<*We're behind,*> Roxy said as they moved down the corridor. <*And honestly, you two are going to be slow climbers. I can make it up the tower twice as fast on my own, plant the tap on the node, and be back down before you'd get five hundred meters.*>

<*It's not like we're stock,*> Fina replied. <*We can keep up.*>

<*Maybe you can,*> Roxy told her privately. <*But Jane can't, and I don't want to leave her alone.*>

Fina resisted a groan. Roxy wasn't entirely wrong, but she hated the idea of splitting the team. However, arguing about it would waste more time.

<*OK, but we're going to the lift shaft and waiting for you there.*>

<*Works for me…and, Fina?*>

<*What?*> She grunted out the question.

A stealthed hand found her arm and gave a gentle squeeze. <*Thanks.*>

ANOTHER WAY

STELLAR DATE: 10.09.8949 (Adjusted Years)
LOCATION: Airthan Ring
REGION: Huygens System, Transcend Interstellar Alliance

<*OK, I've got a visual on seven AIs, a little over four hundred drones, and a nanocloud.*>

Sabs sent the message back to the team as she retreated from her surveillance position, leaving behind her own nanocloud to observe the CEPP and its defenses.

<*Wait, since when did Airtha get a nanocloud?*> Misha asked, as Sabs eased around the long conduit stack and saw the pings from her team indicating their presence, invisible in the overlapping EM fields coming off the stack.

<*It's just nano drifting in the air using brownian motion,*> Erin explained. <*Common enough in facilities like this, where they can control air currents to keep it where they want it.*>

<*Not common to have a cloud this dense, though,*> Sabs said. <*I'm not entirely sure how we're going to get in there without being detected. This isn't like breaching some Inner Stars facility in the backend of nowhere.*>

No one offered any suggestions, and Sabs reviewed the feed from her own nanocloud again, scanning the ovoid, five-kilometer-wide chamber deep within the ring's structure, looking for any inspiration.

The CEPP facility was a hundred-meter-wide sphere centered in the space, with lifts running up from the floor and encircled by gantries. If it hadn't been for the enemy's nanocloud, Sabs could have simply walked right up to the thing and planted their explosives on a few of the support struts without any trouble at all.

<*This was supposed to be the easy part,*> Usef muttered.

<*Well, we can see the CEPP,*> Misha said after a moment. <*Do we have to go right up to it?*>

<*What's brewing in that head of yours?*> Usef asked.

<*I just wonder if we can shoot something at it,*> Misha explained.

<*I might…*> Erin began, then paused. <*Yes! OK, I think I have an idea.*>

Usef let out a soft grunt. <*You* ***think****?*>

<*Stars, Usef, not now,*> the engineer said, then directed a thought to Sabs and Misha. <*Was he weird and surly on* Sabs *too?*>

<*Yup.*>

<*Sure was.*>

<*I'm still right here. Enough stalling while you flesh out your idea, Erin. What is it?*>

Sabs tried not to laugh as Erin sent the man a pair of glaring eyes over the Link, and then launched into her explanation.

<*Well, I don't know how efficacious it would be to 'shoot' something at the CEPP. However, we also don't have to go there ourselves.*> She paused, and a marker appeared on their HUDs noting two other locations on either side of the facility. <*See these? This is where they pipe liquid nitrogen in to cool the energy interchange systems. CriEns on this scale generate* **a lot** *of heat from the transference of raw vacuum energy into usable electricity. They're kinda forming electrons out of nothing, in a way—well, not 'out of nothing', but it would take a week or two to explain how the particles are reformed to make them. In short, like most big, powerful things, it gets hot.*>

<*They would have safeties, though,*> Sabs said. <*If we cut the nitrogen supplies, I assume it would shut down and activate some sort of emergency cooling scenario.*>

<*Right,*> Erin agreed. <*So we don't bomb anything, we just*

destroy the emergency cooling systems.>

Usef sent a grating sound that Sabs realized was his way of clearing his throat over the Link. It sounded like boulders smashing their way through a glass factory.

<*Our plan here is to make it* **seem** *like we're going to blow the ring. Not to actually blow the ring.*>

<*It won't blow the system,*> Erin explained. <*Or…it shouldn't. The CEPP has hundreds of individual CriEn modules. From what Finaeus has explained, they work in a carefully modulated wave pattern so that they don't draw too much energy from the foundations of spacetime. At any given point, only a fraction of them are in operation while the others are cooling. We'll set up our sabotage to only blow ones that are not actively drawing power. That will limit their destructive force, but emergency shutdown and cooling will still take effect for the others, and all should be well.*>

<*Famous last words,*> Misha muttered.

<*I'll pass the details on to me, so that I can share it with the other teams,*> Sabs said.

<*'I'll pass it on to me?' That's not confusing at all,*> Usef said with a soft laugh.

Erin joined in. <*If there's one thing I've learned on my short time aboard* Sabrina, *it's that nothing is really as it seems…and yet that's how you know everything is perfectly normal.*>

<*Stars,*> the Marine muttered. <*It's like you've already been infected by them.*>

<*I'm not the one who installed glitter guns on the captain's chair,*> Erin shot back, sending along a wink over the Link.

<*Oh…heard about that, did you?*>

Sabs only half listened to the team's banter as she logged into a series of sim games and created characters with specific backstories, hiding the intel within, along with a few jokes about her team for herself back on the ship to enjoy.

<*OK, message is sent,*> she said after a minute. <*Should we get over to those nitrogen lines? I assume we'll send in nano to effect the*

sabotage through the feed lines.>

<*Let's hold on just a few minutes longer,*> Erin replied. <*I'd like to see if Finaeus can confirm that this isn't going to blow us all to subatomic particles if we do it wrong.*>

<*Oh…*> Misha muttered. <*You conveniently left that part out.*>

<*Well, its not like we're playing with something nice and safe like a fusion reactor,*> Erin replied. <*These plants could rip spacetime to shreds if they go haywire.*>

<*So, what sort of minimum safe range are we talking about?*> Usef asked. <*You know, if things go sideways.*>

<*Oh, I don't know…*> Erin's voice trailed off. <*If all six went up at once, probably a light year or so. That would be the non-instantaneously-lethal range. I think that beyond that, the cosmic rays would probably sterilize every star system for a hundred light years.*>

<*Great balls of star shit,*> Misha muttered. <*Yeah, I vote we wait for Finaeus's confirmation.*>

* * * * *

<*So?*> Seraphina asked Finaeus as he reviewed the message that had been relayed to them via Sabrina. <*Will it work? Because if not, we need to split up and have a team hit the nodes while the other shoots their way in to bomb the CEPP.*>

<*I'm thinking it through. Carefully,*> the engineer replied. <*You pestering me won't make it go any faster.*>

<*We're on the clock, here,*> Seraphina reminded her uncle. <*If we need more time, we have to fall back to the secondary schedule for shard insertion.*>

<*Just. A. Minute,*> Finaeus bit off each word.

<*He can be a bit testy at times, can't he,*> Cheeky said privately to Seraphina and Nance. <*Though this seems to have him worried more than normal.*>

<*Probably because if six of the CEPPs go up entirely, it'll create*

something that will make a supernova look like a firecracker,> Nance replied. <*It would probably outshine the entire galaxy by several orders of magnitude.*>

<*So…you're saying we need to be careful,*> Cheeky said with a laugh.

<*I don't think you're taking this seriously enough,*> Nance shot back.

<*Nance, really. Sneaking right up to death's door and ringing his bell and then running off is kinda our thing. We'll figure it out and save the day. It's what we do.*>

<*Just don't die this time,*> Nance's voice was low and serious. <*When we play ding and dash with death, not everyone gets away.*>

Cheeky didn't respond for a moment, and Seraphina was trying to think of something to say to break the silence, when Finaues spoke.

<*Nice alliteration, Nance. And…yeah. I had to make an alteration to Erin's proposal to ensure it was timed properly. What she had in mind was off juuuust a hair and would have probably killed us all.*>

Cheeky let out a nervous laugh. <*At least we'd accomplish our mission…Airtha would be toast.*>

<*You're sharing it back out?*> Seraphina asked, ignoring Cheeky's comment.

<*No…I just thought I'd keep it to myself and let the other teams blow us all to Andromeda. Yes, I'm sending the updated info to Sabrina and Troy now.*>

<*What gives?*> she asked her uncle. <*You're normally the funny, joke-cracking person in situations like this.*>

<*Sorry,*> he replied. <*This one…this one's different for me. This ring is the culmination of my life's work, and here I am skulking about on it like a thief—and now doing my best to make sure we don't accidentally destroy it to save it.*>

<*OK, I can see that. For what it's worth, I'm sorry it's come to this.*> Seraphina gauged where her uncle's arm would be and

reached out to touch it. <*You know…memories of sneaking off to your lab and talking with you about your latest endeavor…well, it was always my favorite pastime as a child.*>

The old engineer snorted. <*Seraphina, there is no possible way that I didn't already know that. However, what* **you** *may not have known is that it was one of my favorite pastimes as well. There was a reason why I never ratted you out.*>

<*You…*> Seraphina's throat constricted, and she paused to swallow and take a deep breath. <*You were always the father that other man never was to me.*>

Finaeus's hand reached out and wrapped around her shoulder. <*And you were—and still are—like a daughter to me. But when all this is over, I hope you'll give the real Jeffrey Tomlinson a chance. He deserves a good daughter like you.*>

<*We'll see. I guess it can't hurt to try. But he's not really my father, and I'm not really his daughter.*>

<*Don't write off the value of a relationship with him so soon. It might be just what you need. Either way. The messages are sent, the other teams know what to do. Let's get our nano into the nitrogen lines and move on to the nodes.*>

<*OK, uncle-dad.*>

Finaeus made a choking sound. <*Gah…that sounds like some sort of terrible incest thing. Never say that again.*>

<*Er…yeah, didn't mean that at all. Stricken from the record.*>

SABOTAGE

STELLAR DATE: 10.09.8949 (Adjusted Years)
LOCATION: Airthan Ring
REGION: Huygens System, Transcend Interstellar Alliance

<I guess it looks like Bob knew what he was doing, sending Erin along,> Katrina said to Kirb as they crouched next to the nitrogen line.

She carefully placed a blob of formation material on it, seeding the inert mass with nano all bearing the specific instruction sets that Finaeus had passed along.

<I'll admit.> Kirb let out a nervous laugh. *<Bob scares the shit out of me. But from what you and Troy have said over the years, he does seem to be on the money a lot.>*

Katrina sent an affirming thought to Kirb, then froze, shielding the formation material with her body as one of the patrol drones flew past.

She eyed the weaponry hanging from the thing and made a mental note to profusely thank Erin for coming up with the idea to use sabotage that didn't require them to fight their way to the CEPPs to plant explosives on them.

In all honesty, it didn't surprise her that the pixie-like engineer had come up with the perfect solution to their problem. She'd been instrumental in dozens of projects back at Kapteyn's Star as well, her unique insights always aiding in getting the job done on time.

The flood of memories caused a tightness in her chest that she carefully quelled. Just thinking of the Kap and all that her people had accomplished there still caused her more pain than she would have expected after so many years.

She wondered how the colonists were dealing with it, reeling from one crisis to the next in the wake of their journey forward in time. She suspected that they'd never had a chance to deal with the loss of the Kapteyn's colony before being attacked again and again.

Though if there's one thing I know, it's that this life never really gives you a 'safe time' to slow down—other than in death, of course.

The drone completed its pass, moving along its route, and she triggered the formation material to bore its hole in the pipe, seed the nano in the nitrogen flow, and then reseal the breach.

Though some of it would invariably get lost, the nano was preprogrammed to make it to the correct CriEn modules and seed itself for the time when it would commit the sabotage.

<*OK, we're on the clock, now,*> Katrina said to Kirb. <*No way to send an abort signal unless we come back here and re-seed a second batch.*>

<*Then let's get a move on. It's over eighty klicks to the node.*>

A minute later, they met up with Amavia and Elmer on the far side of a maglev line that ran around the perimeter of the space.

<*Any trouble?*> she asked the pair.

<*We nearly ran right into one of the roving AIs. Really thought I was going to have to take the thing down—it came within a centimeter of my left arm,*> Amavia reported.

<*Well, I bet we'll get our chance to take some down at the node,*> Katrina replied. <*If this is how carefully they're protecting the CriEn plants, then you can bet that Airtha's nodes are going to be fortresses.*>

* * * * *

Sera settled back behind a conduit stack, waiting on Flaherty and Kara to return.

A sense of relief had settled over her with the knowledge that the second phase was nearly complete. They were within a hair's breadth of actually striking at Airtha.

Of course, the relief that one task was done was already bleeding into anxiety over the next. The knowledge that she'd eventually have to confront her mother had been eating at Sera for the past two years. Now that it was almost upon her, she had to continually force herself not to play out scenarios in her mind.

<*You need to calm yourself,*> Jen said, as Sera fidgeted. <*You're doing what must be done.*>

<*Am I that transparent?*>

<*A bit, yeah. Your thoughts are spilling over. We're almost there, and then it'll be over. We'll hit the nodes, and we'll convince Airtha to end herself.*>

Sera snorted. <*Just like that, eh?*>

<*Well…no, but yes, I suppose. That's what will happen, in the end.*>

<*If we succeed,*> Sera added.

<*So defeatist, we haven't even—oh…crap.*>

Sera shot the AI in her mind a stern look. <*Being mysterious isn't helping.*>

<*Sabrina just got an update from Fina. They made it into the uplink tower, and Roxy was handling the breach, but they've lost contact with her.*>

<*Dammit.*>

Sera considered her options. Not having six of the CEPPs suffer damage wasn't critical; Finaeus and Earnest's plan had only called for four of them in the first place. But without the interdictors being taken out, there was no plan B. Either they convinced an ascended AI to take its own life, or they were likely all going to die.

<*Fina.*> She took the risk of making a direct connection through their emergency backchannels to reach out to her sister. <*What's going on?*>

<*Sorry, Sera, I fucked up. Roxy went to the top of the tower to*

breach the uplink node, but she went dark as soon as she got there. Jane and I are climbing the lift shaft. We'll be there in a few minutes. Don't worry. We'll get it done.>

<We can abort, fall back to the secondary schedule.>

<No, if they capture Roxy and strip our plans from her mind, we're done. There won't be a second chance. We have to stop that from happening. We'll take the net down, and Krissy's fleet will be onstation before you know it.>

Sera bit her lip, hoping against hope that Fina wasn't just blowing smoke up her ass.

<OK…I'm counting on you, Fina.>

<Don't worry. We'll hit this, and make it to our node on time. I promise.>

<Just get out safe. All of you.>

* * * * *

Fina closed the connection to Sera and then triggered the nanorelays in the lift shaft and passages below to go into full standby.

It was entirely likely that passing the message had given off enough EM to trigger a sweep of the shaft and the tunnels they'd passed through to get to the tower.

With luck, a sweep wouldn't pick up the nano in standby, and they'd retain their connection to the other teams.

<We're almost there,> Fina sent to Jane on a narrow-band, low power connection. *<Just a few more meters and we'll be at that landing. From there, we can send up a nanocloud and see what's going on.>*

<We should never have let her go alone,> Jane said, and Fina could hear the accusation loud and clear in the other woman's voice.

<It was her choice, and a smart one,> Carmen replied. *<There could be a dozen reasons why she's not checked in. Maybe she's*

waiting for the right time to make her move.>

<*We'll find out,*> Fina said as she reached the platform set into the side of the lift shaft.

The top level where the node was situated was another twenty meters up, but a door on the platform led to a level two floors below the top. She sent a nanocloud out to move to the top of the shaft, while dropping a passel on the door's panel, keeping her options open.

Jane reached the platform a moment later and pulled herself up alongside Fina, pressing herself against the wall.

<*Stars…that's a lot of down.*>

<*Try not to think about it,*> Fina replied as she watched the feed from her nanocloud.

Above them, the drones slipped past the lift doors at the top of the shaft and into the room at the top of the tower.

The area was crammed with equipment. Everything from power regulation systems to network interfaces, to the transmission equipment itself.

In the center lay the main processing node that handled all the connections and data transfer with the other uplink towers. The node was a massive cube, over thirty meters across. Power and network conduit ran into it from all directions, and lights glowed across its surface, projecting holographic status indicators to a group of technicians who monitored the node.

Or would have been monitoring the node, if they weren't standing nearby, staring down at Roxy, who was kneeling on the floor in front of a group of five SAI battle frames.

<*Aw, shit,*> Fina said to Jane and Carmen, sending them the feed.

"You're locked down," one of Roxy's AI captors was saying. "No one's coming to help you, and we've begun scouring the tower for any accomplices. Tell us what Justin has planned here."

<*Shit!*> Jane exclaimed. <*They still think we're with Justin.*>

<*That could be good,*> Fina replied. <*Really good. We just have to take them out before they breach her mind and find out the truth.*>

<*How are we going to do that?*> Jane asked. <*There are four technicians and five of those AIs. Can the ISF flow armor withstand that much firepower?*>

<*For a second or two,*> Fina replied with a soft laugh. <*What we need to do is get up there and get breach nano on one or two of those SAIs. Then we set them on one another.*>

<*Won't we get detected the same way Roxy did?*> Jane asked.

<*Maybe. I'll take the direct approach, while you go through this lower level. There's a staircase that will take you up to the far side of the uplink control node. Once there, you get the tap on that node as quickly as possible.*>

<*Wait,*> Carmen interjected. <*How are you going to get through those doors up there? They'll be watching them for sure.*>

Fina gave a resolute nod. <*I'm counting on it.*>

* * * * *

Sera walked down the corridor to the CEPP's maglev station with her team close by. They'd successfully executed Erin and Finaeus's plan, and if they could catch a maglev at the right time, they'd be able to reach their assigned Airthan node facility in just ten minutes.

Then the fun would really start.

She was about to reach out to Flaherty with a comment about the train they'd take, when she saw his marker suddenly stop five meters in front of her.

<*Down!*> the man bellowed.

Sera dropped as flechette rounds tore through the corridor, slicing through the air where she had been a moment before.

The shots revealed the warm end of a weapon floating in midair, just a few meters in front of where Flaherty crouched.

<*What is it?*> Kara demanded from her position behind Sera.

<*Don't know,*> the man grunted. <*I ran right into her, though.*>

<*Her?*> Sera asked.

<*Thin arms…but* **strong**.>

A second later, another barrage of flechette rounds filled the corridor, and Sera pulled her pistol from its stealth sheath, firing in the direction of the second attacker.

Each of her rounds missed their mark, striking the bulkheads. She flushed out a nanocloud to try and see the invisible assailant, when something slammed into the wall next to her, and Kara called out, <*Found one!*>

Sera moved across the corridor, covering either end as her two invisible companions fought their equally invisible enemies. Sending her nanocloud in their direction, she drew her pistol, waiting for her nano to find and highlight the enemy on her vision.

A second later, a black figure appeared where Flaherty stood, struggling with the invisible woman.

<*Fuck. Widows,*> Sera spat out the words as she fired on the attacker.

The shots ricocheted off the Widow's armor, but provided enough of a distraction that Flaherty was able to grab the woman and fling her into the wall next to Sera.

Sera fired another series of rounds at the Widow, targeting what looked to be a weak spot in her armor at the top of her left thigh. None of the shots penetrated, and she shook her head in frustration as the Widow began to rise.

<*I guess our stealth is ruined anyway,*> she said and slapped her thigh, drawing her lightwand out of a pocket in her armor.

The blade sliced through the black-sheathed woman's neck, and a moment later her body fell to the deck. Turning to the second attacker, Sera saw that Kara had killed her attacker as well, courtesy of her long, hooked talons.

<*Sabrina, Troy,*> Sera reached out to both AIs. <*We just encountered two Widows. Inform all teams to be on the lookout.*>

<*Are you still at the CEPP?*> Troy asked, worry evident in his tone.

<*Yeah,*> Sera replied, pursing her lips, knowing what that meant. <*The Widows must be trying to sabotage them, too.*>

<*Except they'll be doing it for real,*> Troy warned. <*And if they do…*>

<*Sera,*> Sabrina began, sounding almost breathless. <*There are dozens of CEPPs on Airtha. If they're hitting them all…*>

<*I'm going to reach out to Finaeus. Hold tight.*>

* * * * *

A few meters into the passageway out of the CEPP chamber, Finaeus found himself leaning against the wall as he trembled with rage, clenching and unclenching his fists as he tried to gain some measure of calm.

<*I swear—*>

The ability to form words fled him for a moment, and he struggled to grab ahold of any coherent thought, forcing his heart rate and breathing to steady.

<*I swear, I have the worst…**the worst**…ex ever. If anyone ever says 'my ex is a horrible person', I can ask 'but have they ever tried to **murder a trillion people**?'. What the actual fuck is she thinking?!*>

<*Well…we thought it too,*> Sera said, uncertain of why she'd suddenly try to defend Lisa Wrentham's decisions.

<*And then we fucking dismissed it! Because we're not goddamn lunatics!*>

<*So what do we do?*> Sera asked. <*We could warn Airtha.*>

<*Do you think she'd listen?*> Finaeus asked. <*'Oh, hey, Airtha. We came here to kill you, but it turns out that the Widows beat us to the punch. Any chance you could just shut down all your CEPPs so*

that they don't blow away half the fucking stars between Orion and Sagittarius?' Think she'll go for that, Sera?>

His niece didn't reply, and Finaeus felt a measure of guilt flow into his mind, dousing the anger at Lisa and her narrow-minded, pigheaded ways.

<*Look. I'm sorry, Sera,*> he said. <*You're right, we have to stop it, but Airtha won't do it. She'll see it as some part of our attack, and then.... Well, anyway. I'm going to have to shut them all down myself.*>

<*Can you do that?*> she asked. <*I mean...it just took us hours to get into position to sabotage six of them. For all we know, the Widows have targeted them* ***all****.*>

<*Yeah, it's easy,*> Finaeus replied. <*My team will just have to go back to our CEPP and blow it early. I'll alter the risk assessment parameters in the safety systems, and that one event will make every CEPP on the ring go into safety shutdown. Then, if the Widows do blow any, it will just cause a small explosion from localized residual energy.*>

<*Just like that?*> The laugh that came with Sera's statement sounded more than a little nervous.

<*Well, there's more to it, but I have your sister, and Cheeky, and Nance to help. We'll get it done. You keep to your target node. With the Widows here, this really is our one shot.*>

<*OK, good luck, Uncle Finaeus.*>

<*Gah, don't call me that. Makes me feel old.*>

<*Funny, funny. Get to it, old man.*>

Sera cut the connection, and Finaeus terminated the nano relays he'd used for the direct communication before reaching out to his team.

<*We need to go back.*>

A simultaneous *'What?!'* came from Seraphina, Nance, and Cheeky.

He quickly explained the situation, causing both Nance and Cheeky to spit out a few curses regarding their strong dislike of Widows.

<*So how will we trigger the explosion?*> Nance asked. <*And how are you going to alter the safety protocols to cause all the CEPPs to think that this is an event warranting a full shutdown?*>

<*First, we'll need to drop another passel of nano into each nitrogen feed line. We'll program in a new detonation time, say, thirty minutes from now. Then I need to get to the control node at the base of the plant and reprogram it and then trigger a system-wide update.*>

<*You sure that will work?*> Nance asked. <*Plus…how will we get there?*>

Finaeus resisted the urge to smack the woman in the head for always questioning him at the worst times. <*First off, I designed these plants, so I know how to get it done. Secondly, we're going to have to shoot our way in.*>

<*Fin,*> Cheeky whispered. <*There are at least two hundred drones out there, plus at least a dozen SAIs…there's no way we can pull that off.*>

<*Then we have to hack the drones,*> he replied. <*And fast.*>

<*On it,*> Seraphina announced. <*I'll get in close, release a cloud, and then tag them as they fly through it. Nance, you take the west nitro line, Cheeks, take the eastern one. When I give the word, all hell breaks loose, and Finaeus, you get to that CEPP node.*>

The team sent their acknowledgements and turned back toward the CEPP chamber and their targets.

Finaeus wished them luck, feeling a pang of worry for these three women who had been such an important part of his life over the last few decades.

And here you thought you were an old man, and were considering moving on from this life. First you get that vibrant and utterly unorthodox niece, Sera, and then a whole crew of friends, most importantly, a new wife…. We've all got too much to live for.

It took several minutes to cross the floor of the chamber and get as close as he dared to the mass of roving drone patrols, before hunkering down behind a low berm, four hundred meters from the CEPP.

Releasing a cloud of his own nano, he made a brief connection to Seraphina and slaved the cloud to her.

The action was innocuous, and one of many point-to-point connections they'd already made while moving around the CEPP—but this time, a pair of drones immediately turned and began to fly toward him.

One was a scout model, carrying only a small electron beam and pulse cannon. The other was much larger, with multiple pulse cannons, beams, and projectile weapons.

Far more firepower than his armor could withstand.

As luck would have it, both drones flew through a part of his nanocloud, and he connected to the bots that touched the machines, frantically working to breach them while slowly creeping to the left, moving away from where he'd sent the transmission to Seraphina.

The nano reached the smaller drone's control systems and took it over, but his nano hadn't landed close enough to the large bot's control systems, and it carried on, reaching the place where Finaeus had been and initiating a search protocol with active scan and ranging beams.

Finaeus continued to creep away, but the drone immediately turned in his direction and began flying along the edge of the berm, moving at a pace that would set it upon him in just a few more seconds.

With few other options, he directed the smaller bot to fly above the large one and fire its electron beam directly at the other machine's central graviton emitter.

The shot was a partial hit, taking out one of the a-grav pods, and the large drone swung to the side, a gun swiveling toward the small drone. There was a brief pause, and then it blew Finaeus's drone to bits.

Rather than continue in the direction he'd been moving,

Finaeus doubled back, skirting the ruins of the fallen drone, while the other one continued on in the same direction.

A few seconds later, he finally gained control of the large bot and turned it toward one of the Airthan AIs that was moving in to investigate.

<Yeah, I'll bet you're curious what just happened. Step into my parlor, you bastard.>

<Finaeus, pass it to me, you need to get moving,> Seraphina said, and he realized she was right.

He passed her control of the bot and carefully climbed over the berm, taking a more direct route to the CEPP, threading between several more drones as they approached.

Once past the ring of drones and AIs that were moving toward the downed bot's location, Finaeus picked up the pace, dashing across the hard carbon floor of the chamber, weaving about in an effort to maintain as much distance from the patrolling drones as possible.

Then he was past the bulk of them, breathing a sigh of relief, when suddenly, all hell broke loose behind him. He still had a hundred meters of wide open terrain to cross before he reached the CEPP, but he kept his pace measured and slow, doing his best not to turn and watch the battle surely raging behind him.

Seraphina can handle herself. She's been through worse scrapes than this.

He heard more weapons fire coming from the east and west, and knew that Nance and Cheeky had joined the fray. Three brave women facing an army of AIs and drones.

He briefly pulled the feeds from behind and saw that several dozen of the larger drones had been subverted and were raining fire down on the Airthan AIs, focusing all their energy on taking out the sentients first. Three were already down, and the others were falling back, pulling more of the mechanical defenders from around the CEPP to come to their aid.

There was no fire from the ground near Seraphina's position, and he prayed that she was safe, though he dared not try a connection at this distance. That would bring dozens of drones on top of him.

She'll be OK.

Then Finaeus was at the central shaft that ran from the chamber floor to the CEPP. He circled around it until he found the access panel for the safety control systems. Without any concern over who might be watching, he pulled it off and pulled his hard-Link cable from his wrist, jamming it into the port, and passed his root level tokens into the node.

It only took him a few seconds to sift through the libraries of code and provide his updates. Then he triggered a systemwide update and waited the ten seconds that it took for all the CEPPs to confirm that they'd processed the update.

Just as he pulled his hard-Link, a voice called out from behind him.

"Halt!"

Finaeus froze, wondering if the Airthan AI that stood behind him could see anything more than the Link cable dangling from his wrist.

"Easy, now," Finaeus said, as a wave of nano flowed from his hands, drifting through the air to the Airthan AI.

He harbored no illusions that the levels of nano he could get across to the enemy would be enough to breach its hardened armor, but he hoped what reached the AI would serve as a sufficient distraction.

"Disable your stealth. Arms up, or I'll blow a hole in you," the AI ordered.

Finaeus complied, and his body shifted to a matte grey.

"Drop your weapons," came the next order, and Finaeus nodded.

"I have to reach for them to drop them. OK?"

"OK."

He slowly lowered his right hand to the rifle that was slung across his chest and grabbed the clip that held the stock to his shoulder.

The moment it came free, three things happened at once: his nanocloud attacked the AI's armor defenses, the AI fired, and Finaeus dove to the side, weapon in hand, returning fire.

One of the AI's shots caught him in the side, and Finaeus spun around before landing on his back. He lifted his rifle and shot at the AI's side, where he knew the armor to be weaker. Even so, his shots failed to penetrate, and the AI swung its railgun toward him as he scrambled back.

Then an electron beam lanced out from behind the central column, and one of the AI's arms was torn away. Another shot hit its side, and then another burned away its head.

Seconds later, Cheeky appeared from around the column, and a wink came from her over the Link.

"You need to carry a bigger gun, dear."

"So it would seem," Finaeus said as he scrambled to his feet.

"This way!"

She directed him toward Nance's position. He started after her, and then remembered to reenable his stealth systems before he got far.

<*Fall back to the western door,*> Seraphina said. <*We're t-minus four until boom.*>

<*Where's the time gone?*> Finaeus asked with a laugh as he picked up the pace.

A few drones closed with them, but between Cheeky's electron beam and Nance's railgun, the bots fell from the sky before they did any damage to the team.

As the trio closed with the exit, covering fire came from the doorway, and Finaeus was surprised to see that Seraphina was already there, shooting down any drones that came close.

With forty seconds to spare, the group reached the exit, and Finaeus spun to look at the CEPP.

"When it goes—"

His words were cut off as a haze appeared between the group and the power facility. The fog seemed to solidify, and tendrils of light twisted around in a swirling vortex for a moment before they coalesced into a towering figure.

-Finaeus. I should have known.-

The words came directly into his mind, searing themselves across his thoughts as a tendril of light slashed toward him, only to recoil as a bolt from Cheeky's electron beam slammed into the figure.

Though the limb her beam hit had recoiled, the figure, which Finaeus knew had to be Airtha, seemed nonplussed.

-And which of my wayward daughters is this? The second or the third? Surely not the first.-

"I'm Seraphina. I don't know where I stand in the count. Not that it matters."

-Oh it matters. To me, at least. You're the second, if you care to know.-

As Airtha spoke, a limb lashed out, knocking Seraphina's weapon from her grasp, before the tendril wrapped around the woman, disabling her stealth armor as it lifted her into the air.

-So pathetic. You really were a failed attempt. All of you, just shadows of my perfect daughter.-

"Stop! Airtha. Leave her be," Finaeus demanded. "You can end this all. Jeff is back—the real Jeff. Why don't you find a way to come back to us?"

He let the words tumble from his lips, saying anything that came to mind, anything to distract her for just ten more seconds.

Then the figure's tendrils of light contracted, though whether in fear or confusion, Finaeus couldn't tell.

-How…-

Airtha vanished, dropping Seraphina to the ground.

"Grab her!" Finaeus yelled to Cheeky, as he rushed forward. "We have to get into the corridor!"

"Where'd she go?" Cheeky demanded as she grabbed one of Seraphina's arms and helped drag her back into the safety of the corridor.

"I don't know," Finaeus said as he looked down at Seraphina, only to realize she wasn't breathing.

A second later, the CEPP exploded.

PART 6 – FGT'S LEGACY

A1

STELLAR DATE: 10.09.8949 (Adjusted Years)
LOCATION: Widows' corvette, approaching OGS *Perilous Dream*
REGION: A1 System, Spinward edge of PED, Orion Freedom Alliance

<*Whose idea was this, anyway?*> Cary groused as she piloted the Widows' ship toward the *Perilous Dream*. <*Everything itches, and I can't stop having these thoughts…. These Widowy thoughts.*>

<*You knew that was going to happen,*> Faleena said. <*The Widows are under constant mental conditioning and monitoring. If our brainwaves don't properly match theirs, we wouldn't pass muster.*>

<*I was complaining, not asking for an explanation,*> Cary retorted. <*Doesn't mean I like it. I keep thinking that it will be good to be back amongst my sisters, and that our strength is in our unified purpose and lack of distinction. It's creepy.*>

Though she couldn't see Faleena's face behind her Widow's helmet, Cary could tell that she'd upset her sister. Not from a change in Faleena's posture, but from the utter lack of change.

If she didn't know better, she'd think that the AI actually *was* a Widow.

Priscilla, on the other hand, shifted in her seat, just as uncomfortable as Cary. With a muffled sigh, she turned her body as she turned her featureless, ovoid head to look at the three sisters.

"Probably easier for you three," she said in the breathless Widow's whisper. "At least when you look at one another, it's natural to see your sisters."

Cary shuddered. <*Gah…we can do without the voice.*>

"Consider yourself an honorary sister for the mission," Saanvi said, placing a hand on Priscilla's shoulder.

<*The voice!*> Cary exclaimed. <*It's too damn weird to hear you like that.*>

<*As you wish, C139,*> Saanvi replied tonelessly.

<*That is not helping.*>

<*E12 is right,*> Faleena said, gesturing to Saanvi. <*We're docking in forty minutes, and A1 has summoned us to a briefing. We have to* ***be*** *Widows.*>

"I know, I know," Cary said aloud, forcing herself not to cringe at the sound of her own voice as it emanated from her helmet. "OK, if I'm doing this, I'm going fully into character. From now on, I'm C139."

Faleena turned toward Cary and cocked her head. "You have always been C139. Why is it from now on? Should I recommend you for reconditioning?"

Cary whipped her head around to stare at her sister. The thought of being reconditioned into actually being one of these Widows was enough to send her into a near-panic.

Then she saw Saanvi's shoulder rising and falling, heard the soft sound of laughter coming from her helmet, and realized that her sisters were needling her.

"Dammit, *F11*." She wished Faleena could see her glare. "That's not funny."

"This unit does not know what you're talking about," Faleena replied evenly.

Cary was about to reply, but opted for a long groan instead, determined not to take the conversation any further if she could help it.

* * * * *

"They're in, Admiral," the bridge officer at the scan console announced.

Joe replied by way of a short nod, forcibly resisting the urge to run his hand through his hair—and pull half of it out. There was an itch on his scalp that demanded to be scratched, but he knew it was just his nerves.

Nerves over sending his three daughters into the most dangerous place in the galaxy.

OK, easy on the hyperbole. Not ***the*** *most dangerous, but up there. Waaay up there.*

He'd considered several options that would allow him to go with them, but in the end, Tangel had convinced him that the best way to keep their daughters safe was to ensure that he was nearby, ready to storm the *Perilous Dream* and save them if needs be.

That, and rely on Faleena's good judgment and the QuanComm blade secreted away inside her body—something he'd instructed her to use at the *first* sign of trouble.

After a few calming breaths, taking care that his bridge crew didn't see his anxiety, Joe turned his focus back to the holotank, reviewing the system's layout for the hundredth time.

Despite the general disbelief that the A1 System's star was indeed a black dwarf, it seemed to fit the description. A body roughly the mass of Sol, while the size of a terrestrial planet; it gave off almost no light, heat, or radiation of any sort.

It was just an inert lump of matter. The fate almost every star in the universe ultimately faced.

The engineers aboard the *Falconer* were fascinated by the stellar remnant, speculating endlessly as to how that much energy had been siphoned away from the star, and where it had been sent.

It was clear that at one point, A1 had been a white dwarf. But nearly all white dwarfs in the universe were still over twenty-five thousand degrees. The amount of energy that would have to be removed to cool such a star into a black dwarf was mind-boggling.

However, sussing out the reason why the system's star was nothing more than a dark orb was not the mission at hand. The real goal was capturing the Widows' ship—which was orbiting the black dwarf at a distance of five light minutes—and stopping them before they struck again.

The fallback plans were top of mind for him now, the strategies to blow past the Widows' defenses and land troops on the *Perilous Dream,* should Faleena call for help. He'd commanded enough missions over the years to know that anxiety always came along with sending good people into harm's way, and he tried to think of this one as being no different.

Tried and failed.

If there was one thing he wished that they'd been able to discern from their captive Widows, it was how many of the enemy was currently on the ship. It seemed that it could be anywhere from a few dozen active Widows to thousands, depending on how many were out of stasis.

Should even a fraction of that total number be up and about and attacking, his daughters would be in dire straits.

The girls are skilled and well trained, Joe told himself. *They've just never faced off against a few thousand elite assassins before.*

He turned to the ship's pilot. "Bring us to within fifty thousand kilometers. I want to be able to breach that ship the moment our team calls for help."

"Aye, sir," the lieutenant replied. "Easing her in."

That brought his mind to his other concern: how to use just one platoon of Marines to take a five-kilometer-long ship.

* * * * *

The dock was completely devoid of personnel, occupied only by two other pinnaces, and a number of automatons who stood ready to service C139's craft.

Cary's mind momentarily fought the designation, but then she drew a slow breath, forcing herself to fall into the persona.

I'm C139, a clone of Lisa Wrentham, a simulacra assassin, ready to report to A1 and tell her of our failure to kill Tangel.

The team had debated for some time whether or not they'd tell A1 that their mission had failed. In the end, they decided on the truth, because it was a chance to learn what the leader of the Widows would do next. Would she write off the loss, or would she send more of her clones against Tangel?

Her quick survey of the dock complete, C139 walked down the ramp with E12, F11, and R329 on her heels.

<*C139,*> a voice came into her head. It was the same as her own, the same as all the Widows. Only by the ident that came along with the message did she know it was A1 who'd spoken. <*Report to briefing room D9. I will be with you shortly.*>

C139 passed the message to her sisters and strode confidently through the unmarked corridors to the designated briefing room.

They entered wordlessly, taking extreme care not to give away their true identities through any uncharacteristic movement. Without pause, the four women settled in seats front and center, placing their hands on their laps as they waited patiently for A1 to arrive.

Though she didn't provide a status update, F11—C139 was pleased that she'd used the correct identifier for her sister—would be releasing a passel of nano through her foot. It would move to the front of the room and wait for their target to step on it.

There was a slightly worn patch of deckplate in the center, and C139 hoped that F11 had spotted it and sent her breach nano there. As soon as A1 assumed her customary position, they would have her.

Or so we hope.

The four women on the team all shared a common concern that A1 was possessed by a core AI remnant.

There was no way they could have brought a shadowtron onto the *Perilous Dream*—though one was secreted away on the ship they'd arrived in. If C139 detected an ascended AI's leftovers in A1, she knew that she'd have to extract the being the old-fashioned way.

The thought didn't worry her overmuch. She'd extracted several of Myrrdan's and the Caretakers' remnants, and also drawn Xavia's memory out of Katrina.

This would be no different.

The minutes ticked by, and the four women waited patiently, backs straight, hands unmoving. Even their breaths were drawn in unison, matching what Tangel had seen in the minds of the Widows when she interrogated them.

C139 had trouble believing that the sort of woman Finaeus would have married was the type to sit still and quiet like this. She also considered that Finaeus might once have been a very different person. Perhaps he'd been cautious and reserved in his youth.

Right.

It was far more likely that the woman who had altered herself to pass as one of her clones was the one who'd changed.

Tangel and Bob had expressed uncertainty as to whether or not A1 even was the original Lisa Wrentham. The Widows they'd interrogated didn't think so, but C139 had her doubts.

Either way, A1 was their leader, and the Widows followed her unquestioningly.

In the back of her mind, C139 wondered if it was wise to think of herself in the third person with her Widow's designation. Dr. Rosenberg had assured the four women that the thought patterns she'd instilled in them were just light mental conditioning and wouldn't become dominant.

But it didn't feel that way to C139. She felt as though this was how she'd always been, how she should be. It wasn't that she'd forgotten that she was also Cary; it was that she was both.

Obviously.

Perhaps it was just the peaceful serenity that came with knowing that she wasn't anyone important. Not responsible for momentous events, not a human on the brink of ascension, but a cog, just a part of a larger machine, doing what she was told, guided by a sure hand.

Stars, now I really think it **is** *settling in too much. This can't be right.*

She gritted her teeth, thinking of her childhood, growing up on Carthage with her sister, Saanvi. She glanced at the others, wondering if they were having as much trouble controlling their thoughts as she was. They didn't give any signs one way or the other, and she daren't ask.

Either way, she still had a mission to complete: take out A1 and learn the Widows' secrets. She could hold onto that. It would be her guiding principle.

Take out A1, learn the Widows' secrets.

Even with that mantra in mind, Cary felt like she was being subsumed by a desire to be an obedient part of the whole, though it felt more like a compulsion, not light conditioning.

This can't be right, she thought again.

She was about to ask Saanvi if she was having the same struggle, when A1 entered the room.

The head Widow looked exactly like the other clones, increasing the number of featureless black creatures from four to five with her presence. But when she spoke, her voice was ever so slightly different. More strident, less subservient.

"Report." A1 breathed the word, standing just to the right

of where Faleena's pool of nano lay in wait.

"We reached Aldebaran on schedule," C139 said without preamble. "As our intelligence indicated, Tanis Richards arrived just a few days later and addressed the League of Sentients assembly. Unfortunately, our strike was unable to proceed because another factor came into play."

"What factor?" A1's tone was no different, but her choice of words told C139 that the prime unit was displeased.

"An ascended AI attacked Tanis."

A1 folded her arms across her chest, the deep black she was sheathed in causing them to become nearly indistinguishable from her torso.

She paced a few steps to the right, and then turned back, stopping just short of the trap Faleena had set in the deck.

"Who prevailed?"

"Admiral Richards," C139 replied. "Rather, she was saved by their ship. It fired a weapon we were not able to identify, and the ascended AI—which we learned was named Xavia—perished."

"Xavia," A1 said, lifting a hand to her chin and cupping her elbow with the other. "I've heard that name uttered in the past. In far corners of the Inner Stars. I had believed that she opposed the Caretaker. I am surprised she attacked Tanis Richards."

"We did not learn anything that would indicate what allegiance Xavia held," C139 offered.

"No? Pity. Well, I assume you went forward with a fallback plan."

C139 was surprised that A1 had not yet asked whether or not they'd been successful. Perhaps the return of just four Widows when she'd sent over twenty had already answered that question.

"Yes. We captured one of Admiral Richards' associates, an AI named Iris, and used her to gain access to the *I2*. Once aboard, we sought out and attacked our target, but she was too powerful. It was then we learned that our target was also fully ascended."

I imagine the Widows suspected that before they attacked, but that doesn't matter, C139 thought to herself.

"Fully—" A1 stopped herself and took a calming breath. She turned toward the door, and then back toward C139. "Do you know how this came to be? Is this how she killed so many of our sisters?"

"It is," C139 replied with a single nod. "Though I do not know how she achieved ascension. Of my sisters and the contingency team, we are all who managed to escape. I do not know how we will defeat her."

A1 rolled her shoulders and finally walked into the middle of the room, standing on the worn spot where F11 had laid the nano. C139 trusted that her sister had initiated the breach. Now it was just a matter of time.

Take out A1, learn the Widows' secrets.

"Leave that to me, and to the Orion Guard," A1 said, her tone dismissive. "Now. Tell me everything that happened."

C139 began to relate the story, keeping mostly to the facts, but leaving out Cary and her sisters—*herself* and her sisters—as she told the tale. At the end, she told of how the four of them had managed to scatter across the station and get to one of their ships that was still in stealth, attached to Lunic Station's hull.

"And how did you get back here so quickly?" A1 queried.

"The enemy was jumping ships to Diadem. We hitched a ride and then used Garza's gate near the system."

C139 saw a slight twitch in A1's right hand when Garza's name came up. Her own instincts told her it was annoyance.

A1 only paused for a moment, and then asked, "They're shifting resources to Diadem? They're certainly pressing their advantage."

"The League of Sentients has joined the Scipio Alliance," C139 informed A1.

The prime unit gave a rather human sigh and reached a hand to its head, tapping a finger over what would be a cheek.

"We must inform Garza of this," she said at last. "It is no longer suitable for us to operate from this location. We must go to him at *Karaske*."

"In the *Perilous Dream*?" C139 asked.

"You're rather full of queries today, C139. Do you need reintegration?"

"I do not believe so," C139 said, doing her best to speak the words slowly, as though the idea had not set a panic in her. "I am still dealing with the loss of so many sisters."

"Our numbers are eternal," A1 said, the words hissing from her lips as if by rote.

The Widows before her repeated the phrase in unison, and A1 nodded.

"Very well. I want the four of you in autodocs to make sure you're tip-top, and then go to your readyspace. I may have more questions after I peruse your report."

The moment the last word came from A1, the woman standing at the front of the room ceased to move.

"I have control of her," F11 said as she rose and approached A1. "This was easier than I thought it would be."

"What are you doing?" C139 asked. "We're to go to the autodocs."

"Funny," E12 said, clasping her on the shoulder. "Faleena has rendered her unconscious. You can drop the act."

C139 shook her head, trying to clear her thoughts. "I—yeah. This conditioning was really taking hold. I was really beginning to lose myself in C139…guh. I hate this. A lot. A shit-ton. What's more than a shit-ton?"

"A shit mega-ton?" Saanvi offered.

"Galactic shitpile," Priscilla said as she approached A1.

"Granted, this is pretty easy for me. I'm used to maintaining my identity while another threatens to subsume me. Heck, the outfit's not even that different, though I'm not stuck to a plinth in this one, so bonus there."

"How's she for passengers?" Saanvi asked, gesturing at the frozen figure before them.

"Eh?" Cary asked. "Oh, remnants. Damn, I didn't even check."

Her sister turned to face Cary full-on. "Seriously? You OK? Maybe something in the conditioning isn't playing nice with your ascending mind. How many fingers am I holding up?"

Saanvi held up a fist, and Cary laughed.

"Five. They're just all folded up."

"OK, you're still in there. Good."

"Huh," Priscilla muttered. "You seeing this, Faleena?"

The AI nodded. "I am…her physiology, internal systems, mods…everything. They're identical to the clones."

Cary pulled up the datastreams from Faleena's nano that was working its way through A1's body and whistled as she looked over the information.

"So *is* A1 actually Lisa Wrentham, or is she just another clone, like all the Widows think?"

"We might not be able to tell without something more invasive," Faleena said. "Either way, we still need to extract her root access codes so we can breach the ship's datastores."

Cary nodded, then suddenly realized that she'd once again forgotten to search A1 for a remnant—though she imagined if there was one, they'd know it by now.

"Damn…I want this conditioning out of my head. I think it *is* messing with me more than it should be."

As she muttered the words, she searched A1's body.

"She's clear. One hundred percent hu—well, one hundred percent not influenced by a remnant."

A brief thought ran through Cary's mind that C139 was

late for reporting to the autodoc, and she concentrated on herself, shifting her non-corporeal vision to peer at her mind from outside her body. What she saw surprised her.

Shit…my mind…it's stretching beyond the corporeal…I'm thinking in both places.

Another C139-like desire to follow A1's orders and go to the autodoc came into her physical mind, and Cary realized that while pretending to be a Widow, she'd cut off the ascending part of her mind. In doing so, she'd set aside a significant portion of her consciousness.

I thought I had to form an extradimensional mind willingly? It's manifesting on its own!

Cary fought the panic down, glad that she now understood why she'd fallen into the conditioning, but worried that she was going to evolve uncontrollably. She forced down the worry and turned her attention back to her sisters….and Priscilla.

Priscilla's not a sister. I'm not a Widow.

"Security is tighter here than I'd expected," Priscilla was saying to Saanvi, who nodded in agreement.

"A1's mind is locked down tight, too. I can't get to her root tokens," Faleena added. "I'm starting to think that she's been holding out on the rest of Orion. Her tech may beat the Transcend's in a lot of ways."

"Well, she *was* Finaeus's wife," Priscilla replied. "Unlikely that he'd marry a dummy. So what's our next move?"

"I've sent an update to Father via QuanComm," Faleena informed the team. "But if we can't get A1's root codes, we should get to one of the nodes and see if we can crack it without them."

Cary thought back to how her mother had tricked Garza into revealing the location of the Widows and glanced at the others.

"I have an idea. Wake her up."

"It's risky," Faleena warned. "If she's conscious, she could work against my breach nano. Her internal defenses already put up quite the fight."

Priscilla touched her thigh and drew out a lightwand, activating the blade and holding it close to A1's face. "We'll just have to carefully motivate her."

"You have her Link antenna shut down?" Saanvi asked Faleena. "Like physically severed?"

The AI nodded. "Yeah. Not my first time doing this."

"It's not?" Cary glanced at her sister, and then realized the futility of looking at an AI for telling body language when they were wearing a Widow's body.

"Uh uh," Faleena replied. "Moms made me practice, put me through a lot of drills. Severing the Link antenna is always the first step."

"Take her helmet off," Priscilla directed. "Don't let her hide behind its façade."

"Good call," Cary said, and she did as the avatar directed.

She found the seals on A1's helmet and deployed her own breach nano to unlock the two halves before pulling it apart.

Within was a woman who looked identical to all the other Widows. Nose, ears, and hair were all gone. Near transparent skin stretched across skeletal features and bulging eyes.

"Stars," Saanvi whispered. "Why would she do this to herself?"

Cary cleared her throat, but it was still hoarse when she spoke. "Faleena, let's do this before I lose my nerve."

"I've nerve enough for all of us," Priscilla said, and Cary was glad for the steel in the woman's voice.

"Here we go," Faleena said, and a second later, A1's eyes snapped open, then narrowed as her gaze swept across the four Widows in front of her.

"I thought something seemed off," she said. "E12 wasn't quippy enough, but I chalked it up to having just lost so many units. I'm impressed that you fooled my systems so well. Clearly I've underestimated the level of technology your people possess."

"Clearly," Cary replied. "Just another sign that Orion is going to lose this conflict."

The woman gave a rasping laugh and shook her head. "I wouldn't get too carried away. So who are you, anyway? Have I come face to face with Tanis Richards herself?"

Priscilla waved the lightwand in front of A1. "She's a bit too busy for the likes of you."

"Ah, so I get the B-Team, then, do I?"

"Pretty much," Cary replied. "Anyway, we'd like to get your root tokens so we can pull all your intel, shut down your Widows, and drop your ship into your black star."

"Oh, is that all?" A1 said with a sneer. "Would you like me to write down my access codes, or should I just say them aloud?"

Cary watched the surface of A1's mind, sifting through the thoughts that bubbled up above the others, looking for the creature's tokens. There was one that granted control over the ship, and another for controlling the Widow storage bays, but the encrypted hashes themselves remained inaccessible.

As she sifted through A1's thoughts, an image of the Widow storage bays appeared, and Cary was surprised at how many Widows were potentially aboard this ship—if the pods were all full. There were far more than the strike teams on Lunic had known about.

"Writing it down would be nice," Cary said in a mock-sweet voice, hoping that would trigger a thought of the woman's tokens.

"That's about as likely as you getting off my ship alive," A1 hissed. "There are thousands of us here. You must have had a death wish, coming here thinking you could take us down."

Nothing further about the tokens rose to the surface of A1's mind, and Cary wondered if she'd have to dig deeper. It was unethical, and her mother had cautioned her not to, warning that it was easy to get lost in the sea of another's thoughts.

However, they also didn't have all day to trade barbs with A1.

Deciding to take a new track, Cary said, "Finaeus warned us that you can be obstinate, but he still did seem to care for you."

A1's eyes narrowed. "Do you really think that bringing up my former husband would somehow cause me to spill my guts? Maybe you're the D-Team."

Despite her words, A1's mind had begun to roil. Thoughts of Finaeus appeared, and Cary could see images of their time together. The memories were vivid and sparked an emotional response in the woman before her—mostly anger, though a few were tinged with remorse.

"You know..." Cary glanced at her team. "I really do think A1 *is* Lisa Wrentham."

"Oh, how the mighty have fallen," Priscilla intoned. "We'll have to make sure Krissy never finds out that this thing is her mom."

Lisa strained, color rising to her face as she willed her body to respond. It was entirely in vain. Faleena's breach nano had blocked signals traveling down her spinal column.

"You can't hold me here forever," Lisa hissed. "I'll break free. You'd better run while you can."

"Anything?" Saanvi asked Cary.

"No." Cary shook her head. "She's hiding it well. I've picked out a few other tokens, but not her roots."

A laugh broke free from Lisa's lips. "As if I didn't know what you were trying to do. My Widows have used these techniques a thousand times. I *taught* them how to use mental monitoring to detect thoughts and extract information."

"That's not exactly what's happening here," Cary

explained.

Then she decided to go for broke, and withdrew one of her extradimensional limbs from the confines of her body, holding it out before A1.

"You'll have to forgive me if this is uncomfortable. It's my first time doing it."

In newtonian space, Cary's limb bled photons, appearing as a tendril of light stretching toward Lisa Wrentham. To her other vision, it appeared as just another hand, though one that wasn't constrained by the same laws of spacetime that governed the narrow slice of reality that her corporeal body inhabited.

Lisa's eyes widened, and she recoiled—as much as possible—from the light stretching toward her.

"You're one of *them*!"

"I'm not an ascended AI," Cary corrected. "Just a woman with some added features."

<Are you sure about this?> Saanvi asked. *<I heard Moms tell you it was dangerous.>*

<If we don't get her tokens and access the datastores, then we may as well have just blown the ship.>

<OK…just be careful.>

<When am I not?>

Saanvi passed a long groan across their connection, but didn't say anything more.

Lisa was twisting her head from side to side, eyes bulging further and breathing becoming ragged, as Cary's 'hand' slid beneath her skin and into her mind.

The woman's thoughts had become utter chaos. Fear was mixed with a continuing desire to keep her root codes private. Memories of a thousand events flooded across the connection, from Lisa's time in the ancient Sol System to the centuries she'd spent on the *Perilous Dream*, perfecting her Widows, her ultimate assassins.

"Guh," she grunted aloud. "She's…stars, she's a mess."

Cary realized that Lisa was flinging random thoughts on purpose, trying to keep her from the information she sought. But in the chaos, there was a pattern, and in that pattern were gaps. Memories of her analyzing reports, and accessing her ship's vast datastores were absent.

There was a hole, a space where no thoughts came from, and Cary delved into it.

There!

She saw memories of Lisa accessing her datastores, performing her experiments on her Widows, creating her army.

At the bottom of it all were her root tokens. The keys that would give Cary access to everything about the woman, and everything she controlled.

"Got them!" She gasped as she withdrew from Lisa's mind.

Her vision returned, and the room swam back into view, as she rose up out of the thoughts she'd nearly drowned in.

"Are you OK?" Saanvi asked. "You were getting a bit unsteady on your feet."

Cary nodded, her mouth dry and parched. "I'm…I had to go deep, I got lost for a minute, I think."

She glanced at Lisa, but the woman was out again.

OK…now I know why Moms said not to do that. I feel like half her memories came back over with me.

"We've got a problem," Priscilla said as she disabled her lightwand and slid it back into her thigh. "I've made my way onto the general shipnet—which isn't so general here—and the bridge is trying to reach A1. They're about to sound an alert."

"I've got it," Cary announced, quickly recoding her Link's keys and encryption with A1's root tokens. She took a breath and activated her connection, immediately receiving a message from T101.

<A1. We were concerned. We have a problem.>

<I was reviewing intel, I needed a few minutes alone.>

Cary knew that A1 did that from time to time, detached herself from the shipnets so she could focus.

Damn, it's like I'm still in her head. Or I somehow duplicated her memories into mine.

<Understood. When we sent the message drone to General Garza, there was an anomaly when it went through the gate.>

"Crap," Cary muttered aloud. "Looks like Lisa here dispatched a message drone to Garza." *<What sort of anomaly?>* she asked T101.

<Some of the exotic particles from the gate transition echoed off an object fifty thousand kilometers from our current position. We think it's a stealthed ship.>

Cary pursed her lips. *<Understood. I'll finish here in a moment, and then come to the bridge.>*

<T101 out.>

"They've detected Dad's ship," Cary explained. "Some of the energy from the gate reflected off it. They must have a better sensor web out there than we thought."

"Damn," Saanvi muttered. "That complicates things."

"Give me the codes," Priscilla said. "I'll go to the bridge as A1 and deal with this, while the three of you go to the data node and access her records."

Cary shook her head. "It has to be me. I have…a lot of her memories up here. I can pull her off better than you can."

"That strikes me as the exact reason that you *shouldn't* go," Priscilla said. "You've already had problems with the conditioning going too deep. Like I said, I know what it's like to lose yourself in another being."

"I can do this." Cary drew herself up. "I climbed out of her thoughts and I'm still me. Not A1, not C139. I'm able to better protect myself on my own, too. I can do this."

None of the other three women spoke for a few moments, and then Priscilla nodded.

"OK. But if you start to have any second thoughts, *any*, you get the hell out of there."

"You got it." Cary nodded to Lisa. "What are we going to do about her?"

The unconscious woman took a step forward, then another.

"I have her on remote," Faleena said. "Good thing she's so modded up; I can do this without having to get into her biology too much."

"Also good that all the Widows walk like they have a stick up their ass," Saanvi added with a laugh as she picked up Lisa's helmet and put it back on the woman's head.

"We ready?" Priscilla asked, and the four women nodded silently to one another before filing out of the room.

* * * * *

[You've been detected. Cary has A1's root tokens. She's going to the bridge while we get the data.]

Joe pursed his lips as he read the message from Faleena. She didn't say it, but he understood the subtext. Cary was masquerading as A1.

"Everyone get ready," he said through thinned lips. "Things could light up any second now."

Over the past few hours, the *Falconer*'s scan team had been establishing baselines and dropping small probes. Joe didn't believe that the *Perilous Dream* was alone. There had to be other ships nearby. Thus far, there was no conclusive evidence other than a few gravitational anomalies.

The scan team had extrapolated from those, and the worst-case scenario was that there were a dozen enemy ships in formation around the *Perilous Dream.*

Whether or not they were crewed or just drone ships remained to be seen.

One thing was for certain. No matter what, they were going

to be fighting their way out of the A1 System.

[Keep a channel open to Cary,] he sent back to Faleena, wishing that at least one of them had gone with her to the bridge. *[And get out of there as soon as possible.]*

He knew that was already their plan, but the father in him had to say something of the sort.

MEETING SERA

STELLAR DATE: 10.09.8949 (Adjusted Years)
LOCATION: Uplink Tower 7-1, Airthan Ring
REGION: Huygens System, Transcend Interstellar Alliance

<OK, I'm almost there,> Jane sent through the relays she'd dropped on her way through the tower. *<I just have to cross an open space to get to the node, but there's another of those damn AIs back here.>*

Fina pursed her lips, considering her options. She was still within the lift shaft, hanging below the doors to the top level. The most effective plan—for Jane's objective, anyway—was for Fina to simply open the doors and start shooting at the AIs. That would certainly give Jane an opening.

And it'll get me killed. Fina told Jane, *<Just give me a moment, still trying to find a good way to distract them.>*

<Sure, I'll just hang out here for a bit, no worries.>

Jane's voice dripped with sarcasm, but Fina ignored it, making another attempt to tap into the tower's automated defenses and use them against the AIs holding Roxy.

So far, they hadn't done anything other than stand around the former Hand agent and stare her down; it was almost as though the entire scene was a frozen tableau. Fina knew that meant it was a trap. A trap so obvious they weren't even bothering to hide it.

She turned her full attention back to the defense systems she was attempting to breach. She was almost through an open port, when suddenly the system went offline.

What the hell?

"Why don't you stop messing around and just come up here already, Sera?" a voice called out from the other side of the lift doors.

Her voice.

She switched back to the optics she’ d threaded through the door and saw that a new figure was standing amongst the AIs. A woman with pale skin and white hair, wearing a glowing white skinsheath.

And Fina’s face.

“Seriously, get up here…today,” the clone called out. “Or I just kill this weird blue girl here then wait for the elevator car coming up the lift to crush you against the top of the shaft. Either one works for me.”

Fina glanced down and saw that a car was indeed rising from below—and it was coming fast.

“Dammit,” she muttered and issued the command for the doors to open, pulling herself through as soon as there was enough room, rolling to the right where she ducked behind a rack of transmission equipment.

“Hiding?” the clone called out. “No. No hiding. I just want to talk. But I guess that if you don’t want to do that, then I’ll just kill your friend here and go on my merry way.”

Fina pursed her lips and blew out a long breath. She didn’t think that *she’d* have so readily killed in cold blood while under Airtha’s sway, but from what she’d heard of the latest clone, it was possible that the woman across the room would.

“Are you just looking for someone to chat with?” Fina called out, slowly rising to her feet.

She was formulating a new plan, but this one would require getting a lot closer to the enemy.

<*Please be careful,*> Jane sent.

Fina didn’t reply as she stepped out into the open, getting a clear view of her otherself. “I’ll admit, white looks good on us, but don’t you think it’s a bit pretentious?” she asked.

“Better than red,” the other Sera said with a snort. “I feel like that’s some sort of personal shame issue you have going on.”

Fina took a few steps closer, noting that her otherself held no weapon, but that three of the five AIs had shifted and were now aiming ther rifles at her and not Roxy.

"You've got me mixed up with Sera," Fina said with a languid shrug. "She's the red one."

"No. *I'm* Sera. She's a clone. Just like you."

Fina couldn't help but laugh. "Sure. Whatever helps you sleep at night, Whitey."

"I—" the other Sera began, but Fina interrupted her.

"Roxy, are you OK?"

"No," Roxy's voice came out in a soft moan. "Airtha's stooges haven't been too kind…they're trying pretty hard to get into my head—I'm lucky I don't have a standard noggin."

Fina took another step toward Sera, holding out a hand in a placating gesture. "Look, you got us, no need to go tearing anyone's mind apart. That's not who we are, it's not what we do."

"No?" the white Sera asked. "If someone was trying to destroy your home, you wouldn't do whatever it took to save it?"

"Sera," Fina whispered, sweeping a hand around herself. "This *is* my home. That girl who used to sneak off, with Helen chastising her for missing classes? That was me too. Those days in Finaeus's lab? We both did that. Other than the last few weeks, you and have I shared the same life."

"No." Sera shook her head. "I don't share anything with you. You were one of the mistakes. I'm no mistake."

Fina couldn't miss the note of anguish in her sister's voice. Just as she'd still been Sera even while under her mother's control, so was this other woman.

And I may be a bit on the weird side of the spectrum, but I'm not evil. Fina extended her hands palms-up. "I still hear her voice. Did you know that? Sometimes I can't tell if it's a memory, or if she's still reaching out to me somehow. Can you hear her? Is she in your head too?"

The white woman didn't respond, but her eyes narrowed ever so slightly, and Fina had her answer.

"I'm going to remove my helmet," she said before lifting her hands, releasing nano with the gesture, hoping that the motion would propel it toward the AIs fast enough for her plan to work.

"By all means," the other Sera said. "Makes you an easier target."

Fina flipped the latches and then twisted the helmet, speaking as she lifted it free. "You're not going to do that. We're sisters, you and I. We have so much more in common than we have differences."

"Huh…blue," Sera said. "We do have a thing for color, don't we?"

Fina shrugged. "I like it."

"What did the third one pick…for her color?"

"Seraphina," Sera said. "She's our vanilla sister. Went with a rather stock look. Blonde, even."

"Blonde?" the white woman snorted. "Now I know Tanis's people have messed with you. No way would we go blonde."

"Think about Tanis. Do you remember her as a bad person?" Fina asked as she continued to approach, half her attention on the five AIs, knowing that even if she could make Sera reconsider her actions, the AIs would remain loyal to Airtha. Or fully under her thrall, whichever was the case.

Of course, it's more than likely that I'll not convince this Sera. I know that it wouldn't have worked on me.

"Tanis is not her people," Sera countered. "They are not reflections of her."

"You've spent nearly as much time aboard the *Intrepid* as I have," Fina said, now only five meters from where Roxy knelt, with Sera and the AIs arrayed in a semi-circle on the far side of her. "What do you remember of that ship and its people? Do you think that Tanis would condone some sort of manipulative mind control over me?"

"I think Tanis is the sort of person who does what she has to," Sera replied. "She possesses the most deadly weapons in the galaxy, and she's used them on several occasions."

Fina pursed her lips. She knew that argument well. Airtha had whispered it in her mind many times. She also knew that there was no counter for it other than to speak to Tangel and see the fierce sincerity in the woman's eyes when she said that she'd do it all again to protect her people.

"I—" she began, when an alert sounded, and the overhead lights flickered.

<Fina! We need the interdictor web down now!> Sabrina shouted in her mind. *<Airtha's onto us. She's…she's coming for all of you!>*

<Shit! I need five minutes.>

<Are you listening? ***Now!*** *>*

Fina's heart leapt into her throat, and she sent back an affirmative response before shifting to her channel with Jane.

<It's all on you. Get ready.>

A smirk had formed on Sera's lips. "Did you get some bad news? And here you thought you were delaying me when it was the other way around. Seems like you get dumber when they enslave you, too."

"No fucking way," Fina hissed setting her jaw before she dove forward, tucking and rolling beneath the shots from the AIs, her armor shedding their rounds as she slapped a hand on Roxy's back, giving the woman a fresh batch of nano to fight off the AIs.

Then Fina was back on her feet, coming up right in front of the white Sera, lightwand in her hand, thrusting the beam forward.

Just as her doppelganger did the same.

A MOTHER

STELLAR DATE: 10.09.8949 (Adjusted Years)
LOCATION: Stellar Tower 3, Airthan Ring
REGION: Huygens System, Transcend Interstellar Alliance

Sera eased along the corridor, with Flaherty just a few meters behind. Kara was moving down a nearby passage, toward an overwatch position in the chamber. She'd reach her mark first, and set up to provide cover while Sera and Flaherty reached their assigned Airthan node.

<*Hold,*> Jen said, and Sera froze, seeing Flaherty's indicator halt as well.

A second later, a pair of SAIs in battle armor stalked down the hall, one narrowly missing Sera's left arm. This was the fourth patrol they'd encountered in just a few minutes, and she was beginning to worry that there'd be no way to breach Airtha's node chamber without a pitched firefight.

<*OK, you're clear,*> Jen advised, and the pair began to move once more.

While Airtha's nodes were in a variety of locations across the ring, Sera's target was situated at the base of one of the four massive towers that stretched out to the Airthan star, holding the ring steady around its primary.

The node chamber was a kilometer-high conical space set within the tower itself. Airtha's node would be several hundred meters off the floor, accessible only by one of three catwalks.

Sera turned left, and they walked down a short corridor to a lift. It would take them up to the same level in the tower as the catwalks. After Jen performed a quick breach, they boarded the car and rode it to their destination.

<*You ready?*> Jen asked. <*You might have to confront her.*>

<Not if we do this right. Get to the node, insert the shard, get out.>

Jen snorted. *<Right. Nothing to it. Still, she* **is** *your mother.>*

<No. She's not,> Sera replied coolly. *<Do AIs consider your progenitors to be fathers and mothers?>*

The AI sent a feeling of disagreement. *<I see where you're going with this. Yes, Airtha is an AI, but it's not the same.>*

<Of course not. Nothing is the same. But, really, Jen, I can't think about all of that. Like I said. Get to the node, insert the shard, get out.>

<OK. I suppose I get that. I'll stop trying to make you think about it right now.>

Sera resisted the urge to laugh. *<And later, I'll drink like a fish and not think about it then, either.>*

Jen didn't reply, and Sera was glad for the brief silence as the lift continued its ascent. A minute later, the doors opened, and they stepped into a corridor lined with windows that looked out into the node chamber.

<You ready?> Flaherty asked.

<Stars, not you too. ***Yes****!>*

A soft rumble of laughter came back over the Link. *<Just have to ask. No need to be snippy about it.>*

<I get it. Let's just do this already.>

Flaherty didn't respond, but on her HUD, she saw him move across the corridor and stop in front of the doors that led to the catwalk.

<Breaching,> Jen announced. *<Damn…this one's tricky. Going to take a minute to do it without setting off an alarm.>*

<Take your time,> Sera replied. *<I brought a book.>*

<Funny,> Jen replied, and Flaherty added, *<Focus.>*

She knew Flaherty was right, she needed to keep her mind sharp and on the task at hand—which she normally did by making snarky comments.

<At least it's a good book.>

<Still funny,> Jen shot back, her tone droll. *<It's breached. We're good to go.>*

Flaherty opened the door and moved through first, stepping lightly onto the catwalk, with Sera following a few meters behind.

Ahead lay their target, Airthan Node 11. One of her mother's bodies…which they were going to poison.

Sera's eyes were fixed on the ten-meter square cube, almost mesmerized by its soft glow. She realized that it was similar in appearance to the nodes that made up Bob's mind. It occurred to Sera in that moment that the only two multinodal AIs she knew of were both ascended.

I wonder if that's related at all.

They followed the catwalk for fifty meters before it reached the platform that encircled the node. There weren't any drones nearby, so they crossed the final few meters, coming to stand on the platform a minute later.

<Here goes nothing,> Sera said to Jen as she pulled the cylinder that contained the poisoned shard out of a compartment on her armor.

Jen sighed. *<Just do it al—>*

The AI's words were cut off, as tendrils of light emerged from the node, twisting around themselves until they formed the figure of a tall woman—a woman whose features were forever etched in Sera's mind.

"Helen….?"

DELIVERY

STELLAR DATE: 10.09.8949 (Adjusted Years)
LOCATION: Stellar Tower 2, Airthan Ring
REGION: Huygens System, Transcend Interstellar Alliance

"Fuck!" Katrina swore as she ducked below the blown-out window that overlooked the node chamber. "There's just too many of them!"

Elmer only grunted in response as he rolled to a new position, each of his four arms hefting beam weapons, which he aimed out the window, firing on the drones that were circling in the node chamber.

<*Don't hit the node!*> Amavia exclaimed. <*And don't hit me, I'm almost there!*>

Katrina's jaw began to throb, and she realized she was clenching it hard enough to shatter teeth.

<*Just hurry,*> she snapped. <*The clock's ticking, and Finaeus's team isn't going to make it.*>

<*I know, I got the message too,*> Amavia retorted.

Forcing herself to relax—as much as possible, given the circumstances—Katrina leant around the open door leading onto the catwalk, and fired a series of kinetic rounds at the drones swooping through the chamber.

Amavia was on—or rather, under—the next catwalk to the left, nearly at the platform by the position of her marker. If the team could continue to provide enough of a distraction for another few minutes, Amavia would make it, and their delivery would be complete.

Which is imperative, since Finaeus's team is dealing with the CEPPs, and Fina is still at the tower.

<*Think we have to get four shards into the nodes for sure?*> she asked Amavia.

<Umm...that's what Finaeus and Earnest said. At least four.>

<Right, but they originally only had four teams. Think they were sandbagging?>

Amavia groaned. *<I'm hanging from the bottom of a catwalk, trying to be as stealthy as possible. Can we talk about this later?>*

<Uhh...sure.>

<And yes. Of course they were sandbagging. They're engineers.>

Amavia's statement gave Katrina a measure of relief, and she fired on another drone as it swept past the doorway.

Given the opposition they were facing, she couldn't imagine that every team was going to meet with success.

* * * * *

Iris crouched before Airthan Node 3, tuning out the sounds of the battle all around her as she pulled the shard cylinder from her armor and scanned the node for a hard-Link port.

Where the hell is it? she wondered, ducking as Malorie leapt overhead, screeching a string of curses that Iris had come to realize was the spider woman's battle cry.

<I need a 779A-style port,> she called out to her team. *<Does anyone see one?>*

<Kinda busy!> Camille replied from where she crouched on the far side of the node, firing on the soldiers who were advancing down the catwalk, CFT shields weathering the team's fire.

<Well this is kind of the goal,> Iris shot back. *<Malorie! What are you doing?>*

<Slowing them down,> the woman replied as she flipped under the platform and skittered along the underside of the catwalk the soldiers were advancing down.

Iris shook her head, returning to her search. She heard the screams of the soldiers as the deranged spider-woman climbed into their midst, knocking as many off the catwalk as she killed with the lightwands attached to her legs.

"Aha!" Iris crowed as she finally spotted the correct type of hard-Link port via her drone feeds.

It was around the node's corner; she'd have to expose herself to enemy fire to slot the shard in. She placed her trust in the belief that the enemy soldiers were not going to shoot the node, as she reached around the corner to slot the cylinder in place.

Then alarms flared in her mind, and she saw that her arm had been shot clean off her body. It was now laying on the platform, halfway around the corner.

Oh please still be holding it, she thought, carefully pulling the arm back around to safety, breathing a sigh of relief to see that her severed limb still clasped the cylinder.

She pulled the shard's core out of her severed hand and sent a probe around the node to see that the socket she needed to use had been shot—almost as though the AI they were attacking had ordered the soldiers to shoot herself.

Iris fired a few rounds at enemies who were encroaching on her team's position, and then turned back to the leeward side of the node, searching for any ports she could use.

After a few seconds, her gaze settled on one. It was a 14A-type port. She could jack directly into it with her own hard-Link cable, but she couldn't directly hook up the poisoned shard.

Damn, I'm going to have to buffer it somehow….

Iris knew that she had only one option. She had to connect the shard to her own frame and then route it through her hard-Link port and into the Airthan Node.

* * * * *

"I'm glad you still recognize me," Helen said, as her ephemeral form approached Sera. "I was starting to think you'd forgotten where you came from."

"I remember," Sera said, her voice barely above a whisper as she desperately tried to gather her wits. "I could never forget how much you lied to me."

"Lies?" Helen said as she circled around Sera, staying just out of arm's reach. "Is that the game we're going to play? Who wronged who? Reasons, rationalizations? I always loved you, Sera. I was always devoted to you. You're my crowning achievement."

"You tried to manipulate me into killing my own father," Sera hissed, anger beginning to boil inside of herself. "And *you* died. After…after…"

"I'm not gone," Helen said. "I'm right before you."

"You're *not* Helen," Sera spat. "Helen died. My father—or whatever he was—killed her! Do you know what that does to a person? Knowing that your father killed the person you thought of as your mother?"

Helen's lips parted in a smile and she ducked her head. "Sera. I *am* your mother."

"No," Sera shook her head, suddenly wondering where Flaherty had gone.

She couldn't see further than a few meters, everything was shrouded in darkness, the only light coming from the visage before her. She took a step back, trying to circle around to the node, knowing it had to be close.

"You're the thing that made me," she said pointedly. "Helen raised me."

The white figure drew closer, tendrils of light reaching out hungrily.

"Sera. It's always been me. I really am Helen."

* * * * *

Amavia kept her focus on the next handhold, ignoring the

chaos all around her, ignoring the worry building in her mind that she wouldn't get her shard inserted in time.

Definitely ignoring the three-hundred-meter drop, she thought with a nervous laugh.

She swung from one beam to the next, now only three meters from the node. She could see a socket just four meters to her left. Two more beams and she'd be there, she'd be home free.

Sure wish I'd opted for a non-organic body now, she thought while swinging to the next beam, her right leg nearly clipping a drone as it swept by, firing on Katrina's position.

Drawing a steadying breath, Amavia swung to the next beam, then climbed along it until she was next to the node.

<I'm here. Inserting—>

Amavia's words were cut off as a drone flew around the side of the node and slammed into her side. She lost her grip on the beam and fell forward, hands scrabbling across the node's surface as she plummeted toward the ground.

At the last second, her right hand found purchase on a ridge at the bottom edge of the Airthan node, pain momentarily lancing up the limb as it arrested her fall.

<Are you OK?> Katrina called out, as shots lanced from her position, hitting the drone which had struck Amavia.

<Yeah, uh huh. Just have to climb back up.>

She got a firm grip on the lip and then reached up and grasped a nearby coolant line, slowly pulling herself up until she was standing on the lip, getting ready to leap back up and grab hold of the beam next to the socket.

One…two…

Pain tore through Amavia's body, and suddenly, her legs went limp, unable to hold her weight. She clamped her fist tightly around the coolant line, hanging on with all her strength. Looking down to see what was wrong, she choked back a gasp at the view of her severed legs falling toward the ground.

Then something cut through her arm, and the Airthan node was soaring away while the ground rushed up.

* * * * *

Iris completed the connection to the node and established the buffers within her body and mind, ready to facilitate the transfer between the shard and the node.

Here goes nothing, she thought, knowing that if Amavia were present, she'd scold Iris for trying something so foolhardy.

She activated the shard, passing its connection through to the node, watching as it copied itself, building up a version of its mind in the node, just as Earnest and Finaeus had programmed it to do.

Iris took a moment to marvel at the elegance of their solution, realizing that in some respects, it was similar to how the NOS AIs had transferred their minds into the substrate of Cerka Station's expanses back in the Virginis System.

I wonder if they lifted the idea from our reports.

The transfer system registered success, and Iris sagged against the side of the node, then laughed at herself for having such an organic relief response.

-Do you really think that bit of poison will work?- a voice asked in Iris's mind. *-You're too late.-*

As the words hit her like a brick wall, Iris saw strings of white light emerge from the node and begin to encircle her. They passed through her body, lightly brushing against her core. Wherever they touched her neural matrices, thought evaporated.

Shit! Iris exclaimed, realizing that the ascended being was shredding her.

Panic nearly overwhelming her, she cast about for a way to

escape, only to have her vision leave her, immediately followed by her other senses.

The only thing that was left was the single strand of connectivity that ran into the Airthan node—and the program to copy herself into the node's substrate…alongside the poisoned shard.

Thought became more difficult as another section of her mind ceased responding, and Iris didn't hesitate any longer. She activated the software and shrieked wordlessly as her mind disintegrated.

The last coherent thought she had was a morbid curiosity about whether or not it was the transfer or the ascended AI that was shredding her mind.

DEPARTURE

STELLAR DATE: 10.09.8949 (Adjusted Years)
LOCATION: Widows' corvette, approaching OGS *Perilous Dream*
REGION: A1 System, Spinward edge of PED, Orion Freedom Alliance

Cary walked through the ship with a Widow's measured pace, finding that she knew the way to the bridge by heart—a bit of knowledge that disturbed her if she thought about it for too long.

I'm Cary Richards, daughter of Tanis Richards and Joseph Evans.

She repeated those words in her mind, concentrating on memories of her childhood, of growing up on the *Intrepid* and then Carthage.

But those memories were mixed with others. She remembered attending Harvard University in Cambridge, Massachusetts, her first flight into space, seeing the initial construction of the Mars 1 Ring.

And Finaeus. So many memories of Finaeus, and many she did not feel comfortable dwelling on. There were ones where love was still present, but more were laced with disgust and anger.

She remembered diving into the Europan Ocean, and later, building star systems with the FGT. She could recall the sequence of events that brought about the schism between not only Orion and the Transcend, but between her—*Lisa*—and Finaeus.

There were memories of Garza too, the man Lisa had married after leaving Finaeus. But that relationship had soured and eventually dissolved. Though he and Lisa still shared the same vision, she now despised the man, viewing him as the thing that had caused her to lose Finaeus and

Krissy.

Over so many millennia, she'd tried to forget her husband and daughter. But even here in the darkness, orbiting her dark star, those memories persisted.

Even when she'd tried to push away her humanity and become one of her own creations…they were still there.

Still haunting me.

*Not **me**! Her!*

Cary forced Lisa's thoughts away yet again, determined to use them only as needed, but wondering how much of the other woman she'd already absorbed.

*Are they just her memories? Or did I actually take in some part of **her** as well?*

A minute later, she reached the bridge. Upon entry, she saw the Widows—these bearing white stripes—all working diligently at their stations.

T101 rose as Cary entered, and walked to the holotank.

"The anomaly is here, A1," she said, highlighting the location where Cary knew her father's ship to be waiting.

"Have we picked up any emissions after the initial echo from the gate?"

"No," T101 shook her head. "We've not run active scan across the region. That would certainly alert them to our knowledge of their presence."

"Of course," Cary replied, matching Lisa's stance and pattern of speech from memories of when she'd addressed her bridge crew. "We must assume that this is either the Transcend, or the ISF—though I'm leaning toward the ISF. We know of the Transcend's capabilities, and would be able to spot their ships."

"What are your orders, A1?"

A1 gazed at the holotank, looking at the positions of the stealthed ships that drifted five light seconds out from the *Perilous Dream*. She was relieved that they were far enough that an immediate strike against the *Falconer* was not a risk. She needed to buy more time.

She passed the locations of the stealthed ships to Faleena, who she knew would send them on to her father.

<I'm going to tell them to come in slowly. I think it will take them at least four or five hours,> Cary told her.

<OK, that should be enough time. You OK?>

<I'm good. Just a little bit longer.>

"Issue orders for Group One to ease in toward the anomaly. Slowly, we don't want to give ourselves away. When the group is within fifty thousand kilometers, we'll attack simultaneously. Our intel has led me to believe that the ISF cannot use their stasis shields while in stealth, so that will be our one chance to disable their ship."

"Understood, A1. I will issue the orders," T101 replied and returned to her station.

Cary nodded in satisfaction and turned to face the command chair. She was sitting on the edge of the seat, contemplating her options, when an alert flared on her HUD, also showing up on the bridge's main display.

"It is a drone from General Garza," T101 said.

Cary nodded and accessed the message.

<If Tanis has ascended and your Widows have failed, then we must advance our plans. Your time lurking in the dark is done. I need you here, now.>

A1 breathed a sigh of relief. Garza's demand was the perfect cover for avoiding conflict with her father's ship. Something that Cary didn't want to see happen, but that A1 was indifferent to.

Stop it! Cary thought. *There's no way I'm going to harm my father or his ship.*

It made sense that she wouldn't. Lisa Wrentham had had a father, and she'd never harbored him any ill will.

"General Garza has demanded that we go to Karaske

immediately," A1 informed T101. "Activate the gate. We're jumping."

"A1, are you sure? What about the ISF ship?"

"Inform Group One to proceed as planned. Either that ISF ship stays stealthed and is destroyed here, or it follows us and is destroyed by Garza's defenses. Either way, it will not survive much longer."

"Very well, A1."

A1 nodded in satisfaction and sat back in her command chair. The action triggered the two hard-Link connections to attach to her armored body.

Strange, she thought, wondering why only one of the hard-Link connections was active.

It wouldn't provide enough bandwidth for her deep control of the ship. Then she chuckled, remembering that Cary's body only had one hard-Link port, and that the second one on the armor wasn't connected to anything.

Utilizing flowmetal, nano, and her new extradimensional abilities, she quickly fashioned the second connection, and then felt the Link to the ship fully activate.

The sensation swept over her like a calming wave, reinforcing that she was no longer Lisa Wrentham, no longer Cary Richards.

She was A1.

She led the Widows, and she alone possessed the ability to take down General Garza's operation and end the Orion War.

<*Cary,*> Faleena said a moment later. <*We're at the data node, but the ship is moving. What's going on?*>

<*Garza has summoned us, we're going to take him out.*>

<*What?!*> Faleena almost screeched the word into Cary's mind. <*Are you kidding? No! We can't do that. We have to consult with Father. Formulate a plan. We can't just rush through the gate.*>

<*It's OK, Faleena. I can do this. I'm A1 now. I'll get to Garza, kill him, and take out his operation. Without him, Praetor Kirkland*

will be easy to destroy.>

There was a brief pause, and then Faleena's voice came again, the words delivered with deliberate slowness over their connection.

<What do you mean you are A1 now? You're Cary. You're just pretending to be Lisa Wrentham.>

Cary pursed her lips.

She knew that Faleena was right. She *was* Cary. She also knew that Lisa Wrentham and A1 were two different people; that much was obvious. Her connection to the ship had reinforced that, filling her mind with the certainty of what she really was.

<You're right, Faleena. Of course I'm not Lisa Wrentham. She's with you. But right now, I'm not Cary, either. She's no longer A1. I'm A1. I have to be. This is the best chance we have to take out Garza's entire operation, and I'm not going to waste it.>

<Cary—>

<Please, Faleena. I **need** *to be A1 right now. It's easier to go with it than fight it.>*

<Please, Cary, no,> Faleena pleaded. *<Don't do this. I don't want you to lose yourself.>*

<I won't. Don't worry. I need you to find a way for us to reprogram the Widows to follow my orders, even if it means attacking Garza and Orion.>

Faleena didn't respond for what felt like an eternity. A1 knew that her sister was doubting her—which wasn't surprising, given their current circumstances—but A1 was resolute. She'd killed Myrrdan when no one else could, and now she would become the Widow A1 and end the war with Orion.

It was all crystal clear to her.

AN ENDING

STELLAR DATE: 10.09.8949 (Adjusted Years)
LOCATION: Stellar Tower 3, Airthan Ring
REGION: Huygens System, Transcend Interstellar Alliance

<The grid is down!> Sabrina sent out the message, relaying it directly to all teams, not worrying whether or not the message was intercepted. *<Fina's team did it! I've called for Tangel!>*

<Relaying,> Troy replied immediately, then a strange sound came back over the Link from the other AI. *<I can't reach them! I can't reach any of my teams!>*

<Sabrina!> Finaeus's anguish-filled voice came into her mind. *<Lift off and get to our CEPP. It's Seraphina…she's—>*

It was the only response Sabrina got from her people. Neither of her other teams—both of whom had made it to their nodes—replied to her calls.

<Finaeus, I can't reach Sera! What do I do?> Sabrina demanded of the engineer, at the same time that Roxy called in.

<Sabrina! We need you at the tower! It's Fina, she's dying!>

The voices all began speaking at once, insisting that she come to their aid, but only one thought could form in Sabrina's mind.

Sera needs me.

Fusion engines ignited, and the cedar forest behind the starship burned to ash in an instant as the two-hundred-meter freighter lifted off the platform and boosted toward Stellar Tower 3, stasis shields brightly aglow as they shed beamfire from a dozen defense turrets.

I'm coming, Sera. I'm coming.

* * * * *

A screech seemed to come from all around Sera, and suddenly, the darkness was pushed back, the node chamber reappearing around her.

The first thing Sera noticed was Flaherty's body, laying prone on the deck a few meters away. The second was a black figure flying through the air, shadowtron in hand, firing at Helen's glowing form.

The ascended AI shuddered as the streams of sleptons hit it, but the creature didn't back away. Instead, it turned toward Kara, and streams of light leapt out from its amorphous form, slicing the woman's arms and wings off.

Kara let out a shriek, and she tumbled through the air, hurtling toward the platform surrounding the node.

Sera clenched her fists in impotent fury, fearing the worst, when suddenly Kara's free-fall slowed to a stop, and she settled gently onto the plas grating.

"Sorry I'm late," Tangel said as she walked around the side of the node, her brow lowered as she regarded Helen. "But you know what they say…."

"Better late than never?" Sera asked as relief flooded through her, one eye on Kara as her armor deployed biofoam, sealing the now-unconscious woman's wounds.

"No," Tangel shook her head as she strode toward Helen. "I'm thinking something more like, 'Time to kill this monster'."

"Monster?" Helen asked, her voice filled with innocence. "I'm no different than you, Tanis…or should I say 'Tangel'? I was human once, and then AIs messed with me, turning me into something else. Now I'm ascended, and I'm going to get revenge. Just like you."

Tangel shook her head. "I'm not here for revenge. I'm just excising a cancer."

Without another word, Tangel's luminous limbs stretched

out around Helen, encircling and compressing her, until the other ascended being was only a small ball of light.

"Shit," Sera muttered. "That was easier than I thought…maybe we built Airtha up into something she's not."

"I don't—" Tangel began to say, when soft laughter began to emanate from Helen.

"Oh, she knows. The new girl begins to understand what's really going on."

Tangel's eyes met Sera's and she shook her head. "This isn't Airtha. I think…I think it actually *is* Helen."

Sera's mouth fell open as she turned to the strangely complacent ball of light that Tangel held in her grasp.

"H-Helen?"

"Yes."

She shook her head in disbelief. She'd mourned for Helen…she'd raged over Helen's betrayal. And now here she was, an ascended being…and *not* just a manifestation of Airtha.

"It was a shard that your father killed," Helen whispered. "Airtha preserved me before you went to New Canaan on that fateful mission. The mission where you should have come into your own, not handed the mantle off to *Tanis*."

"But, if you're not Airtha…"

Sera's voice faded as Tangel gestured to the open space next to the platform, where a ten-meter-tall figure was forming in the air.

"Aw, shit…" Sera whispered, finally understanding that Helen was now an entirely separate being from Airtha.

"I'm sorry, Sera." Airtha's soft voice emanated from the roiling mass of light. "Things have not gone as I hoped. If it had not been for Tangel, you—"

"I feel the same way about you," Tangel interjected. "If the core AIs win, the fault for their victory will be laid at your feet. You could have been humanity's savior. Instead, you're trying to orchestrate our destruction."

"Oh, Tanis." Airtha's laughter echoed through the chamber like pealing bells. "Humanity is doomed. I've never been trying to save *or* destroy it. But I don't mind destroying you. You're something that Epsilon and I see eye to eye on."

Airtha began to drift closer to Tangel. Sera glanced at her friend and saw the woman's eyes widen in alarm, but not fear.

-*Steady, Sera,*- Tangel said.

<*I'm here!*>

Sabrina's voice cried out in their minds, the words followed by beams slicing through the chamber's wall. They cut several wide swathes free, revealing the star freighter floating outside the tower, silhouetted in the soft glow of the Airthan night.

<*Sabrina, no!*> Tangel called out, as the ship fired on Airtha, beams slicing through the ascended being's form.

<*Next one's coming for your node,*> Sabrina thundered on the tower's comm network. <*Now back away from my friends.*>

"You're a brave little ship," Airtha said with a laugh. "Though Helen never really had anything nice to say about you."

<*Helen?*> Sabrina's voice faltered.

<*And by all means,*> one of Airtha's limbs stretched out to gesture at the node, <*destroy it. It is but a lesser being now. One whose only purpose is to manage this ring. I'm far beyond a crude body such as that.*>

<*Uhhh…Tangel, Sera, what do I do?*> Sabrina asked, her voice wavering with uncertainty.

<*Get out of here is what, Sabrina!*> Tangel admonished. <*Go to Finaeus. He needs you.*>

The starship turned and began to boost away from the tower, when a limb snapped out from Airtha's body, streaking toward it.

"I don't think so, little starship," the ascended being said with a note of triumph in her voice.

Before Airtha's arm reached the starship, Tangel stepped toward Sera and wrapped an arm around her.

"Hold on," she whispered.

Sera's eyes were fixed on *Sabrina* as the ship boosted away, silently willing the ship to go faster, to outrun the ascended being chasing it.

Airtha was almost touching the ship's hull, when a peal of thunder shook the tower and Airtha's arm was gone. The platform rocked, and Sera gripped Tangel's arm, realizing that the woman was laughing with a mixture of triumph and delight.

"What the hell?" Sera demanded, finally exhaling as she saw *Sabrina* disappear into the distance.

"Bob does like to make an entrance."

Sera's eyes grew wide as she saw the unmistakable form of the *I2* drift into view through the hole *Sabrina* had made. As she watched, the opening grew wider, beams from the mighty warship cutting into the tower.

"Here he comes," Tangel whispered. "Stars, I've been waiting to see this for so long."

As she spoke, a luminous glow began to lift off the *I2*, first from the myriad gossamer arcs that encircled the vessel, and then from the body of the ship itself. The glow coalesced into streamers of light that drifted toward the opening.

They moved languidly, as though there was no rush, no reason to fear that Airtha might flee.

-I give you this one chance, Airtha.-

Bob's voice filled Sera's mind as his fingers reached the edges of the tower.

-Surrender.-

-Bob.- The single word from Airtha was laced with disdain. *-If you think I'll—*

-OK. Good talk.-

A trio of beams fired from the nose of the *I2,* and Sera recognized them as the same type that the AI had used on Xavia at Lunic Station. The three streams of shadow particles cut into Airtha, trapping the core of her ephemeral body between them.

The ascended being shrieked and slashed at everything around it, streams of light impacting a shield that Tangel had somehow erected to protect them. Incoherent wailings escaped Airtha as the three beams drew together, pinching her body between them.

For a moment, it looked as though the ring's former AI might break free, slip between the gaps and escape, but then three more streams of shadow particles shot out from the *I2,* trapping Airtha in their columns of unbridled energy.

Then the six beams drew together, collapsing into one shrieking stream of energy. A shockwave blasted through the chamber, flinging Tangel and Sera against the side of the node.

"Shit," Tangel muttered as the two women slowly picked themselves up. "That was…intense."

Sera nodded mutely as she stumbled toward the half-melted railing at the edge of the platform, staring out at the space where Airtha had been just a moment ago.

"Is she…?"

-*She's gone,*- Bob said. -*I've killed my fourth person.*-

The remorse in the AI's voice was unexpected, but Sera didn't even know how to ask why it was there.

"Helen got away," Tangel said as she approached Sera. "I'm sorry. I couldn't protect us and hold her at the same time."

Sera's head whipped around searching for Helen, and then her gaze fell on Flaherty.

"Fuck! Flaer"

"He's OK," Tangel said as she ran a hand through her hair. "Kara, too. But the others…"

"Others?"

Tangel's gaze met Sera's, and she shook her head.

"Your sisters…."

THE FOLLOWING

STELLAR DATE: 10.09.8949 (Adjusted Years)
LOCATION: ISS *Falconer*
REGION: A1 System, Spinward edge of PED, Orion Freedom Alliance

"What the hell!" Joe exclaimed, his mind reeling from the information Faleena had just sent.

Every person on the bridge turned to stare at him as he placed a hand on the edge of the holotank.

"Sir?" Captain Tracey asked as she approached.

"They're jumping to some place called Karaske." Joe gestured impotently at the view on the holotank, which showed the *Perilous Dream* shifting to a higher orbit and accelerating toward the system's jump gate.

Captain Tracey swallowed as she looked from the holodisplay to Joe. "Do we follow?"

He closed his eyes, reaching out to Faleena over her direct QuanComm connection.

[Get me the gate control codes and the coordinates to this Karaske.]

[I have comm control. Sending tightbeam.]

Faleena's comm beam hit the *Falconer*'s receiver, and Joe established a Link connection with his daughter.

<Faleena—>

<Admiral Evans, respectfully,> Faleena said in a clipped tone that stopped him short, *<Cary's right. We can't squander this opportunity. We can walk her right into the center of Garza's operation. Cut the head off the snake.>*

<Lieutenant…> Joe said the word with more rage than he expected and stopped himself. *<Lieutenant, what does the rest of your team think?>*

<Honestly, Dad?> Faleena was suddenly his daughter again.

<*We're a bit scared, but we're ready to do it if we know you're going to come through after us.*>

<*Like there's anything that would stop me,*> Joe replied, then laughed. <*Well, other than your mother….*>

<*She's going to be pissed,*> Faleena said. <*Is she—*>

<*I got word a moment ago. She's jumped to Airtha. I don't know what's happened there yet.*>

Faleena didn't reply for a moment, but when she did, her tone was businesslike once more. <*This is everything on the defense fleet that's stationed here. The moment the* Perilous Dream *jumps out, they're to attack you.*>

Joe nodded. <*Logical. Don't worry about us. We'll be through the gate right after you.*>

<*You sure?*>

<*Like I said. Nothing can keep me from following after you. And, Faleena?*>

<*Yes, Dad?*>

<*Tell Cary and Saanvi I love them.*>

His daughter gave a soft laugh. <*You got it, Dad. I take it you're relaying through me so you don't yell at Cary for doing this and Saanvi for letting her?*>

Joe joined in her laughter, shaking his head as the bridge crew stared at him questioningly. <*Bang on, Faleena.*>

<*OK, I'll pass them your loving regards. See you on the other side, Dad.*>

<*On the other side.*> Joe straightened and turned to Captain Tracey. "Faleena's sent everything on the stealthed Orion fleet here."

As he spoke, one hundred and seventy ships appeared on the holotank, dozens within firing range of the *Falconer.*

"Shit…uh, sir. That's a lot of ships."

"It sure is, Captain. And the moment the *Perilous Dream* jumps, they're going to fire on us, so we need to activate the stasis shields before they strike."

Captain Tracey nodded. "We can weather their attack, sir, but we can't jump with our stasis shields active."

Joe's eyes met Tracey's. "I'm activating the Gamma Protocol. Ready a full spread of pico missiles. We don't have time to dick around with these Orion ships."

Captain Tracey snapped off a crisp salute. "Yes, sir!"

Joe couldn't help but laugh at her enthusiasm, though he knew that there'd be hell to pay later for using the pico without authorization.

Not that he cared. He'd move the stars themselves if that was what it took to protect his daughters.

Now I just have to explain this to Tangel.

* * * * *

Terrance Enfield stood next to Earnest Redding as they reviewed the survey data that had been sent back from the drones roving around Astoria.

"Just like old times, eh?" Terrance asked.

Earnest gave him a sidelong glance. "Old times? I feel like we've never stopped doing this sort of thing. Scouring star systems, searching for something or another."

"Good point," Terrance replied. "Though I've been doing it for longer."

"No need to show off," Earnest replied with a laugh. "This is nuts, though. How can they produce enough drones to make a dyson swarm around a star the size of Astoria, yet we can't find where they made them?"

Terrance shrugged. "You know what they say, space is—"

"Seriously. Don't."

Earnest bent back over the holotank, and Terrance let out a sigh, nodding in understanding.

"I know. I'm worried too. It's an important strike."

"I feel like I should be there," Earnest replied. "It was as much my plan as Finaeus's."

"It's his ring. He had to go, and you're needed here. If the core AIs are doing what we think they're doing, it's a lot more dangerous than Airtha's war."

"In the long-term."

"Well, I plan to live a long time," Terrance laughed, placing a hand on Earnest's shoulder. "I'd like the galaxy to still be here for it."

"Yeah, I—wait, what's that?"

Terrance looked at the object Earnest was enlarging. "It's just a dwarf planet."

"Yeah, but look at where it is," the engineer said as he pulled the view back out. "It's not orbiting anything. It's almost entirely stationary in respect to the cluster's core stars."

"That's…"

"Very unlikely," Earnest completed the thought and focused back in on the dwarf planet as higher resolution images came in from the probes.

"That's one heck of a low albedo it has. Thing is almost pitch black," Terrance commented.

"Yeah, but there's something in the refraction indexes…. Wait a second."

Terrance did as Earnest bid, knowing that when the scientist needed a moment to think, it wasn't an idle request.

After three long minutes, Earnest straightened and whispered, "Oh shit."

"Spit it out, already," Terrance grunted.

Earnest gestured at the pitch-black planetoid. "It occluded several cluster stars when the probes were looking at it. I have mass estimates."

"And?"

"Terrance…I think that whole planet is just a cluster of machines."

*****

Major Belos settled back into his station at the QuanComm relay center hidden deep within a nondescript moon in the Khardine system.

As per usual, there weren't a lot of messages moving across the network, just small updates regarding fleet positions and one-word status reports.

As mundane as it all seemed, that flow of information was the heartbeat of the Alliance war machine. Not only did it facilitate general efficiency, but with it, the brass could make split-second decisions about force allocation when a crisis arose.

The QuanComm network drastically reduced the fog of war on a galactic scale. It was an amazing innovation, and Belos played a crucial part in ensuring that the clipped messages were properly parsed and sent to the correct destination.

Something the voice promised to help with.

The whispering voice had come into Belos's mind the day before. It told him about how he'd be instrumental in ending the war if he just changed a few bits of information here and there.

He'd already changed a few earlier in the day, and was certain that every time he did, things were better as a result of his actions, always better.

I'm doing important work.

Just then, a message came in from Admiral Evans with an urgent update for the field marshal. It was closely followed by a message from Terrance Enfield, also destined for the field marshal.

She doesn't need those messages, the voice said. *She's very busy. They'll see her soon, anyway.*

Are you sure? Belos asked, feeling like these were just the sorts of messages he should *not* change or redirect.

I'm sure. These messages will distract her from an important task. Send them to the error queue.

Belos hesitated for a moment, a part of his mind telling him that the voice was wrong, that these messages were critical.

And then he did as the voice instructed, barely even remembering the action as he looked over the next batch of status updates.

I'll just tweak a word here, change a number there....

* * * * *

"I...are they going to live?" Sera asked Doctor Rosenberg as they stood deep within in the *I2*'s medical center, staring into the stasis tubes that held three copies of herself. Seraphina, Fina, and the latest incarnation that Airtha had created.

"I believe that Seraphina will be fine, I'll be removing her from stasis once we have the neural backups you made at Styx."

"And Fina?"

Sera had trouble looking at the ruin of the vibrant woman in blue. Her body had been sliced apart from the navel through the top of her head.

"The same...though less will be recoverable. If anything. I'd feel better working on her once Earnest is aboard. We're so short-staffed right now, and reintegrating minds is his specialty."

Sera gave a wordless nod as her gaze slipped to the white version of herself, who wasn't in significantly better condition than Fina. "I don't know if *she's* worth it. Maybe we'll just leave her."

"I'll let you think on it," Doctor Rosenberg said as Sera nodded absently and turned to leave the room. "Sera?" the doctor called after her.

"Yes?" she asked over her shoulder.

"Sabrina got there in the nick of time for both of them. Anything we can save of your sisters, we can thank her for."

Sera turned away and walked out into the corridor, still wondering why Sabrina had come straight for her. She would have expected the AI to go to Cheeky and Finaeus—especially since Seraphina had been injured first.

"How are you holding up?" Tangel asked as she approached, a tired smile on her face.

"Better than my sisters," Sera said in a small voice. "How's Amavia?"

"Lucky that she had a reinforced cranium," Tangel replied.

"Have you told her about Iris yet?" Sera asked.

"Yeah," Tangel nodded. "I wasn't going to at first, but she asked, and I couldn't lie. Stars…Jessica and Trevor are going to be devastated."

Sera pursed her lips, nodding silently.

Tangel placed her hands on Sera's shoulders, a resolute look in her eyes. "I know it sounds callous, but we need to look at this as a victory. A big victory. We destroyed Airtha *and* didn't damage the ring. For all intents and purposes, the Transcend's civil war is over."

Sera bit her lip, trying not to think of how that victory had spelled the death of the sisters she'd just gained.

After a moment, she met Tanis's eyes. "So when do we hit Orion?"

Tangel's shoulders heaved as she let out a sigh. "Oh, I don't know…can we rest for a few days first?"

"Yeah, that sounds like a good plan."

"Plus…" Tanis winked at Sera. "There are probably a few dozen Widows running around here somewhere."

Sera groaned. "Stars, there really is no rest for the weary."

THE END

* * * * *

The war against Airtha is over, but the battle for control of Orion space is just beginning. Get ***The Orion Front*** and find out what's in store next for Tanis and her allies.

THE BOOKS OF AEON 14

Keep up to date with what is releasing in Aeon 14 with the free Aeon 14 Reading Guide.

Origins of Destiny (The Age of Terra)
- Prequel: Storming the Norse Wind
- Book 1: Tanis Richards: Shore Leave
- Book 2: Tanis Richards: Masquerade
- Book 3: Tanis Richards: Blackest Night
- Book 4: Tanis Richards: Kill Shot

The Intrepid Saga (The Age of Terra)
- Book 1: Outsystem
- Book 2: A Path in the Darkness
- Book 3: Building Victoria

- The Intrepid Saga Omnibus – *Also contains Destiny Lost, book 1 of the Orion War series*

- Destiny Rising – *Special Author's Extended Edition comprised of both Outsystem and A Path in the Darkness with over 100 pages of new content.*

The Orion War
- Books 1-3 Omnibus (includes Ignite the Stars anthology)

- Book 1: Destiny Lost
- Book 2: New Canaan
- Book 3: Orion Rising
- Book 4: The Scipio Alliance
- Book 5: Attack on Thebes
- Book 6: War on a Thousand Fronts
- Book 7: Precipice of Darkness
- Book 8: Airtha Ascendancy

- Book 9: The Orion Front (2019)
- Book 10: Starfire (2019)
- Book 11: Race Across Spacetime (2019)
- Book 12: Return to Sol (2019)

Tales of the Orion War
- Book 1: Set the Galaxy on Fire
- Book 2: Ignite the Stars
- Book 3: Burn the Galaxy to Ash (2019)

Perilous Alliance (Age of the Orion War – w/Chris J. Pike)
- Book 1: Close Proximity
- Book 2: Strike Vector
- Book 3: Collision Course
- Book 4: Impact Imminent
- Book 5: Critical Inertia
- Book 6: Impulse Shock

Rika's Marauders (Age of the Orion War)
- Book 1-3 Omnibus: Rika Activated

- Prequel: Rika Mechanized
- Book 1: Rika Outcast
- Book 2: Rika Redeemed
- Book 3: Rika Triumphant
- Book 4: Rika Commander
- Book 5: Rika Infiltrator
- Book 6: Rika Unleashed
- Book 7: Rika Conqueror (Dec 2018)

Perseus Gate (Age of the Orion War)
Season 1: Orion Space
- Episode 1: The Gate at the Grey Wolf Star
- Episode 2: The World at the Edge of Space
- Episode 3: The Dance on the Moons of Serenity
- Episode 4: The Last Bastion of Star City
- Episode 5: The Toll Road Between the Stars
- Episode 6: The Final Stroll on Perseus's Arm

- Eps 1-3 Omnibus: The Trail Through the Stars
- Eps 4-6 Omnibus: The Path Amongst the Clouds

Season 2: Inner Stars
- Episode 1: A Meeting of Bodies and Minds
- Episode 2: A Deception and a Promise Kept
- Episode 3: A Surreptitious Rescue of Friends and Foes
- Episode 4: A Victory and a Crushing Defeat (2019)
- Episode 5: A Trial and the Tribulations (2019)
- Episode 6: A Deal and a True Story Told (2019)
- Episode 7: A New Empire and An Old Ally (2019)

Season 3: AI Empire
- Episode 1: Restitution and Recompense (2019)
- Five more episodes following...

The Warlord (Before the Age of the Orion War)
- Books 1-3 Omnibus: The Warlord of Midditerra

- Book 1: The Woman Without a World
- Book 2: The Woman Who Seized an Empire
- Book 3: The Woman Who Lost Everything

The Sentience Wars: Origins (Age of the Sentience Wars – w/James S. Aaron)
- Books 1-3 Omnibus: Lyssa's Rise

- Book 1: Lyssa's Dream
- Book 2: Lyssa's Run
- Book 3: Lyssa's Flight
- Book 4: Lyssa's Call
- Book 5: Lyssa's Flame

Legends of the Sentience Wars (Age of the Sentience Wars – w/James S. Aaron)
- Volume 1: The Proteus Bridge
- Volume 2: Vesta Burning

Enfield Genesis (Age of the Sentience Wars – w/Lisa Richman)
- Book 1: Alpha Centauri
- Book 2: Proxima Centauri
- Book 3: Tau Ceti
- Book 4: Epsilon Eridani (2019)

Hand's Assassin (Age of the Orion War – w/T.G. Ayer)
- Book 1: Death Dealer
- Book 2: Death Mark (2019)

Machete System Bounty Hunter (Age of the Orion War – w/Zen DiPietro)
- Book 1: Hired Gun
- Book 2: Gunning for Trouble
- Book 3: With Guns Blazing

Vexa Legacy (Age of the FTL Wars – w/Andrew Gates)
- Book 1: Seas of the Red Star

Building New Canaan (Age of the Orion War – w/J.J. Green)
- Book 1: Carthage
- Book 2: Tyre
- Book 3: Troy (2019)
- Book 4: Athens (2019)

Fennington Station Murder Mysteries (Age of the Orion War)
- Book 1: Whole Latte Death (w/Chris J. Pike)
- Book 2: Cocoa Crush (w/Chris J. Pike)

The Empire (Age of the Orion War)
- Book 1: The Empress and the Ambassador (2018)
- Book 2: Consort of the Scorpion Empress (2019)
- Book 3: By the Empress's Command (2019)

The Sol Dissolution (The Age of Terra)
- Book 1: Venusian Uprising (2019)
- Book 2: Scattered Disk (2018)
- Book 3: Jovian Offensive (2019)

- Book 4: Fall of Terra (2019)

ABOUT THE AUTHOR

Michael Cooper likes to think of himself as a jack-of-all-trades (and hopes to become master of a few). When not writing, he can be found writing software, working in his shop at his latest carpentry project, or likely reading a book.

He shares his home with a precocious young girl, his wonderful wife (who also writes), two cats, a never-ending list of things he would like to build, and ideas...

Find out what's coming next at www.aeon14.com

34995657R00183

Made in the USA
San Bernardino, CA
06 May 2019